Praise for *So Far Back*

"Durban writes about the South . . . with the critical, objective eye of an outsider and with the empathy of an insider."
—Melissa McIntosh Brown, *The Commercial Appeal* (Memphis)

"Durban combines well-drawn characters with a deft evocation of both the old and the new Charleston."
—Mary Ellen Quinn, *Booklist*

"Durban's carefully managed cast of characters—antebellum aristocrats, slave families, and their descendants in the modern South—are drawn with subtle grace, producing a narrative of compelling intensity."
—*Publishers Weekly*

"Absorbing . . . moving . . . [Durban's] patience and compassion make her fiction very attractive—and worth paying attention to."
—*Kirkus Reviews*

"A realistic picture of Charleston, South Carolina, past and present."
—*Library Journal*

Also by Pam Durban

The Laughing Place
All Set About with Fever Trees

So Far Back

[a novel]

Pam Durban

Picador USA
New York

This is a work of fiction. Names, characters, places, and events have been
imagined by the author or are used fictitiously. Any resemblance to actual
persons, living or dead, events, or locales is entirely coincidental.

www.picadorusa.com

For information on Picador USA Reading Group Guides, as well as ordering, please
contact the Trade Marketing department at St. Martin's Press.
Phone: 1-800-221-7945 extension 763
Fax: 212-677-7456
E-mail: trademarketing@stmartins.com

Library of Congress Cataloging-in-Publication Data

Durban, Pam.
    So far back : a novel / Pam Durban.
        p. cm.
    ISBN 0-312-26869-6 (hc)
    ISBN 0-312-28347-4 (pbk)
    1. Charleston (S.C.)—Fiction. 2. Mothers and daughters—Fiction. 3. Single
women—Fiction. 4. Women slaves—Fiction. 5. Diaries—Fiction. I. Title.

PS3554.U668 S6 2000
813'.54—dc21   00-040657

First Picador USA Paperback Edition: October 2001

10 9 8 7 6 5 4 3 2 1

This is for Wylie

Why? God, why does she have to live so far back? . . .
The answer to that is as hard for me as is the answer
to everything else. It was ordained before I—before
father—was born—that she should live back there.
So why should I try to understand it now?

—Ernest J. Gaines
"Just Like a Tree" from *Bloodline*

acknowledgments

In preparing to write this book, I did research in several major archives. I would like to thank the staffs of these collections for their guidance:

The South Carolina Historical Society in Charleston, South Carolina, and especially Steve Hoffius for directing me to the Mary Lamboll Beach letters and the John Bennett collection, among others.

The South Caroliniana Library in Columbia, South Carolina, for guiding me to the Louisa Minot letters and to the "Anonymous" heading in the card file, where I found a rich collection of letters and documents.

The Southern Historical Collection in Chapel Hill, North Carolina, where I found the John Mitchell letters and the diary of Caroline Laurens, whose riveting narrative of a husband's death almost caused me to miss a plane.

The Charleston Library Society in whose collection of ante-bellum pamphlets, sermons, newspapers, and articles on agricultural and medical theory and practice I happily rummaged.

I would also like to thank the following people and organizations:

Teresa Jones, a diligent and effective research assistant in the early stages of the writing of this book.

Carl and Susan Cofer, for their generosity in allowing me to use the guest house at their farm.

Deb and Edith Wylder, who are sustaining friends and ideal readers.

James Allen, for good talks about Southern history and for his gift of a copy of *Advice Among Masters*.

Anthony Tambakis, for helping when it mattered.

Robert Sattelmeyer, chair of the English Department at Georgia State University, and Ahmed T. Abdelal, Dean of the College of Arts and Sciences, for their support.

Frank Hunter, without whose patience and faith this book could not have been written.

The National Endowment for the Arts, for grant support.

NATIONAL
ENDOWMENT
FOR THE ARTS

So Far Back

Walking Tour of the Historic District
Charleston, South Carolina
Site No. 1

⁂

This is the Fireproof Building, current home to the South Carolina Historical Society. Designed in the Classical Revival style by the young architect and native Charlestonian Robert Mills, and completed in 1827, it is a fine example of the late-eighteenth-century and early-nineteenth-century ideals of balance, order, and harmony. Notice how every element is repeated and complemented by another—gracefully curved steps on the left and right climb to a porch topped by double doors of rosewood—and in this way, symmetry is achieved, symmetry and repose. Place each element of this building on the pans of a scale and when it was done, the whole would hang, perfectly balanced.

Beauty, permanence, safety: Those are ideals this building was designed to express. The building is fireproof—stone floors, walls, ceilings, stone window casements and sills—because fire was a constant threat in this city in the Colonial and antebellum eras and well into modern times. Imagine this narrow peninsula crowded with wooden buildings. Imagine candles and lanterns and oil; open flame was, of course, the only source of light and heat in this city for close to two centuries. Imagine paper and straw, drunken sailors, the careless and unruly poor, the campfires of plantation Negroes who traveled here on authorized and unauthorized errands. Imagine braziers in the market, cotton on the wharves, torches and strong winds from the Atlantic to fan the flames. The great fire of 1740 destroyed 334 buildings in less than four hours. The fires of 1835 and 1838, and the colossal fire of 1861, also caused widespread damage. Some of these fires were deliberately set. We are speaking of arson here, deliberate and calculated acts of destruction. Imagine a city of slaves (antebellum census figures show a city more black than white) who slipped through the streets after curfew. (How to keep them all safely confined to their masters' houses and yards? How to know their whereabouts, their activities?) Imagine also a large population of free blacks in whose homes and illegal grog shops the slaves could hear about the success of the slave revolt in Santo Domingo, or study the Bible with Denmark Vesey, that notorious inciter of mayhem, who glossed for them the twenty-first verse of the sixth chapter of the book of Joshua: "And they utterly destroyed all that was in the city, both man and woman, young and old, and ox, and sheep, and ass, with the edge of the sword." Imagine the city burning, the entire peninsula from the Ashley to the Cooper rivers in flames and the Fireproof Building untouched in the middle of the inferno; at worst, it would lose only its utterly replaceable roof, doors, window sashes.

Now, at this same building that has stood so long and served so many so well, you climb the curved steps and ring the bell beside the rosewood doors, which open, and a young man asks, "Yes?" bowing slightly, smiling. Not "Come in," or "Welcome," but "Yes?" a question you must answer. What is the answer? If you've been brought up in the South, you will know instantly that you are being sized up. If you are not from the South, you will still recognize, somehow, that though this door leads to an institution, there is something *personal* about the way you've been greeted, as though this were still someone's home and the maid had been told not to let in a Fuller Brush salesman or a Jehovah's Witness or any other pushy individual with a hustle and a smile, and you will understand that this is being decided about you as you state your business.

Inside, you sign the guest book on the hall table; nonmembers pay a five-dollar admission fee. As you hand over your money, you may feel the need to smooth the bill, perhaps to blow on it discreetly or to wave it in the air to dry it; it is damp, isn't it, from being folded in that nylon wallet and mashed against your flesh all day? It might even be a little soiled; one person's money is not the same as another's, and even if it were, you could have all the money in the world and still not belong here. You can't buy your way into this town.

Our memories, you see, are very long, and we refresh them regularly, and in that way, the line remains unbroken, and the circle, too, which is why we love the old stories with their rounded edges, their completeness. It is why we love spring as well, when all is reborn and renewed. Spring is clean; spring is light and sweet—the season this city was made for. It is bougainvillea and wisteria, tea olive and the azaleas all in bloom against the pastel houses. Sometimes in spring, the air snows blossoms and, passing a garden behind a brick wall, you will hear the trickle of a fountain. Spring gives us back the sweet landscape in which the old story unfolds; it is the stage on which the beautiful old drama plays again.

Notice the flag in the sealed case above the stairwell. That is the Banner of Secession, famous flag of defiance. To this day, there is a dinner given for the descendants of the signers of the Ordinance of Secession, that momentous and incendiary document. Housed within these thick stone walls, down in deep and spacious acid-free boxes, rest some of the most significant collections of documents and memorabilia in this state's history. These are the rules: Only pencils allowed in the reading rooms. All bags and coats are to be stored in the lockers provided. We have had our share of thieves and vandals, even here. Please present your requests one to a card, with call numbers and other descriptive information clearly and correctly printed. A young man or woman will take the card and bring back the box you requested and hand it to another young man or woman at the desk in the reading room, who will then check out papers, photographs, et cetera, to you, *one item at a time*, each item to be returned and checked back in before you will be allowed to check out another.

Please handle all papers briefly and carefully, as the oil from your fingers will damage the fibers. *Close the lid of the box* each time you remove or replace an item, in order to keep sunlight from fading the papers. This is not a preserving climate. Salt air, thick heat, and glaring light all work to hurry the downfall of things we'd like to keep. This is a softening climate, a loosening, rotting climate. Every living being—man born of woman, for example—and whatever is made from a living thing—paper and wood, cloth and thread—is subject to its laws. Among the ancient coastal tribes, whose sea-level existence made burials difficult, it is said that a man was appointed bone picker, his job to strip the flesh from the bones of the dead. But let us not dwell on heat and illness, on death and despair. Let us return to the comforts of permanence and solidity. The irreducible elements still keep their shapes, even here, as do elements hardened by fire. The slate of old sidewalks. Potsherds and arrowheads. Oyster shell. China and bone. And even the perishable can be rescued and fixed if the climate in which it is stored is controlled. Control is the key to preservation, always.

Gravity
(Louisa Hilliard Marion, 1989)

Whenever she visited her mother in the last weeks of the elder's long life, Louisa knew that if an aide had turned Mother's wheelchair to face the Cooper River bridges, she would be asking for Mamie again. She'd been in the home for two months now, since January, and yet the ebb and flow of clarity and confusion by which they'd lived for the last few years had kept its weekly rhythm—lucid days at the beginning and end of each week, bracketing the confused middle—and the private nursing home up on Society Street was in a house so familiar, though it was a larger Georgian to their double house, that sometimes it seemed to Louisa her mother had simply moved to another room in their house. Quiet and clean, her mother's new home smelled of the same citrus and apple potpourri that scented the air of their house. Downstairs, ticking steadily, stood a tall clock like their own that had crossed the ocean on an English ship. A twin to their own handsome breakfront made in Thomas Elfe's Charleston workshop dominated the front sitting room of the Society Street house. Throughout the house, there were familiar mantels and crown molding and portraits and wide floorboards covered with Oriental rugs.

Upstairs, in five large, bright rooms, the old people dozed and fretted, wept and puttered, and the people who fed and cleaned and quieted them were courteous, almost invisible, old-style colored people such as you seldom found working anywhere anymore. Which was fortunate, Louisa thought, because on her mother's bad days, she saw Mamie in every black woman's face. The nurse, the woman who fed her or helped her to the bathroom. If she was black, her name was Mamie.

Also, any footsteps might be hers. "Mamie?" Her mother's voice would meet Louisa out in the hall as she walked toward the room. "Mamie?" Her mother would be watching the door, a bright, hopeful look on her face until she saw her daughter and the brightness dimmed. On her lucid days, she laid down her search for the actual Mamie (dead fourteen years that spring), and told a story about Mamie, the same story, over and over again: Mamie and the Cooper River bridge. In her mother's last months, Louisa began to think of that story as a lighthouse beam: Whenever her mother sailed out of sight of land, she swung toward its light and traveled home.

Not that these urgent interests were recent. Over the past few years, Louisa had gotten used to being blown by her mother's whims. If in the middle of the night Mother had needed to see the silver stand that held the cut-crystal cruets or another piece of their china or silver, Louisa had pulled on her robe and gone downstairs, rummaged in drawers and sideboard cabinets until she'd found the item and taken it up to her. Once the thing had been found and delivered, it stayed put. For a year before her mother went into the home, the top of her dresser had collected saltcellars, gravy boats, cups and saucers. Even their famous silver pitcher had ended up there. It had been made in Santo Domingo by Louis Boudo and carried his stamp on the bottom, and the spout was shaped into the face of the wind with its fat, puffed cheeks and streaming hair. The pitcher had come to Charleston from Barbados with Isaac Hilliard, sea captain, merchant, and planter, early in the eighteenth century, and it had sat on the sideboard in their dining room for almost two hundred years, minus a one-year absence when it was hidden in the attic of the house upstate in the Pendleton District, where the family had waited for the end of the Civil War. Looking at it had made her mother smile. Now it was Mamie she wanted.

No one in Louisa's lifetime and, as far as she could remember, no one in her mother's lifetime, either, had ever been curious about Mamie. Curiosity was not a family trait, and the important facts were settled: Mamie Jones's family had been with the Hilliards here on the coast of South Carolina since time was. "Time was" was her mother's name for a length of time so long, it had no beginning; its clock had been ticking when the sun was lit, the earth began to turn. It was a species of eternity, then, and, like eternity, it was empty. Lacking cause or beginning, it was also innocent, entirely neutral. Whatever had been happening since time was was not good and it wasn't evil; it simply was, and always had been.

Everything that mattered here had been going on since time was: Their family had been in Charleston since time was, and down through the generations, in slavery and in freedom, right on up through the civil rights days, Mamie's family had worked for the Hilliard family. Mamie's mother, Kate, had been born in a room over the kitchen house in their backyard, and so had Mamie. Maum Harriette, Kate's mother, had been born and raised a slave at Fairview, the Hilliard plantation on the Edisto River south of the city, and her mother, Abby, and Abby's mother had been slaves there, too. So the families had moved through time together, until the day when Mamie's sixteen-year-old granddaughter, Evelyn, whom Mamie had raised since her mother, Mamie's daughter, Yvonne, had died when the girl was two, left the Hilliards' backyard kitchen house apartment and went to live with relatives out on Edisto Island. Every day for two months after that move, Evelyn traveled back into Charleston to work for them. First she came at ten o'clock, then she came at noon. Finally, one week, she did not come at all. No one at the phone number Evelyn had given them knew where she was, and that was the end of the Jones's service to the Hilliards.

Why Mamie? It was early on the Friday morning before Palm Sunday in the spring of 1989 when that question first moved through Louisa's mind. She could pinpoint the actual day and hour that it came, because the question had started turning in her mind on the same morning that two other events happened that marked off her year. Just that morning, as she did every year at the beginning of the tourist season, Louisa had hung the sign on the brick gatepost beside their wrought-iron gate. KINDLY ADMIRE THE GARDEN FROM THE STREET, green words painted on gray slate, the letters twined with flowering jasmine to sweeten the message: Stay on your side of the wall, please, and we will stay on ours. She'd hung the sign, picked up the hose, and was watering the ferns that lined the brick walk that curved through their yard when she'd heard the sound of the first horse's hooves and carriage wheels in the street in front of her house, and just at that moment, the question had arrived, so that always after that day, it was as if the question had pulled up in the carriage with the first tourists of the season.

From there, the question had branched. What was her mother looking for, telling her Mamie story to anyone who would stand still long enough to listen? And why, out of all the stories she could have told about Mamie's life with their family, did she choose the one about the Cooper River bridge? As Mamie had moved through their lives, they had known her by the names of her work and its outcomes. She was the girl with the quick broom and she was the sound of pots and pans in the kitchen early in the morning, the hymns that rose above the vacuum cleaner's roar; she was the smell of cinnamon rolls, sweet hair pomade, and bacon, the faint crackle of a starched and ironed blouse, the stuffy apartment they'd made for her in their old kitchen house, where she lived with her pictures of Jesus, the gas space heater blazing, even in midsummer, because she was always cold or afraid of getting cold, touching off a flare-up of misery in her knees.

She was also the sum of her useful parts. For close to eighty years, one Hilliard or another had totaled her. "A good pair of black hands," Louisa's mother had called her. "The laundress and housekeeper and cook." Finally, when the useful part of her life was done, she became "the family retainer," who lived out her days on their property. How old was Mamie? No one knew. No white person anyway. "They destroyed my dates," was all Mamie would say if you asked her, then set her jaw as if she'd clamped a plug of words between her back teeth. Prodded, she would add, "I be just born, time of the shake." Other stories would follow then: a garbled account of dates written in a family Bible, a fire that only she remembered, a slave ancestor who'd run away and whom Mamie sometimes confused with Maum Harriette, her own grandmother, who'd never left Edisto Island. But at least one date in that knotty mess was fixed by something other than an old colored woman's memory: the shake, the earthquake of 1886.

"Our little historian," her mother had begun to call Louisa after her daughter graduated from Converse College in 1945, moved back home, and developed an interest in family papers and history. She was still calling her that in 1989, when she was ninety and her daughter was sixty-five and the job of collecting, sorting, and donating the family archive was almost done. The Hilliards were wordy people, and they'd recorded their lives in blanket books and ledgers, in letters and journals and sketches — in Louisa's opinion, they'd never thrown away a piece of paper with a word written on it — and now these papers and books and drawings were stored down in the vaults of the Fireproof Building, safe from acids, moisture, oils, light, or fire.

Sometimes Louisa imagined her life as finished history, too, her own set of papers and memorabilia, safe in their archival boxes. Home and Family (55 items). Love (1 item). Needlework (12 items). Civic Accomplishment (25 items). Duties and Joys (175 items). Contains typescripts of seventy-five class outlines from Sunday school classes taught by Miss Louisa Hilliard Marion at St. Philip's Episcopal Church, 1959–1970. Includes "The Mustard Seed and the Mountain," "The Fearful Disciples," "Quieting the Waves," "The Miracles of Jesus," "The Woman at the Well," "Psalm 143: My Heart Within Me Is Desolate—and Beyond." She was no longer curious about missing family Bibles or the fires that had blazed in Mamie's memory. She was finished with curiosity, the way she was finished with so many things. Something in her had closed; she'd felt it shut. When? Ten, fifteen years earlier? Where does it begin, the feeling that your life is finished? Slowly, the way single stitches build a design; slowly, the way family papers are sorted and filed away. The way a life turns in one direction, leaves another, and only later, looking back, do you see the way it has gone. But now there was the Mamie question, and under it, a prickling restlessness and curiosity. There was something uncomfortable about this curiosity; it was like an itch under the skin, down in the nerve endings, too deep to scratch, or a foot that's gone to sleep coming back to life, bristling with pins and needles.

Out in the street, the tour guide pulled the carriage horse to a stop and draped the reins loosely over one hand. A college boy, she guessed, like the ones she used to train. He wore a gray Confederate army cap on his head and a fringed red sash tied around his waist. The carriage horse, a muscular chestnut Belgian with a bright blond mane and tail, dozed with one back hoof cocked on the pavement. Then she heard a familiar voice, a woman's voice, begin to speak and she ducked down and looked out through a section of open work in the brick wall to see Ann Simmons Culp, her goddaughter and the oldest daughter of her best friend, Susan Simmons, standing in the front of the carriage. She wore a straw hat with a wide green ribbon for a band and a linen dress the same green as the hatband. As Louisa watched, Ann Culp began to speak:

The Hilliard house, Ann said, was one of the oldest examples of a typical Charleston double house still standing. Built long instead of wide and set gable end to the street, with piazzas up and down to catch the prevailing winds and a garden tucked behind an old brick wall, its architecture was West Indian. Specifically, its influences could be traced to Barbados, from which string of Windward Isles many of the early planters made their way to the Colonial city of Charleston, Isaac Hilliard among them. Louisa flinched at her goddaughter's accent, the sprawl of vowels. *Pay-ant the bo-at*, indeed. She was laying it on thick for the tourists. Oh, Ann, Ann, Ann. If Louisa were still training tour guides she would have put a stop to that accent, which was this city's, but exaggerated into parody. Louisa was known for the rigor of her history lessons, her refusal to accept less than sober accuracy with facts. Now there was carelessness everywhere, a casual shrug of an attitude to be endured with patient resignation, like so much of life. Now it was entertainment they were after, a pageant, a show. Her goddaughter, it seemed, had caught this local virus; she was feverish with it now.

"Please note the ornate ironwork of the gate," Ann said, "handmade by local artisans, and the *chevaux de frise*, a bristle of iron spikes set along the top of the brick wall as protection against the pirates who once roamed and pillaged through these streets." Pirates, Louisa had noticed, were a recent favorite theme. Anything racy or salacious that could be accented with a wink and a nudge. There were tours of the State Street houses that had once been pirate brothels and taverns. Once she'd passed Ann in the street, leading a group of tourists on a hunt for Stede Bonnet's grave. That famous pirate had been hung and buried in a marsh that had long since been filled in and paved over; it was said that his bones lay under White Point Gardens on the Battery.

"Notice the bricks of which the house and its wall were constructed," Ann went on. "They were fired in the brickyard at Fairview, the Hilliard family's plantation out on the Edisto River.

"Now the Hilliard family," she said, "as was the custom with wealthy rice planters of their day, owned this house in town and the plantation house at Fairview, between which residences they divided their time. In late winter, they came into Charleston for the balls and races of the social season, then left for the plantation in time to oversee the planting of the rice crop in the spring. During the summer, the sickly season, they lived in town, or on the beaches, or in the up-country, then journeyed back to the plantations for the fall harvest and stayed there through Christmas."

Yes, yes, almost done. And one Hilliard descendant—the last of the line—still living here; she would say that soon. Even though Louisa was a Marion, her father's name and fine in its own way, with Francis Marion, the "Swamp Fox" of the Revolution, among the ancestors, they'd always lived here in the Hilliard house and she and her mother had thought of themselves as Hilliards first. Matriarchal as the Navajo. She pressed the black dirt of her yard with the toe of one bone pump, brushed a mosquito off her cheek. She had so much to do: sit with her mother, then off to the Ladies Altar Guild meeting and back to meet the plumber at one o'clock about the dripping faucet in the upstairs bathroom, then out again to read to her second graders in the elementary school over near the projects. Without her mother to care for, her days were busier than ever, full of duties. The squares of her kitchen calendar stacked with lists and appointments. "Keeping busy," she would say crisply when one of her friends squeezed her hand and asked how she was getting along without her mother.

Now Ann had reached the part of the story where the plantation-made bricks were carried on flats along the river and through the smaller creeks to the Charleston wharves. She told how Hilliard labor had unloaded the bricks from the boats and loaded them onto carts and trundled them from the wharves over to this house on Church Street, which was a main thoroughfare of the early city. She described how Hilliard labor had built the house and hung the piazzas and walled the yard, all of this building and digging and hanging begun in the year 1741 after a fire destroyed the original wooden house built on this site in 1725, making it one of the oldest dwellings in the city to be continuously occupied by the same family. Then she paused to let the date sink in, and above her, the sky was a light, clear blue and over the carriage hung a seagull, making no headway against the breeze blowing inland from the harbor. "Once," Ann said, "households such as this one were small compounds: main house, stable, kitchen house, and slave quarters, one big family sheltering within these fine brick walls. This is one of the few houses in the old city with an original kitchen house still standing. Typically, the kitchen house is a square brick structure divided into two rooms—laundry room and kitchen—with a central fireplace that heated both rooms. Such houses are historically significant, but as this is a private residence, unfortunately, we cannot go in. However, if you'd like to take a peek . . ." Then there were faces looking over the top of the wall. Louisa stepped back into the shade of the tea olive tree and stood very still.

Finally, it was over. She heard the creak of springs as Ann settled back into the carriage seat; then the boy in the Confederate cap clucked to the horse and the carriage moved on. Soon, Ann's bright voice trailed away and what was left was a drift of horse smell in the warm air and a pile of golden droppings in the street. Soon, she knew, the small, white city truck would drive down Church Street and stop beside the pile. Men in white coveralls would jump out and scoop up the horse droppings and then the truck would drive away, round and round like that all day, following the carriages. Closing the iron gate behind her, Louisa stepped carefully over the slate flagstone sidewalk in front of this house that Hilliards had built, where Hilliards had lived forever.

That spring, she was sixty-five; she'd given up pretending to less. She avoided Chalmers Street now, paved with old ballast stones from the sailing ships, treacherous as a rocky streambed. Crossing the uneven flagstone sidewalk in front of her house, she was conscious of her ankles, her brittle spine and hips. Sometimes at night, she imagined the calcium sifting out of her skeleton, as though her body were dissolving, bone by bone. Soon, she thought, she would be rounded and soft, like the bricks of this house or a tabby foundation, after a few centuries out in the weather.

Still, thanks to a daily dose of estrogen, to willpower and to upbringing, she kept her back straight as she walked up Church Street, a tall woman with a wide, quiet face, a sweep of white hair, held back with two silver barrettes, a raw silk shirtwaist dress, teal, coordinated with a scarf swirled with teal, fuchsia, and gold. Not many of her friends walked anymore, and those who did carried pepper spray in little cases on their key rings, which they clutched as they moved warily along. But she had promised herself and lectured them: She would not give in to fear. It was her city, too, and she would live there as if she believed that. She was forever telling people that the city had been laid out for walking, and so she was going to walk. That spring, her face and eyes were clear; she was still fine in vein, bone, and tendon: something wind-driven, prowlike, swift about her. She carried a soft tapestry bag full of sewing supplies and she walked with her head held high and quiet on a long neck, enjoying the subtle prickle of salt air on her face, the smells from the gardens she passed, the sound of trickling water, the cries of gulls, a perfect spring day.

At Market Street, she turned and walked toward East Bay Street and the harbor. Passing the market, she spoke to the vendors by name as they set out their buckets of flowers and unshuttered their stalls. The Customs House came into sight, like a temple, she thought, a temple on its own hill of high steps, with a deep columned porch at the top. On East Bay Street, the door to the ship's chandler's shop stood open and she inhaled the oily, hay field smell of rope that drifted from the narrow door. Inside, she knew, there were spools of thick anchor cable, charts for all the local rivers.

She looked up the tall green side of a freighter in the harbor to the flag that flew above its bridge: a red cross on a white field. She studied this one through the pair of small folding binoculars she carried in her bag for such sightings, then pulled out a leather-covered binder and added another check mark in a line of them beside the flag's country: Denmark. And right there, it happened, a moment so rooted in place and time, a historical marker could have been placed there. *On this spot in 1989, Louisa Hilliard Marion experienced a regret so sharp, it rocked her and she put her hand to her heart to steady herself.*

It was a particular kind of regret that had filled her—as though something inside had been suddenly exposed to bright, painful light—and it happened when she saw a ship's flag or sometimes when she studied the list of flags she'd kept in the same notebook for thirty years and saw how neatly and carefully she'd printed her list, in large letters that a child could read. And there it was. Her list was something a person shows to children, wealth one hoards to give to them. The flags of almost sixty countries! Of the world, in and out of the port of Charleston! Look, there's the flag of Guinea-Bissau. Where is Guinea-Bissau? a child asks, and you're off to the atlas, to the library. You people the world. You call in Shakespeare to speak of discovery. "O brave new world / That has such people in 't." To fly such flags. Every time she wrote down a flag, the bones of her hands felt lighter, as if they remembered the time when the future had peopled itself with her children and her hopes hadn't been just a young woman's gauzy dreams. When she'd started her list, there had been an actual man, a possible future. Now, noticing flags and writing them down was a habit, a routine, and that a habit, a simple daily act, should cause such complicated pain was a betrayal, a kind of mystery that had caused her to give up on curiosity in the first place. But here it was again; *it happened on this spot*, and then she walked away from it.

At the nursing home, Louisa tiptoed up the stairs and down the hall until she came to her mother's room. "Good morning, Mother," she sang as she stepped through the door.

Her mother turned her head. This being Friday, her wheel-chair faced the window and the bridges over the Cooper River. The strong sunlight came through her hair; it looked like mist rising from her head. "Mamie?" she said. A bad sign, middle-of-the-week confusion seeping into the week's end.

"It's Louisa, Mother. Here we are," she said, as she always said, as though they'd arrived together at some destination. Her mother shook her head and sighed, disappointed as ever, but Louisa was used to this. Her mother hadn't forgiven her for putting her here, and she never would. "Well, I'm going to kiss you anyway," Louisa said, aiming for the small pink patch of bare scalp on the crown of her mother's head. Kissing the bald spot, Louisa breathed in, felt her shoulders drop in relief. Baby powder and lotion; she hadn't wet or soiled herself yet. There would be no struggle about that this morning, though many fights had begun with Louisa's reaching down the back of her mother's gown, running a finger into her diaper the way you do with a baby, finding her mother wet and calling an aide to change her. She could sit all morning in a wet diaper, smile and nod, hold out her hand to visitors, and believe that she was still the tiny cut-crystal woman flashing fire, whose big, doting husband had lived to dress her in cashmere and drape her with pearls. Her body would never convince her that she was anything less than she'd ever been.

Louisa pulled a chair close to the wheelchair and lifted her project out of her bag — Pax and the Paschal Lamb — that she was stitching on the linen banner that would hang beside the altar in St. Philip's Church on Easter Sunday morning. Every year since she'd come back to Charleston after college she'd sewed new banners for the church, one at Christmas, another at Easter. She perched her glasses halfway down her nose, smoothed the chain that held them. Mother glanced at the cloth, humming high in her throat, and turned back to the window. "Today is the Friday before Palm Sunday, Mother," Louisa said. "Easter is almost here. The first tour came by this morning." Her mother sighed and shook her head, while Louisa crossed her ankles, straightened her back, smoothed her face. Today, she would practice forbearance. The road to the quiet soul, as she'd told her Sunday school class, lies through the disciplined practice of virtue. And the quieting of the soul is one of life's only real accomplishments. If she had kept a list—"Virtues Mastered"—she could have written *acceptance* there.

Soon the bundle of pink quilted satin with a failing heart and lungs inside, and a brain misted over and full of holes where white light burned and silence whistled, this bundle that was her mother began to stir. She had room in her and breath enough, but just enough, to tell her story. "The Cooper River bridge was the bridge we had to cross, you see . . ." she said, pointing at the bridge outside the window. Dutifully, Louisa looked, too, pushed her needle through the linen, knotted the last of the Lamb's woolly fur, then threaded her needle with green thread and began to stitch the grass under his feet. As she sewed, she relaxed into the rhythm of the backstitch with which she made the grass. The needle drawn up a bit ahead of the last stitch, leaving a gap, then the thread carried back over the gap to close it and the needle brought up through the cloth ahead of that stitch. And so on and on, a slow progress made by reaching back and pulling forward.

Maybe, Louisa thought, the old soul (the words made her see something tarnished and heavy, smooth and nearly round, like an old iron egg) told the story of Mamie and the bridge because it was the only story she remembered that could still carry her out and over the water, away from her present life. Or maybe she was simply drifting. Once, browsing through newspapers in the reading room of the Charleston Library Society in search of a mention of some nineteenth-century Hilliard, she'd come across this advertisement in a copy of the *Charleston City Gazette* published in the summer of 1820. "$10 Reward. Drifted from Haddrill's Point, a CANOE, painted red or a bright Spanish brown, branded with my name in several places, has locks for 6 oars." That is how she thought of her mother's mind: a ninety-year-old bright Spanish brown canoe of a mind, drifting here, drifting there, stranded on an oyster bank when the tide was low, then lifted off again by the rising tide, drawn by the tides and currents always back toward Mamie and the Cooper River bridge.

"The Cooper River bridge was the bridge we had to cross, you see, to get from the Charleston peninsula over to our beach house on Sullivan's Island. We spent our summers there, away from the city's heat," she confided to Louisa with a flash of the old haughtiness, as if her daughter were another tourist, a stranger, a member of the audience at one of her talks on Charleston history, manners, and customs. In the twenties, Louisa's mother had given dramatic readings—performances, really, from a book written by her husband's mother: *Life in Old Charleston*, by Mrs. Arthur Marion, A Lady of That City. The book had been published locally and reprinted three times, and it was full of belles and beaux, jolly Negresses, outrage at some piece of eighteenth-century gossip about Francis Marion, the "Swamp Fox." Sometimes, even now, Louisa felt that her mother was acting out scenes from this book when she talked.

Now, the Cooper River bridge was not always the wide highway of a bridge it is today: A chunk of Interstate 26 lofted over the river, with reversible lanes and walls to keep you from looking down or sailing off the edges. Crossing the new bridge, you might as well be flying over the river in an armchair. The old bridge, however, which still stands beside the new bridge and carries traffic one way into the city from the north, was once the only bridge, coming or going. A narrow two-lane steel-girder bridge with rusty open railings (like some rickety roller coaster at a county fair) through which you could look down onto the wings of gulls and onto barges, sailboats, tankers, and, sometimes, the periscope of a sub-marine heading downriver from the navy base toward the harbor and the open ocean beyond. That was the bridge in her mother's story, the bridge that Mamie was required to cross with their family every summer on the way to Sullivan's Island.

"Well, old Mamie had an absolute and utter terror of that bridge," Mother said. She was launched now, Louisa saw; there would be no turning back. What amazed Louisa (and on her own bad days made her want to jump up and scream, "Get to the point, for God's sake, Mother") was how the story never varied from telling to telling by one detail, pause, or inflection; how it seemed to be asking a question, by which construction a person might as-sume that the story had an answer, a point, a destination. How, though it traveled in that direction, it never seemed to arrive.

She pushed her needle harder through the stiff linen, relaxed her mouth. Pressed tight that way, it turned her face to stone, and she did not want to become a woman whose face announced its disappointments to the world. "Something about being high up in the air like that, crossing water, scared her so much that when I told her it was time to get ready to go to the beach, those little bitty pigtails would practically stand straight out from her head, and she'd drop to her knees right there on the kitchen floor and start wringing her hands. 'Lord, Missis,' she'd wail. 'Lord God. Leave I back behind on solid earth. I too old. Be crossing that water soon enough.' I'd tell her I'd carry her petition to my husband, but I knew it wouldn't do any good. He never would put up with non-sense from the colored. 'She'll ride with us, as usual,' he always said. 'I'm not going to inconvenience my family to accommodate Mamie's superstitions.'"

Then she stopped, as if the story were done, folded her hands and stared out the window.

Louisa rested her sewing on her lap and looked out at the bridges, too. What *was* this story her mother was trying to tell?

Was it perhaps a story of injustice, historic and ongoing? The thought made her smile. In the 1960s, when the concept of injustice had finally forced its way into their world, her mother had been outraged. "Injustice?" Mother would say, revolted by the taste of the word. She came from the generation whose childhoods had touched the outer rim of the time in which conclusions about race still felt like certainties. "What injustice? When was Mamie or any of her kin ever mistreated by a member of this family?" In her mother's eyes, the only possible injustice was personal, an individual act of cruelty or neglect. Get her started on the subject of injustice and you'd get a long and vehement tour through history. Now, though the old woman watched the bridge and did not speak, Louisa heard her mother's voice leading the tour again.

"The Hilliards were good masters, kind masters, who'd seldom found it necessary to raise the whip to their people, and so, after they were freed, their slaves had stayed with them at Fairview or here in Charleston. Cuffy and Nancy, Scipio, Daniel and Abby, Maum Harriette, Mamie's grandmother. My own mother was born there and cared for by Mamie's mother, under that system of mutual care and affection and an acknowledgment of God-given differences that has peacefully carried the races in South Carolina through three centuries together.

"Now, the Hilliards always cared for their own. Take the time that Mamie's husband, old King Jones, got his boat confiscated by the Harbor Authority for blocking a freighter." He'd fished with the Mosquito Fleet, Negro fishermen in boats as frail as pods, sailing out past the bar, out of sight of land. He'd kept them in good fish as long as he lived. *"Who went to court and got his boat back? My husband, of course, with a word to the judge in chambers.*

"Mamie's granddaughter, Evelyn, her daughter's girl, grew up in our yard, and after the daughter died, we allowed Evelyn to stay. We didn't have to do that, or let Mamie live out her own life in our

kitchen house, rent-free; free, for that matter, of most obligations and troubles. We could have turned her out any time, but did we? We did not. And when Evelyn graduated from South Carolina State, who drove Mamie up to her granddaughter's graduation?"

"I did," Louisa answered her mother's voice that was speaking inside her head. "And I followed the hearse carrying Mamie's body to Edisto Island, and sat through the service in that stifling little church and stood beside Mamie's grave."

"So who was loyal to whom? Please answer me that."

Louisa listened, but this time, no answer came. Round and round the stories went, round and round like miraculous wheels that rolled through time and never warped or splintered as they rolled.

When the civil rights movement came and the hospital workers went on strike, Louisa remembered, demonstrators had lined King Street, singing and chanting, holding their signs: FREEDOM NOW. WE SHALL NOT BE MOVED. Her mother had been personally hurt and affronted that blacks should have seen themselves injured by families they'd been part of for so long. Once, in a bitter mood about the city's handling of the protests, after his fifth trip to the cut-crystal decanter of port on the dining room sideboard, Louisa's brother, Hugh, had said, "Keep Mother away from the windows, Louisa. She's liable to ask Martin Luther King if he's looking for yard work." She might have, too. Their mother was as impervious to the idea of injustice as a turtle latched in its shell. And through it all, Mamie had gone right on living in their kitchen house, watering her little patch of four-o'clocks, raising her sunflowers into enormous bowing gods, hoarding crusts of bread to feed to the pigeons.

Louisa had reached her own conclusions about the race question. She'd listened, she'd thought it over and prayed about it in church, and she'd never told anyone what she thought. "Keeping your own counsel," her lawyer father had called this. He lived by

it and he recommended it as a way of life. If anyone had asked—
and they hadn't; not once had anyone solicited Louisa's opinion
on race—she would have said that discrimination was wrong, but
the past was the past. It was over, done and finished; you couldn't
change it any more than you could change human nature, the
habits of centuries, or the facts of native ability and intelligence.
There were basic human rights that should be granted to
everyone, the right to vote and to receive a decent education,
among them. In the fifties, she'd written checks on her private
bank account and sent them to Septima Clark's citizenship
schools. In the sixties, she'd written letters to the editor of the
Charleston Courier calling for calm and reason, decency and justice, and signed them "A native citizen."

She was proud of the way her city had yielded to integration
and of its steady progress. Now there was a black police chief,
Reuben Greenberg. A black Jew with advanced degrees from
Berkeley, no less! A portrait of the Reverend Jenkins, who'd
founded the Negro orphanage, hung now in the city council
chambers among the Pinckneys, signers of the Declaration of In-
dependence and every important document since. But integration hadn't worked. The schools were a shambles and more
segregated now than ever: When the black children arrived, the
white children left. The housing projects were swamped with
drugs. Given the choice, the races preferred to live separately.
The older black people said so, too. Mamie herself had said so.
During Jim Crow days, bad as they'd been, the community had
been more solid, more resolute, the people more committed to
taking care of one another. Now, by law, anyone could live anywhere. And the races still lived apart, as both preferred.

Her mother was talking again. "Mamie sat in the back between
you and Hugh. As soon as we started up the bridge, she'd grab
the door handle with one hand and the rope across the back of

the front seat with the other. Remember that big black sixteen-cylinder Buick we owned, your father's pride and joy? Those little ropes across the backs of the seats? Up we'd go onto the bridge, Mamie hanging on to that rope for dear life, with her eyes squeezed shut, praying, 'Sweet Jesus. Lord have mercy. Great God! Do, Jesus, Great King.' I think she used up every name they have for their God before we'd gotten over the first span. She'd start off low, grumbling and muttering to herself—she knew your father didn't want to listen to her carry on—but before we'd reached the top of the first span, she'd practically be shouting. Of course, I'd see what was coming by the way your father scowled into the rearview mirror, and then all of a sudden, '*Mamie,*' he would say, so quietly, *I* almost couldn't hear him, and I was sitting beside him in the front seat, but Mamie would jerk straight up like he'd yanked her. 'Do I need to remind you that you are riding in my family car, you are not at some camp meeting out in the Congaree Swamp?'

"'No, suh,' she'd say, 'sure don't,' and all the while she'd be studying the floor with her old bottom lip poked out about a mile. Mamie was light-skinned. 'High yellow,' we called those kind, much lighter than your blue-black Negro, with more refined features and a few freckles across her nose and cheeks. She had light brown eyes, almost golden. But she sure prayed like an African. Well, after your father spoke to her, she'd simmer down and mumble her prayers to herself until we were safely across the bridge and down into Mt. Pleasant. Old Mamie. Didn't she make the best biscuits?"

And right there, her mother stopped, as she always stopped, as though the thread had all run off that spool. She nodded—*there*—smoothed the skirt of her bathrobe over her knees and stared out at the bridges until her eyes began to droop. This was Louisa's signal that the story and the visit were done. Mother would not talk again that day. It was time for Louisa to put away the linen banner—three folds and a skimming spank to smooth it—and tuck it in her bag along with her embroidery floss and the small silver scissors, with handles shaped like the curved necks and outstretched heads of flying cranes, that had once belonged to Eliza Hilliard, her ancestor. She was another spinster seamstress, author of the Hilliard christening gown, which was famous among textile archivists throughout the South for its French knots and drawn thread work, the precise delicacy of its joining stitches. Every Hilliard baby from Eliza's time forward had been baptized in it and now the gown was permanently housed on a pedestal inside a tall glass cube in the Low Country room in the Charleston Museum, together with photographs of the Hilliard babies, each dressed in the gown on the day of his baptism.

Now it was time to get her mother into bed, to draw the covers up around her neck, kiss the pink scalp, and tiptoe out of the room, closing the door behind her. Time for a word to the help: Please see that her diaper gets checked three times a day. She'll tell you she's not wet when she is. Time to walk out into the nursing home parking lot, into the smells of fish and oil and sun on water, and to remember so suddenly that it frightened her, how the water had looked from the top of the highest span of the old Cooper River bridge: like a floor, hard and glittering, swept with light.

However, it was not her mother's drifting Spanish brown canoe of a mind that had carried her to the nursing home; it was her body, a frailer boat. One night in early January, Louisa had waked to her mother's call. Though her voice had thinned, it was still sharp as a needle, and like a needle, it had pierced Louisa's sleep. "Louisa, Louisa, I need to tee-tee."

Sleep-clogged, stiff, Louisa had dragged herself out of her canopied bed. In the bedroom next to hers, she'd found her mother propped on pillows on the chintz-covered chaise longue where she slept sitting up in order to ease her breathing. Oxygen tubes ran up her nose; a canister of oxygen on wheels sat at her side like a loyal spaniel in a portrait.

"Hello, monkey," Louisa said under her breath. She meant no disrespect when she thought of her mother as a monkey. At ninety, that's what the old woman had become. A little withered monkey paw and a little monkey head with a busy, whiskery mouth and small bright eyes. Sometimes that winter, watching her mother nibble toast, watching her lips purse, grope for the rim of the coffee cup, and delicately suck the hot liquid in, an act that whittled her cheekbones to blades and outlined a skull beneath the mottled skin, Louisa had decided that to call her mother a monkey (in private, of course, only to herself) was simply to state a fact, and it was with facts that Louisa had made her life's most enduring relationships. Still, she was amazed at herself for looking at her mother this way. There was something primitive and cruel about it, but something affectionate and protective as well. As if calling her that were a way of sidling up to oblivion, tickling it under the chin: *Hello, death, you funny little monkey.*

As her mother's body had shrunk, her stubbornness, her imperial selfishness (this much resentment Louisa would allow herself) had ballooned. Even when she could no longer walk, she wouldn't agree to a wheelchair or allow Louisa to hire someone to help them after Mamie died. Absolutely not. No. Whatever she needed, Louisa could get for her. If the silver tip of Mother's cane marred the floors, Louisa would arrange for the floors to be refinished. Once a week, Louisa helped her down the stairs for a tour of her first-floor rooms and kitchen. Twenty minutes down and another twenty back up, with a long breather on the landing for both of them. Her mother's demands and Louisa's sacrifices were a family tradition. Juliana Hilliard (Elizabeth's mother) had cared for *her* mother in this house, setting up the sickbed in the front sitting room (while her husband withered away in a bedroom upstairs, attended by a nurse); Elizabeth had nursed Juliana through her last illness; now Louisa would care for Elizabeth. In that way, the generations would hold and a bright vein of loyalty would run through dark and crumbling time.

The night of the bathroom call, Louisa knelt and forced her mother's feet into the only bedroom slippers that would fit her: size-ten mustard-colored corduroy loafers from Woolworth's, the kind that Mother had never allowed Mamie to wear around the house because they slapped against her heels with such a slovenly sound. Looking at her swollen feet in the ugly slippers, her mother often wept. Heart, lungs, kidneys: They were all breaking down. At her mother's last appointment, the doctor had spoken plainly. "If we're lucky," he said to Louisa as her mother sat in the waiting room while he wrote a prescription for a stronger diuretic, "her heart will give out before her lungs and she will not drown. That is a terrifying death, Miss Louisa, and we do not wish it for your mother." He could talk that way; he'd known them all their lives, had delivered Louisa and then Hugh in their mother's bedroom, had been the first one called when Hugh senior had collapsed on Broad Street. He knew them so well, he included himself in those who would be relieved by death's mercy.

Hoisting her mother, Louisa said "Upsie-daisie," just to hear the cheerful buoyancy of those words rising through the dark. Each time Louisa lifted her, her mother felt lighter, so light that Louisa imagined air inside her bones instead of marrow. Louisa rolled the oxygen tank with one hand, kept the other arm around her mother's waist while her mother held on to her with both arms around her neck. Together, they moved toward the bathroom at the far end of the hall. Louisa felt her mother's damp armpits and clammy neck; she heard her mother's breath whistle past her ear. Her mother leaned on her; she was light but complicated; she clung to Louisa like a burr, stuck to her in many places. "Where are we going now, dear heart?" she asked, turning her face up to her daughter's.

"To the bathroom, Mother." Unless we fall, Louisa thought, and felt the beginning of a panicky tightening in her lungs.

"Well, all right," her mother said, brightly, patting Louisa's arm, *humoring* her in the old maddening way. Caring for her mother, Louisa had come to believe that of all the mysteries that moved the world, this was one of the deepest. You'd think that as a person moved closer to death, the maddening shell of a personality inside which they'd rattled all their lives would crack and fall open, letting a brighter, more spacious spirit unfold. Instead, as the body failed, the shell grew brighter and harder, while the spirit stayed as folded and elusive as ever.

But they didn't collapse in the hall. They made it all the way to the bathroom, and then, as she tried to ease her mother down onto the toilet seat, holding her around the waist with one arm and maneuvering the oxygen tank while Mother grappled with her underpants, Louisa's feet slipped on the throw rug in front of the toilet and they both went down. When Louisa couldn't get her up, and her mother could no longer hold back her water, Elizabeth Hilliard Marion had peed on the bathroom floor in the house where the Hilliards had traveled their high or low, prolonged or shortened arcs from birth to death for more than two centuries. When her mother was done, Louisa picked up the wet towels and dropped them down the laundry chute in the bathroom closet. But when she tried to lift her mother, the old woman went limp and sagged back onto the floor, and at that moment it seemed to Louisa that something had been punctured in her, the strength all drained out. "Help me, Mother," she said, but her mother looked at her in helpless confusion, then frowned. "Louisa," she said, "there is perspiration on your upper lip."

She propped her mother against the toilet and held her small, frightened face between her hands. "I'll be right back," she said slowly. "Don't you move." From the phone in the upstairs hall, she called 911. "My mother has fallen in the bathroom," she said, "and I can't get her up."

Back in the bathroom again, she sat down on the floor, leaned against the toilet, and held her mother, waiting. And as her mother dozed in her arms, she knew that she'd crossed from the end of one part of her life into the beginning of another. Sitting on the bathroom floor, she knew that she would date some darkening and acceleration of time from this night when she'd laid three of their thick monogrammed towels on the floor, then stepped out of the room and stood in the hall with her hand on the heavy glass doorknob while her mother wet the towels. Before that night, she'd hadn't thought of herself as old. Before that night, in cold rainy weather, her knuckles swelled and ached. On winter mornings, her hips felt stiff. Some days the smell of her pillow—like gray iron—startled her. Or the smell that rose from her mouth when she flossed her teeth, that carried her back to her grandmother and what had been on her breath. How foreign and alarming it had seemed then, how familiar now. There were the migrating patches of numbness and constriction, the fine lines around her mouth, into which her lipstick spread and climbed. The caution on uneven pavement. Signs of aging, true, but never overwhelming, never all at once.

That night on the bathroom floor, though, she felt old all over, as though age had swamped her, or she were curing in it, like the nineteenth-century Hilliard Madeira and peach brandy still curing in barrels down in the cellar. Both of them, herself and the liquor, steeped in time, which caused the collapse of one and deepened the flavor and doubled, then tripled the value of the other. They'd been offered one thousand dollars each for those barrels. And she wept for the two old women they'd become, two old women with their stains and flows. Two old women who could no longer keep up with the laundry, and the younger, who was herself, unable to help the older, who was her mother, up from the bathroom floor or to pull her nightgown out from under her body and cover the underpants and withered thighs and ugly slippers that no stranger should have seen. That was the night that Louisa laid her cheek down on her mother's head and whispered, "Mother, don't you think it's time to move on?"

Later, she wondered if her mother had heard her that night. It was January when she'd put her in the home; August when the owner called in the middle of the night. "Miss Marion," she said, "I'm sorry, but I must tell you that your mother has passed away." Even while the woman talked—fifteen minutes ago, she said, peacefully, in her sleep—Louisa felt restless. Hugh needed to know that their mother had died, and she was the oldest; she must make the call. Besides, the news of her mother's death had gone into her and started growing, pushing everything else out, until there was a spinning hollow place inside, and she was in danger of dropping into that place without another soul to know it with her. "I'll be right there," she said, "but first I must call my brother."

She switched on the gooseneck lamp on the telephone table in the hall and took her address book out of the drawer, thumbed through the book, looking for Hugh's page, while fear rose inside her, hissing softly like Mother's oxygen. She had to find his number before the fear filled her and she was lost in it. This terrified Louisa over every other terror—to be lost, to look and not to recognize, to lose her bearings. To walk out into the city as in the vague terror of a dream in which everything is suddenly foreign, a menacing riddle that must be solved, and quickly, the strangeness made familiar again in order to save yourself from harm. By the light of the small lamp, she found her brother's page. "HUGH," she'd printed in block letters across the top. His addresses, entered and crossed out, filled the entire page. The apartment on King Street that he'd moved into after he dropped out of law school at the University of South Carolina. The house on the marsh on Isle of Palms where he'd lived one summer while he rented floats to swimmers from a shack on the beach. The apartment near the Navy Yard in North Charleston where it was never quite clear what he did.

When the state law-enforcement agents set out to stop the drug smuggling along that part of the coast, they'd gone to the real estate agencies in Charleston that sold houses in the historic district and collected the names of people who'd made large cash down payments. They did the same at marinas and luxury car dealerships. Hugh's name came to them from the Mercedes-Benz dealership in North Charleston, but they never did catch up with him; he moved too fast.

Then she was fully awake and Hugh was dead, as he'd been for twenty years. She hung up the phone, closed the address book and put it back in the drawer, turned off the lamp, and, with one hand on the wall, found her way back to her room. There was no one, no one she wanted to call. Her oldest friend, Susan, was off visiting one of her daughters in Richmond, and the thought of the concern she'd get from her church friends, the fluttery, hovering kind that brushed you like moth's wings, made it hard to breathe. The room was hot and stifling, as if the heat were piled in it layer on top of soft, smothering layer. No one to blame but herself now, she thought, and almost laughed, still dutifully living by her mother's rule that the air-conditioning units in the upstairs bedrooms must be turned off promptly at eight o'clock, the windows opened even if the heat was so thick that, as on this night, it came through the screens like fog through a sieve.

She closed her window, twisted the knob on the air conditioner to High Cool, and sat down on the bed in front of the cold stream of air. Since childhood, she'd plaited her hair into a single small pigtail before going to bed, and now she brushed the bristly end of the familiar braid against her cheek and swung her feet and rocked a little, getting ready. The dark from the hall seemed to flow into the room. It smelled of old wood and wet air, something green and moldy trailing through it. The smell of ghosts, Mamie always said. At night she wouldn't go up into that hall where the ghosts crowded and jostled one another. "Black and white, all jam up together," was how Mamie described what happened in the hall at night. Once, Mamie said, a plat eye in the shape of a cat had jumped her in the hall and ridden on her back all the way down the stairs and out into the yard, where it disappeared in a flash of fire. Louisa remembered being up in the hall with Mamie, the feel of Mamie's fingers plucking at her sleeve. "Walk over this side the hall, Miss," she'd say, and Louisa would know that they were detouring around one of her ancestors, or Mamie's. You wouldn't want to disrespect a ghost, Mamie had warned; they might turn spiteful or vengeful. She'd find Mamie standing on the sidewalk in front of the house, broom in hand, staring up at the chimney. "They pouring out now, Miss," Mamie would say, meaning, Louisa knew, the ghosts, pouring out like smoke.

It happened quickly, the owner said, as she opened the front door and let Louisa in, steered her by the elbow toward the stairs. Three A.M. and the woman's hair was combed. She wore glasses, low-heeled pumps; she carried papers in her hand, as though she'd been at work for hours. Louisa was grateful for the woman's efficiency, for her kind, calm eyes and firm handshake. No bathrobe, no straggling hair or slack, bewildered face to show that death had surprised her. "I'm going to let you talk to Hannah, the aide who was on duty when your mother passed away," the woman said as she and Louisa climbed the stairs. A woman like herself, Louisa thought, the unmarried daughter of a family like her own, going about the work she'd found to do in this married world, placing her considerable energies at the service of others.

Walking down the hall toward her mother's room, Louisa caught herself listening. *Mamie?* It was quiet except for the sound of their feet on the carpet, the rustling of sheets, the groans and sighs of the sleepers in the other rooms. The full moon cast the shape of the window at the end of the hall ahead of them as they walked.

In her mother's room, the bedside lamp was turned low. She did not look at the bed, but at the woman who sat in a rocking chair beside the bed, humming to herself. She stood up and smiled when Louisa came in, smoothing down her uniform. Louisa saw a broad, kind face, a quick smile that showed a gold tooth, neat braids pinned across the top of her head.

"This is Mrs. Marion's daughter, Hannah," the owner said, and went out of the room, closing the door with a click as she went.

Hannah. Hannah. She had heard that name before. The last time Louisa had visited, she'd found her mother holding the woman's hand, a worn Bible open on the bed. "This is my good friend Hannah," she'd said. "Such a pretty name," she'd added as Hannah had turned to go, laying her cheek against the black woman's hand. "Come back to see me again soon, won't you?" That night, Louisa had sat up, wide awake and frightened in the dark by the thought that her mother would die soon; she was halfway gone already, changing from the woman she'd always been into this stranger who told a black woman she had a pretty name.

"She was a sweet, fine lady," Hannah said. "She didn't suffer, thank the Lord." She touched the dead woman's cheek. "Some just struggle and fight." She'd checked on Mother at midnight, then gone down the hall to look in on someone else, and when she'd come back at 12:45, Louisa's mother had died.

"So she didn't say anything?"

"Not as I am aware of." Hannah turned to go. "Sorry to hear your brother been passed," she said at the door.

"My brother? Yes, thank you." So Mother had told Hannah that story, too, the other one she couldn't stop telling. She made a mental note: Leave a check for Hannah. It was one of the true mysteries and miracles of life here, and a tribute to their way of life, that it had produced such kind, decent, upright black people, the most trustworthy people on earth. The older ones anyway. The younger ones would just as soon rob or kill you as look at you.

"Thank you, Hannah, for all you've done," Louisa said, and when the woman had gone, she sat down on the edge of the bed. Her mother lay on her side, with her eyes closed, her hands tucked between her knees. They'd disconnected the oxygen tubes from her nose and rolled the oxygen canister into a corner. On her mother's upper lip, Louisa saw the mark of the tape that had held the tubes in place. She licked her thumb and moved to scrub, then stopped. Let the undertaker clean those away, she thought; that was his job. Let him clean all the marks of life away. Now there was only silence in the room, silence and the sound of her own breathing, the small rustle of the sheets when she shifted her weight, the soft batting of a moth against the shade of the bed-side lamp.

Her mother's face looked peaceful. In fact, she was smiling the same dreamy smile that she'd smiled when the story was over and Mamie was safely back in their kitchen again, rolling out her bis-cuits. It occurred to Louisa that at the very moment of her death, her mother might have been dreaming of Mamie's biscuits. She could almost feel one herself, firm and warm in the hand, dissolv-ing like a buttery cloud when you bit into it. If that had been her mother's last memory, she was glad for it, a fierce gladness that brought tears to her eyes. It was comfort that her mother had been looking for, telling that story, she thought, comfort and consola-tion and certainty. And she hoped that the memory of Mamie and her biscuits had carried her out and set her down easy, wherever she'd landed.

Louisa felt she'd entered a world of silence and stillness that lapped out from the body on the bed and surrounded her. It was the stillness that she could not bend her mind around. She almost said, "Mother?" the way she used to do to wake her, but she smoothed back wisps of hair from the high widow's peak and kept still. Seeing that whatever life is it visits the body, then goes, taking nothing you could catch and store in a bottle, press or keep under glass. Taking nothing you could see or name and taking everything. And she remembered a darkened room stuffed with summer heat, wooden shutters latched over the windows, a black fan with a frayed cord that had pushed the heat aside for a moment every time it swung toward her, and herself sick with diphtheria on the canopied bed, the cool feel of her mother's fingers rubbing a hand cream that smelled like almonds on Louisa's lips. The last person who knew her before she knew herself, who could say, "When you were a baby . . ." and tell her a story about who she was before she knew what it meant to have a story, to be a self.

Through the window of her mother's room, Louisa saw the lights of the Cooper River bridges. She thought of Hugh driving north across the new bridge and onto Sullivan's Island. She thought about how he'd let himself into Waveland, their beach house; how he'd rummaged in drawers, drunk half a bottle of port, sat in every chair and lain on every bed. For weeks, the restless twist of his body had stayed in the white chenille bedspreads. She thought how he'd driven his dark blue Mercedes up onto the dunes in front of the house, until the tires sank in the sand, then shot himself in the head.

She sat beside her mother's bed till dawn, remembering these things, and when the first pink light came into the sky, she called the funeral home, then waited in the alley behind the house while they loaded her mother's body and drove away. When the hearse turned the corner, she felt fear open inside her, like something she'd fallen into. In the early-morning light, a few cars with their headlights on were crossing the Cooper River bridge, and she reached to claim the comfort of her mother's story. She remembered crossing the old bridge, all of them together in the car, lifted high over the water. She remembered Mamie's fears and prayers, her father's outburst, then the quiet, everyone safely put back where they belonged, while Mamie hummed low to herself and rocked, holding on to the velvet rope across the seat back with both hands.

She had come this far, many times, with her mother and they had laughed together at Mamie's old colored woman terrors, so much more primitive and obscure than their own. But now she was the only survivor of those who had lived that story. It was her story now and she was still traveling. Looking at the bridge, what she remembered was how that story had gone on. How her father had grown morose and philosophical after he'd silenced Mamie. Glancing down at the water, he'd tell them every time how water would feel hard as stone if you fell into it from that height. What she remembered was that her father had silenced Mamie, and it was still a long way to the water. And how that knowledge had mixed with the silence and become the silence and had ridden with them to the other side, grudging and sullen as one of Mamie's ghosts.

Box No. 15
Love (25 items)
Contains Miscellaneous Letters, Dance Cards,
Watercolors, Birding Lists, and a Story

"Horsey" had been her mother's description of Louisa, her explanation for Louisa's singleness. That long nose, and those big teeth, those eyes that shone with dark, equine clarity: Everything about Louisa was too large and striking to be called beautiful. Handsome, yes, but handsome does not mean beautiful. Not here. Handsome is one of those words that seems to pay a compliment but actually names a defect or a failure in a woman. *Handsome. Unusual. Colorful. Outspoken.* The local patois is stuffed with them. Then there was Louisa's mind. As a child, she'd been too smart for her own good, brought home Unsatisfactorys in conduct from Ashley Hall, along with the As. Where did those big bones, that outspokenness come from? Certainly not from her mother. Hilliard women were lush and petite; the Marions, though, were fleshy. Every generation of that family had produced a few unusual women, most of them spinsters.

A dance card from Louisa's debutante year, from her St. Cecilia ball. A palm-sized book, just the right size to tuck into a satin evening bag. Note the weight of the paper, the fine silk ribbon marker, the deep bite of letters on the cover. Those words are *engraved*, not embossed or printed. Her escort's name—Pinckney—was as old as hers, but all the names on her dance card are crossed out, scribbled over with other names. *You. Now you. No, not you; him. I shall never dance with someone so rude.*

A group of old photographs. Louisa on the garden bench in a white satin gown, a cameo on a ribbon around her neck, holding a magnolia blossom as big as a dinner plate and smiling a smile that sharpened the handsome geometry of her face. This photograph has been tinted: her lips and cheeks brushed pink, to soften her, but even in dim sepia, her eyes shine. Louisa as a student at Converse College, a winter guest on the Wofford College campus: marcelled hair, a playful smile, saddle oxfords and thick socks, holding a snowball. Converse and Wofford, for women and men, are upstate in the Piedmont, where it snows.

Letter from LHM to Frederick Holly, Conway, South Carolina, August 14, 1944. Written on the letter: "Fred was serving his country in the Coast Guard, off the SC coast."

> *Dearest Fred,*
>   *I received your letter of last week and was relieved to hear that you were not too badly shaken in the storm your ship was forced to weather in the open ocean. I hope that*

you will continue well in your Coast Guard duties. I must
write to you now, Fred, of a decision I have lately reached
after many sleepless nights and anguished days spent con-
templating the future, our future, dear, and what it holds.
I have the utmost respect for your integrity, your honorable
nature, and the fine qualities of character and conscience
that have made you dear to me. I shall always reserve
for you a special place in my heart and cherish the memo-
ries of our association, even though I can continue no
longer with plans to marry you. Our paths, I fear, would
prove too divergent over time to bring about the true har-
mony and oneness of mind and will that is the mark of a
successful marriage. I wish you all the best and trust that
you will find a true companion to travel the road of life
with you.

> *With dearest love,*
> *Louisa*

Who was Fred Holly? A boy from Conway, South Carolina, a
careful, formal boy with a broad, open face and a bald spot already widening on the crown of his head, who wore suits and
freshly shined wing-tip shoes to class every day, whose manners
were by the book. Escorting Louisa, he kept one hand cupped
around her elbow, and when she talked, he leaned toward her
with the same serious expression on his face whether she was discussing Shakespeare or joking about the coffee in the Converse
dining hall. Meeting him at a dance at Wofford in the spring of
her sophomore year, she'd thought he was a divinity student, but
he was on his way to law school, his father the head of the
Farmer's and Merchant's Bank, the largest bank in Horry County.
Someday, he told her on the night they met, when the lights were
turned low for the last slow dance, he would be a judge.

In the fall of their junior years, he asked her to marry him and she said yes. That spring, they went with his family to the Carolina Cup horse races in Camden, where they ate chicken and potato salad from a picnic basket on the tailgate of the family station wagon, and he toasted her ("my bride-to-be") with an heirloom silver goblet his mother packed in the picnic basket for the occasion. The next weekend, she took him home to Charleston to celebrate the engagement with her family. That's when the steam went out of their relationship. He'd visited once before and they'd tolerated, rather than welcomed, him, but Louisa hadn't worried then; they were always standoffish at first, with anyone but family or family friends. By the end of that second weekend, though, she knew; she knew by what had not been said or offered—fresh-squeezed orange juice at breakfast, a second drink before dinner—that Fred Holly lacked something essential that her parents expected her to find in a husband. Family, perhaps, social stature. She would not let her parents down; her outspokenness ended where their authority began. Besides, she trusted them to know what was best for her.

On Monday, she sat down at the ladies writing desk near the window of the front room on the second floor of her parents' house, and with her back very straight, her legs crossed at the ankles, she wrote that letter. As she wrote, the bells of St. Michael's Church two blocks south across Broad Street, had rung the hour: five o'clock on an early-summer afternoon, with all the windows open so that the breeze could travel through the house. From the room's front window, she could look down the street and see the harbor. The sight of the ocean that day—restless water under the sun— had looked like her future; her husband was out there and someday, if she would just be patient and wait, she would see his sail. Maybe that's what she was thinking about when she wrote out the lyrics and music to this song, to pass the time until he arrived: *Shrimp boats is a-comin'. Their sails are in sight. Shrimp boats is*

a-comin'. There's dancin' tonight. Why don't you hurry, hurry,
hurry home? Why don't you hurry, hurry, hurry home?

A portfolio of watercolors, local scenes painted on note cards and
initialed LHM. Their house with its scrollwork gate set in the old
brick wall, the door that opened from the street onto the first-floor
piazza. An old vegetable peddler pushing his cart past the pastel
houses of Rainbow Row. Also a transcription of his call: *Bean,*
bean, good sivvy bean, Missis. Sails in the harbor. An oak limb
heavy with Spanish moss draped over a mossy brick wall. A fountain seen through an elaborate iron gate. Flower vendors and basket weavers with their goods spread on the sidewalk near St.
Michael's Church. A Negro fisherman casting a net from the bow
of a bateau on a tidal creek. An ancient Negro woman with wily
eyes (their Mamie, late in life), her head wrapped in a white turban, smoking a pipe. A horsey woman with binoculars around her
neck and a thermos at her feet, sitting on a shooting box beside a
creek, this one titled *Christmas Bird Count on Bull Island.*

That was a self-portrait: Louisa at the annual Audubon Society
bird count on Bull Island. She'd joined the society right out of
college and gone on every bird count since with a goal and a plan.
That year, she'd reached it: over four hundred birds recorded on
her life list and the honor of leading this count. They'd come
across to Bull Island in boats in the cold, thinning dark just before
dawn. She'd posted her spotters, found her own place, and settled
in. She had her binoculars, her father's old dented green metal
thermos full of coffee, and his shooting box with the cracked
leather cushion on top. She wore a weathered green suede jacket,
a thick cabled fisherman's sweater, slacks, and leather lace-up
boots that she'd owned since college and kept saddle-soaped and
oiled so that even now, fifteen years later, they still looked new.

She wasn't there to shoot anything; she was there to watch and wait. By first light, she'd counted ten egrets, three red-tailed hawks, and four flocks of red-winged blackbirds.

She'd set up her observation spot on solid ground near a creek. To the east, across the marsh, long bands of light sloped through a dark line of oaks. The tide was coming in, and as she watched the water turn blue as pearled steel in the rising light, she thought about how she would like to paint a winter marsh at daybreak, how she would catch the golds and browns of the grasses and set them against the dark trees at the marsh's edge, pile the sky with pale thunderheads above a pink horizon. *Time Was*, she would title that painting. The stillness of a marsh at daybreak always brought that expression to mind. The marsh had been here since time was. South Carolina had been South Carolina since time was. She'd been sitting in the marsh on her father's shooting box, watching the rising sun flash on an egret's wings, since time was.

Lately, it had begun to seem that she had been the same person since time was and that she'd go on being that person forever. Only when she was quiet like this did it come over her: the whole picture, not a glimpse or a corner. Herself at thirty-five, still living in her parents' house, sleeping in the same bed, its four tall posts carved with heavy bowing heads of rice, that had held Hilliard sleepers for two hundred years. She could step outside of her bedroom and drink her morning coffee in her own private corner of the second-floor piazza. It would be her house someday and she was willing to wait. Waiting was what she did best. Waiting and watching. She fixed the coffee every morning, cleaned spots from her father's ties, sent Hugh straight to his room when he came home drunk, organized the family papers, shopped for groceries.

Watcher, listener, daughter, friend, busy all the time. Recording secretary for the Junior League, the Altar Guild, president of the local chapter of the Audubon Society, her life full of *Madame Chairman* and *Respectfully submitted*, written in her careful, elegant hand. Smocker of dresses for girl babies, crocheter of blue booties for the boys. The busiest seamstress in the Altar Guild. Godmother to Susan Simmons's daughter, Ann, and serious about that obligation, too. She'd been to Ann's pageants, recitals, graduations, and before her wedding, Louisa had given the brides-maids' luncheon. Weekly volunteer at the St. Philip's Church Bargain Shop; chair of the Christmas stocking project; organizer of the Watch with Me One Hour vigil on Good Friday; deliverer of wheelchairs and walkers and food baskets to the poor. Some-times when one of the younger men at church went overboard with his manners and made a big show of calling her *Miss* Louisa, she wanted to ask him, "Why do you call me Miss like that? I haven't missed so much."

She'd just poured hot coffee into the cup on top of the thermos and was raising it to her mouth to blow on it when she'd looked up and seen a man she didn't know crossing the marsh. The stranger was dressed in a black jacket and held a small folding stool against his chest. He walked slowly, looking down, as though he were looking for something he'd lost. When he saw her, the re-lief on his face was instant, comical.

He waved and she saw black leather gloves. Then a black beret with brown hair curling out from under it, and then—he was close now—his deep brown intelligent eyes and Roman collar. A priest. Whatever had fluffed up in her at the sight of him smoothed out and flattened. A pair of expensive binoculars hung around his neck and he held a leather-covered notepad in one hand. Her first thought was that he looked like the young Anton Chekhov, minus the pince-nez. "Is this where the Audubon Soci-ety convenes?" he asked.

"I believe that's one creek over," she answered, and they both laughed.

Later, after they'd settled in to watch for birds, he told her he'd been tiptoeing across the marsh because he was obsessed, nearly paralyzed, by the fear of stepping on a snake. Since he'd come to the Low Country, his fear of snakes had gone past sensible fear and become a heart-pounding, sweat-popping phobia. She told him that the snakes were all denned up this time of year, down among the roots of the pines, but he said reality had nothing to do with it. He was ashamed of the lack of faith in God this fear implied, but he couldn't master it. Every time he tried, something happened that convinced him all over again that he was *right* to be terrified and vigilant.

Once when he'd thought he had his fear under control, a parishioner had invited him to his weekend place up on the Cooper River for Sunday dinner. On the path that ran along the bank of one of the old rice ditches, the man's spaniel had flushed a water moccasin out of a clump of saw palmetto. By the time they got there, the dog was barking hysterically at the snake where it rested on the path, coil on top of heavy gray coil. Its mouth was open, showing the cottony insides and the ugly fangs. The dog's owner had called the dog, and as the spaniel turned away, the snake struck, the dog shied. When the dog ran up to them, two drops of venom shining on the top of its head, the priest's knees had buckled. He would have fallen if his host hadn't caught him. And when the terror of that incident had eased, he'd forced himself to go out into the garden behind the rectory to trim the elephant ear plants. The first dead leaf he'd snipped had revealed a king snake stretched out in the shade there—half out of its skin! As far as he knew, the clippers were still lying out where he'd dropped them, rusting in the weather. That was the day he knew *they could live anywhere*. Even in Charleston, he wasn't safe. Even there, he paused on sidewalks and looked down through cellar grates to the damp steps and brickwork below, then stepped over in one anxious stride.

They talked all morning while birds flew around them and the other spotters came to report their sightings. The wind blowing across the marsh was cold and it ran up her sleeves and chilled her face. At noon, they traded sandwich halves; her turkey for his roast beef. The tide turned and started out and the water in the creeks began to fall; the gray mud banks glistened in the sun. By midafternoon, they had a standing joke between them: A bird would fly overhead and one of them would raise their binoculars and watch it pass. "There goes one." Then they'd go on talking. He'd been at St. Mary's for six months, transferred from a parish in Connecticut. He came from New Jersey. He'd grown up riding horses; at Thanksgiving this year, he'd been to Aiken and blessed the hounds, ridden in the drag hunt there. She noticed how he cradled the cup from her thermos with both hands, as though it were a fine bowl.

And herself? he asked. There was something careful about the way he asked and how he listened as she talked about her family and her work, which was her life's work now, gathering and sorting the family papers, donating them to the Historical Society. She told him how she believed that the rhythm of tides got into people's blood and made them look at time differently. She'd never told anyone her idea about the tides before, and for a moment she felt caught out in the open, exposed.

As she talked, he sat very still and listened, hands cupped and still around the thermos cup. He listened, not with Fred Holly's studious, furrowed attention, but with a kind of intensity that reminded her of the way Hugh gulped his first highball of the evening. She saw him watch her mouth, her hair. It was beautiful then, red-brown and thick. When it blew across her face, she waited before she brushed it away, and saw him watch her hands. She watched him, too, the careful way he set his cup down on the ground, the way his knuckles stood out when he folded his hands around one knee and leaned back, laughing, the layers of brown in his eyes.

By the end of the day, they were freezing and neither of them had written down a single bird. It was Louisa's idea to make up a list. "I'm a priest, Miss Marion," he said, blowing into his hands, then spreading one hand over his heart, "I can't lie like that. There's no such thing as a harmless lie. Not one that doesn't weaken us and make the next one easier to tell." He didn't say it sternly, but she could tell he meant it.

"But it's not really a lie," she said. "These will be the birds we *would* have seen if we'd been looking." It sounded so thin, after what he'd said. Then she'd bent over her clipboard so he wouldn't see the color creep up her neck, flood her face. She couldn't believe that those words had actually come out of her mouth; whatever her flaws, they didn't include bold-faced dishonesty. She never even slipped fifteen cents out of the cash register at the St. Philip's Bargain Shop to buy herself a Coke, the way some of the younger volunteers did. If she didn't have the money for a Coke, she drank tap water. And he never agreed to the dishonesty, exactly, but when she asked, "How many pileated woodpeckers would you like?" he studied the sky and said, "Two," and then she said, "Oh, take three."

"All right," he said, "give me three." Later, looking back on it, she knew that that was the moment when they'd both said yes to what was coming.

She'd never felt this way before, certainly not with Fred Holly, and not with anybody else, either. Fred had been careful to ask permission to hold her hand, put his arm around her, press his dry, cool mouth against hers. Years after she'd said good-bye to him, she'd gone to a party with someone she didn't remember now and gotten drunk, deliberately, and gone to bed with him afterward. There'd been a few others, nothing memorable. Now this.

As they gathered up their things, she formed a committee of the Audubon Society and named them its only members. First, she told him, they would study the problem of the yellow-crested night herons that had roosted in the live oaks in Washington Square Park in downtown Charleston. Then their committee of two would draft a proposal to protect the birds' nesting grounds and satisfy the city, which wanted them driven out of the park, where old men sat on benches under the trees and tourists were revolted by the meaty, ammonia stink of the rookery, the brick walks spattered with bird droppings. As she talked, he buttoned his jacket, picked up his stool and held it to his chest, and looked over to where the boat that would take them back to the mainland had arrived and the other spotters were gathering. Then he set the first meeting of their committee for the following morning, at the rectory.

Every day for two weeks, she went to the rectory to work on the proposal. He had a housekeeper, a stooped old black woman who let her in when she arrived and locked the door behind her when she left and otherwise stayed back in the rectory kitchen, reading the paper, peeling potatoes, or watching bubbling pots on the stove. Three days a week, the parish secretary, a tall, quiet woman who wore a large silver cross and almost never looked directly at anyone, worked in an anteroom off his study, filing and stamping, answering the phone and scheduling appointments. His office was dim, and it smelled faintly of an unfamiliar spice. In one corner, a large Bible rested on an ornate carved wooden stand; a silver crucifix hung on the wall, and a worn red Oriental rug covered the wide boards of the floor. They sat opposite each other across his walnut desk, passing papers back and forth. When she asked, he told her that the spice was frankincense; priests burned it in a special incense burner on a chain, called a censer, to purify the church before High Mass. He kept a big bag of the resiny lumps in a drawer of the desk. She took some home and put it in a small bowl on her bedside table, and the smell of the spice called up his face, his voice, his hands and how they seemed to sense the contours of whatever they touched.

The day the heron proposal was finished was the housekeeper's day off. He walked her to the door. She said she wanted to take religious instruction, become a Catholic; then, before he could answer, she took his face in her hands and kissed him. Until the day she died, she would remember the way he shut his eyes, as if he were about to be hit and couldn't avoid it, and pressed his palms against her arms, with his fingers held wide apart, as if to close them around her arms, to come that close to her body, would pull him into a current he couldn't swim out of. She would remember how his lips had felt corkscrew-tight, then softened, opened, warmed, as though the heat of his body had all rushed to his mouth. How she'd pressed against him and how he'd taken her by the arms and walked her back a few steps, then bent over, head down, his hands braced on his knees, as though he'd been running and stopped to catch his breath. Then he'd pulled her back into the study, closed the door, and kissed her again. This time, his fingers followed her jawline, traced her ears, her neck, as if he'd already touched her in his mind and knew where he wanted to touch. Her hands followed their own imaginings, up into his thick hair, and down his spine from neck to hips. He was all sinew and bone, like a dancer.

He pulled away, sat down in his chair across the desk from her, put his face in his hands, and took a deep, shaky breath. Then he began to talk. "That morning on the marsh?" he said. "I walked toward the sight of your hair in the sun and the minute I saw your face I started to imagine kissing you, and I haven't stopped since." His head was down now; she saw that he had two swirls of hair on the crown of his head; she would kiss those soon, too, she thought. He scratched with his fingernail at a spot on the desk.

"I keep that frankincense you gave me on my bedside table," she said, "and when I smell it, I see your face and I hear your voice."

He folded his hands and looked at her then. His eyes were darker than she'd ever seen them. "But, you see, the difference between us is that by having those thoughts, you are not breaking any vows, and I am. I should write a letter to the bishop now, today, and renounce my ordination."

She reached across the desk then and pried his hands apart, held on to both of them. "I'll help you," she said.

Then it was Lent, time of repentance and denial, and for forty days he wouldn't see her. Finally, on Holy Saturday night, she went to the vigil at St. Philip's, as always, and helped to set out the supper in the Parish Hall. Afterward, near midnight, she drove to St. Mary's, his church, for the lighting of the new fire. She sat in the last pew of the dark, chilly church. The doors at the back were open and the air smelled watery and clean. Then she heard his voice sing out from the church door, "Christ, Our Light," pure and clear, not at all like his speaking voice. She turned to watch and a fire blazed in a brazier and there was his face, lit up by the fire, as he lit the Paschal candle, held it high and led the procession down the aisle toward the altar. She loved the purity of his face then. Soon, it would shine on her, and she would shine on him, and they would both be changed.

When she asked him to come out to Waveland to see her the week after Easter, he came. This time, he closed his hands around her arms, his arms around her body. She led him through the house to her room at the front, where the curtains blew in at the window and the sheets on the bed were damp from the salt air. After they'd made love, he held her and rocked her and wouldn't let her go. "I have taken the wrong vows," he said. His calling was to love her. That week, she went to the rectory on Thursday when the housekeeper and the secretary were off, and he dictated and she typed ten different letters to the bishop, renouncing his vows, then tore up every one, because none of them had said exactly what he needed to say. That's when she told him again that she wanted to take instruction, become a Catholic. Not from him she wouldn't, he said. It would be the most obscene hypocrisy, after what they'd done, for him to teach anyone about the faith. Instead, he sent her to an old priest in Mt. Pleasant whose study smelled of wool blankets and milk.

They would be together. She'd never felt surer of anything. She didn't tell him this, but she knew; she saw it all: They would leave Charleston, marry, have children. They would bring the children back for visits to the city where their parents had met. They would walk them through the old streets, feed them creek shrimp and grits, okra and benne-seed wafers and pecans roasted in butter. Walking home from the rectory the day after the first night they'd spent together, she'd felt her children waiting, ready to step into the world; she'd seen the flags on the ships in the harbor and started her list, for them. "Children," she'd say to them someday, "these ships came here from all over the world and they've been coming into this harbor for centuries."

Sometimes she wouldn't see him for days. He was forever necessary to parish work, and sometimes he stayed away, just to see if he could. That April, they spent every evening at the beach house in bed, with all the lights out, in case anyone should drive by. Every evening was the same: fiery lovemaking, then prayer and agony on his part, prayer and patience on hers. After the first time, when he'd held her for hours while they'd talked about how he would renounce his vows, he got up right away and dressed, then knelt down beside the bed to pray. He was like Jesus in the Garden of Gethsemane, she thought once as she sat on the bed in her slip, watching him. Any minute, he might begin to sweat blood. That night, with his folded hands pressed hard against his forehead, he'd prayed to know why God had forsaken him, why he was numbered among the fallen. Fallen. At first, that word had pricked her; then it had made her proud: He had fallen, and she was the cause, potent as Eve.

Before Henry, prayers for her had always been something to read from the Book of Common Prayer; now she found her own words. While he prayed for help and forgiveness, she prayed to God, who felt like a radiant will to happiness glowing inside her. She prayed to be pregnant; she prayed that he would mail the letter to the bishop; she prayed that this would never stop. It felt as though she'd begun to be another person, just hatched, more powerful and more beautiful than she'd believed she could be. In late April, they wrote another letter to the bishop, stamped it, laid it on the chest in the rectory foyer to go out in the morning mail.

When he took the letter back and began a novena to the Virgin

Mary, she should have known, but she wasn't a Catholic yet; she couldn't have known about Mary and the priests. She didn't know that to a priest, Mary was the ideal woman: humble, modest, chaste. The Blessed Mother. The Blessed Virgin Mother of Christ. They loved her for each of her titles; they loved her as a son loves his mother, honors her, and looks to her for wisdom and protection. When impure thoughts tempted them, they prayed to the Blessed Virgin and she blew the unclean thoughts out of their minds with her Holy Mother's breath.

Every night during the last week of April, Louisa sat in the back of the church and watched him rehearse the little girls for the May procession. May was the Virgin Mary's month, and on the first Sunday, the girls would dress in their white organdy First Communion dresses and veils and march through the church, carrying flowers for her altar, a crown for her statue. He was strict with the little girls, and their mothers liked him for that. No giggling, no fidgeting. He was a tyrant about the marching and clapped out the beat—step, PAUSE, step, PAUSE—while they marched and sang. *Oh, Mary, we crown Thee with blossoms today, Queen of the Angels, Queen of the May.* One misstep and he sent them back to the church doors to start over.

Louisa covered her head with a white lace mantilla and sat among the mothers, studying Mary's statue. The downcast eyes, the globe on which she stood wrapped tightly in Satan's coils, Mary's bare foot crushing the serpent's evil head. She took it all in as she waited for practice to be over so that they could speed over the Cooper River bridge and on to Sullivan's Island, pull the car far into the shadows under Waveland, and fall into bed. She thought about how she'd stroke and squeeze him until he gasped and moaned and how she'd welcome his fingers and then his cock inside her, how she'd lift her hips against him to push him deeper and how she couldn't ever seem to get him deep enough inside her.

Sometimes, they fell asleep and didn't get back to the city until dawn. Once, he missed a deathbed call in the middle of the night. Another time, the altar boy was lighting the candles for the seven o'clock Mass when he ran in. She became a fearless liar, invented Audubon Society business all over the state. She became a spy, an expert at listening behind and around conversations, second-guessing when her parents might be planning to go to the beach house. Sometimes, she stayed on Sullivan's Island all day, waiting for him. She walked on the beach and swam in the surf, let the ocean roll her and drag her hair across her face.

That spring, she began to feel as if she were living in two worlds. In one, she wrote out sales slips at the Bargain Shop, smocked dresses, chaired meetings. At home, she ground and brewed the household coffee, squeezed a drop of benzene on a mayonnaise spot on her father's tie and rubbed the spot in a small circular motion until the stain disappeared. She shopped with Susan, played Monopoly with Ann, her goddaughter, moved her needle through cloth. Meanwhile, the other world, the secret world, was a country of green light, like the light she saw behind her eyelids sometimes when they were in bed together, a country of fingers and tongues and pleasure in waves, of reckless lying and scheming. Her father had always insisted that everybody had a secret life. As a lawyer, he'd meant it as a warning not to trust anyone or entirely believe them, because what people said was always a combination of what they wanted to be true and what they were trying to hide. But that spring, Louisa came to believe that the secret life had to be secret because it was new; no words had been minted yet to describe it; you had to be quiet until you learned a new language to name its possibilities and pleasures.

He didn't mail the letter. Instead, in June, he made a pilgrimage to the Virgin Mary's shrine at Lourdes, and when he came back, he confessed his relationship with Louisa to the bishop, who ordered him transferred to a mission church on the Pima Indian reservation in Arizona. He was to leave immediately. He told the parish council and the congregation that he loved them all, that the church needed him for a special mission to the Indians, but when Louisa came to his study, he stayed on one side of the desk, kept her on the other. Boxes of his books and papers were stacked around the room. He cleared off a chair for her. "Sit down," he said. "Please, will you sit down," he asked, rubbing his forehead like the exasperated father of an angry child. But she wouldn't sit, so he stood, too, to keep her from looming over him.

He told her that he'd known all along that he was too worldly; that had been his downfall; that was the road Satan had taken into his heart. He should never have joined the Audubon Society, or tried to be a parish priest and believed he could live in the world; he was too weak for that, he said. He should have chosen the monk's life, the cloister, a vow of silence. As he talked, he looked out the window, down at his folded hands, anywhere but at her. She said it sounded like a speech he was reading her. There was a prissiness about him that she hadn't noticed before. "Did the bishop write that for you?" she asked when he was done, and surprised herself with the harsh croak of her voice. A crow on a winter day. She thought she must look that way, all in black, with shining eyes. Surprised him, too, because he looked up quickly then, and she saw that his lips were thinner than they'd felt as he'd kissed her mouth, whispered over her breasts. Satan? His heart? Once he'd said that his heart was so full of her, it was about to spill over. Now she was Satan's tool? He held up his hand, shook his head. When he spoke, his voice was thin and tired, as though he'd been sick and was still getting his strength back.

"I have been instructed by my superiors not to discuss these matters with you further," he said, but she wouldn't stop, rained questions down on him. How could he keep his vows, now that they'd been broken so often and so completely? How could he pretend to recover chastity, virginity? What kind of hypocrisy was that? What about his vows to her? Finally: "We love each other, what about that?" She held out her hands, and when he wouldn't take them, she pulled them back and hid them in her skirt. But no tears. Tears wouldn't move him; she knew that. He listened to it all in his penitent's silence and stared at the floor. "Please, Louisa," was all he said, and that, barely.

His name was Father Jerome, after a fifth-century scriptural genius, a righteous battler against the errors of his day. They'd talked about his given name—Henry—which he would take back when he left the priesthood. "Henry," she said, the name she always called him when they were alone. "Henry, I thought you were a spiritual man."

Then she turned to go and and he came around the desk as suddenly as he'd always moved to hold her. When she reached for him, he held her by the wrists, said, "Louisa, I have to tell you something. It's only right that I do. Maybe it will ease your pain to know that you're not the first." His hands on her wrists trembled, but there was no weeping, no Garden of Gethsemane now.

Not the first. She mouthed the words but no sound came. She saw him at a distance, his mouth moving, saying something about a woman in Connecticut, but all she heard was *not the first* and how he must try, one final time, to be true to his vows; if he couldn't, he would come back and find her.

He left Charleston for Arizona on the first of July, and the next day Louisa started walking. Some mornings, she would leave the house when it was barely light, before her parents were awake, and she wouldn't come back until midafternoon, and then only if it were too stiflingly hot to walk. On cooler days, she stayed out past suppertime, ate chicken, shrimp, rice, anything, with her fingers, out of bowls in the refrigerator, while Mamie stood at the sink and washed up the supper dishes and did not ask where Louisa had been, just shook her head and muttered. Once, tired of the muttering, Louisa said, "Don't start with me, Mamie," then looked up from her bowl of rice, to see Mamie laying knife, fork, folded cloth napkin on the kitchen table.

"Sit down here, Miss," she said. "Don't be messing up my clean floor."

One time, her mother came downstairs, dressed in a pale pink bathrobe and slippers, and stood in the kitchen with her arms folded, watching Louisa eat.

"Where have you been?" her mother asked.

"Here and there," Louisa said. Mamie and Evelyn, who'd been helping Mamie with the dishes, cleared out when they heard that answer.

But Louisa wasn't trying to be smart. *Here and there* was exactly where she'd been. What was important then was *not* to have a plan. She carried no paper or pencil, no checkbook, money, or keys. In fact, whatever smelled of plans, she swerved away from. The thought of plans took her to the brink of panic, as if something were going to be asked of her that she couldn't do or pretend to do. Purpose appalled her. It was not curiosity that moved her, but the feel of her body moving through space. The smell of the wind, the heat that rippled up off the pavement and sidewalks. The sensual world. Her body had led her into this; now it would lead her out. It was that simple. She wanted to go where her body led her, as if aimlessness were the slack that followed the cutting of the tight cord of desire. She was as aimless now as she'd once been intent on him. If she'd had a boat, Hugh's bateau, say, she would have thrown away the oars, unbolted the motor, dropped it over the stern, and drifted, just to see where the current carried her. Something important had happened to her; she needed to know what and where it had left her. If she wanted anything.

One day, she would walk up King Street; the next, she would follow East Bay Street north into Ansonborough. If she saw a friend or an acquaintance coming, a bright, expectant face that seemed to say, How are you today? Let me help, she ducked into a doorway or down an alley. Their smiles, in particular, appalled her. "The little smile," she'd called it, when she'd believed she was on her way to another kind of life, in which she would never smile that way again.

For a month, her mother put up with Louisa's eating with her fingers out of bowls at night. She tolerated her wandering until people began to notice. Not just her hard, knotty calves, her tanned face and arms, but something more alarming. One day, Mrs. Manigault saw Louisa walking across the Cooper River bridge. By the time the story got back to her mother, Louisa had stopped at the top of the highest span and was leaning way out over the railing, looking down. Her hair was a mess, sticky with salt. (The brother, that drinking, you know.)

She hadn't planned to jump; she didn't want to die. To plan to die was a plan, and she had no plans then. She was looking down at the water to see what it had to tell her. If it had told her to jump, she might have. After that, her mother pulled the story out of her: She'd gotten involved with a married man, and he'd gone back to his wife. This was a story her mother would recognize, one that wouldn't frighten her. And it was almost true, except that the man had gone back to the Mother of Christ; he might as well have been *married* to this mother. With the story out, her own mother took action: She talked with Susan, and the two of them signed Louisa up for a bus tour of New England, to see the fall leaves, and Louisa agreed to go, since it didn't matter what she did.

So many suitcases allowed, all tagged with the bright blue-and-white tags of the tour company. An itinerary. Destinations, meals, and activities on a schedule, not much free time to indulge yourself in your troubles. That was her mother's prescription. Most of the people on the tour were older, recent widows and widowers riding away their loneliness. She sat next to them on the bus, ate with them at the cafeterias where they stopped for meals. To keep from talking, she said she was a widow, too, and after that they left her to her knitting. She'd brought along fine-gauge needles, thin as fish bones, and fine white cotton thread. Square by square, she knit a bedspread. Knitting was good because she did not have to look up and because it kept her so busy—the pattern was very complicated and she had to keep strict count of the stitches—no one would think of starting up a conversation. If they tried, she held up the needles and the knitted square and moved her lips to show that she was counting. Sometimes, if she got distracted and dropped a stitch or lost count, the square came out lopsided and she had to unravel it and start over. That was satisfying, too, in its own way; as though by knitting, then unraveling a square, she was making visible some hidden truth about the world, giving it shape and form.

In Vermont, the trees looked like licking flames; the sky was a hard and brilliant blue, like color under clear varnish. She could imagine tapping it with a fingernail, enjoying a hard crack of sound. Seeing that landscape for the first time, she thought, No wonder they are so sure of themselves, those New England people. No wonder their judgments are so clear and sure. Clear as the air and the color of the sky. Definite as their seasons. Out in the country, their houses and their barns were joined into one long building so that in winter they never had to go outside. No wonder they believed that crystals moved through their bowels. No bloody flux here. In the South, you could never forget that you were flesh, and flesh rotted.

He'd asked to be transferred back to New England. Instead, they'd sent him to Arizona. There was a pleasing symmetry about it, a beautiful arc of rightness, that he would be sent from one snake-infested world to another. On the bus heading north, counting stitches, she thought about the snakes in Arizona, big rattlers the color of earth and rock, their perfect markings, their stillness. *Not the first.* Why should that matter? But it did. It mattered that she was just another—what were the Church's words for it?—*occasion of sin*, the cause of a weak man's latest fall, not the first, the one that toppled the world.

That September, an envelope arrived addressed to her in his handwriting. It carried no return address, only an Arizona postmark, and inside was a blank sheet of paper with a mustard seed taped in the middle. The tiny mustard seed of faith that could move mountains. He'd said that was the kind of faith they'd need to carry them out of their present lives and into their future together. She planted the seed, but it never came up, and that was satisfying to her, too, in the way that unraveling the knitting had been. This, at least, was true: The seed went into the ground and nothing came up. That was the whole story. He wanted her to have faith, to believe the seed's promise, but she preferred the truth of the bare ground, and years later, looking back, she came to see that this story had crossed and closed some distance between who she was and who she became: a believer in finality, in boxes and doors and the locks that close them.

❧

Box No. 20
Welcome Home (55 items)

Contains Daybooks, Household Inventories,
Voices, Familiar and Mysterious,
Sketches of Disaster,
Wind

Her mother died in August; in September, Hurricane Hugo blew in. On the day of the night the storm was due to make landfall, Louisa found herself loaded onto a stuffy school bus, along with other stubborn, confused, or defiant citizens, and evacuated from the Charleston peninsula. For hours, as the sky darkened and the wind rose, the bus inched north on I-26 in a slowly advancing traffic jam toward the storm shelter, a high school gymnasium in the town of Goose Creek. Louisa held a folded Kleenex in one hand, and from time to time she blotted perspiration from her hairline. She was dressed in pressed slacks and polished loafers, a linen shirt and a yellow windbreaker, a yellow scarf neatly tied around her neck. She sat up very straight, held her portmanteau in her lap with both hands and tried not to jostle her seatmate, a tiny old woman,

eyes smoky blue with cataracts, who carried her belongings in a paper sack and who looked as if she'd break if you bumped her.
Louisa had boosted the woman up the bus's high steps and settled
her into the seat next to the window. Whenever the driver geared
down, the engine popped, and once it backfired and her seatmate
jumped and threw up her hands. "Good God!" she said.

"Looks like we're going to have a storm," Louisa answered
quickly.

"Yes'um, sure do."

"I hope your family are all safe."

"My son, he stay out to John Island," the old woman said, looking straight ahead.

"Well, we'll be at the shelter soon, don't you worry."

"Yes'um."

A *shelter?* she could hear her mother say; she could almost see
her mother draw back from the word as though from an unpleasant smell. A *shelter is a place where the homeless go, Louisa. Are
you homeless?*

No, Mother, she answered in her mind, patiently, out of a long
habit of answering her mother's questions.

Why did you never marry, Louisa?

Why do you stride when you walk?

What do you see in him? In her?

If you are not homeless, Louisa, why are you going to a shelter?

She rested her chin in her hand and leaned her elbow on the
ledge below the window and watched the landscape creep by:
head-high pines planted evenly in rows in the sandy fields. It was
stubbornness, really, Mother, she answered the mother in her
mind who was not dead and never would be. Her voice was still
strong, so recently dead. Over time, it would drop to a whisper,
then seem to disappear, though it would only have dissolved into
Louisa's voice so completely that, hearing it, Louisa would come
to accept it as her own. Plain old garden-variety pride. Surely you
understand that. And impatience, Mother, with the person I've

always been, the thoughts I've always thought, the care I've taken to stay safe. Imagine, Mother, and at my age, too, the excitement of not knowing for once where I was going or what would happen when I got there. That, you wouldn't understand, and I don't, either, but here I am.

Well, what are you doing on a public conveyance? her mother wanted to know. Louisa had ridden a bus, a *public conveyance*, on the trip to New England, of course, but never a city bus or a school bus. How to explain? To trace the decision back to its source. She was on this bus on her way to a shelter because she wouldn't go to Columbia with Susan Simmons. That was a good place to start. The night before the storm, as usual, they'd walked down to the Battery together. They'd studied the clear evening sky and talked about how the weather was always like this before a hurricane, so quiet and ordinary, you couldn't believe a wind was coming. Out in the harbor, the lights of Fort Sumter had appeared, and across the harbor, the lights of Mt. Pleasant. They'd watched a big ship loaded with barrels come slowly into the harbor while sailboats with bright sails tacked back and forth. On the Battery, the palmettos rustled; terns and gulls coasted by. White Point Gardens was full of joggers and children playing in the bandstand, same as on any night.

As always, Susan had led and Louisa had followed, her hands clasped behind her back, like a magistrate. Susan was sixty-five now, too, the same as Louisa, but after five children, six grandchildren, and two more on the way, she'd stayed skinny, kept her hair blond. She wore citrusy perfume, blue jeans and a pale yellow silk shirt, little woven shoes. She had gray eyes, a bright mouth, incredibly white, straight teeth. Three men had wanted to marry her since her husband died. Compared with her friend, Louisa had always felt like the burro kept in the stall next to the high-strung thoroughbred to steady the valuable horse. Until now. And that, she supposed, as much as anything else, was why she was on the bus to Goose Creek. Because since her mother had died, she'd been impatient with that attitude; lately, she'd begun to understand—though it was more like waking up and recognizing where you were—that they were *both* thoroughbreds; it was just that she lacked the thoroughbred's ambition to ripple and shine.

Susan had sashayed along the wide sidewalk that ran along the seawall, the tips of her fingers stuck down in the small front pockets of her jeans, talking in her bright voice, and Louisa had walked with her hands clasped behind her back, listening. Susan, Ann, Amelia, and Sara, her three daughters who lived here, were going to her son Wesley's house in Columbia, and Louisa was going with them. That had been Susan's plan. Susan had told her what to pack and where they'd go shopping in Columbia and how they'd put a TV in the guest suite over the garage, where Louisa would stay.

But she didn't really know she was staying until after the walk. At home, instead of packing, she'd broiled a piece of grouper, heated up leftover rice and succotash from last night's supper, and set herself up in front of the television in the reception room to eat and watch the news.

It was all about the storm, of course. The mayor was on the screen, backed by other city officials and police. Behind them was a big satellite picture of Hugo and a red dotted line that showed the storm's projected path. It was out in the Atlantic off of Cuba now, gathering speed, moving fast. The next night, around midnight, if it stayed on course, the storm would make landfall right here. "This storm is a killer," the mayor said, looking straight into the camera, "the likes of which has never threatened this city. We're asking all our citizens to remain calm and leave," he said, "or there will be significant loss of life. We expect the storm surge to flood the entire peninsula. You must leave now."

When Susan called at nine o'clock to say they were on their way to pick her up, her heart beat hard. Most of the time, she welcomed Susan's bossiness—it was as familiar to her as the sound of her own name—but as they talked, a picture jumped into her mind of the single bed in that clean little room over Wesley's garage and herself with the covers tucked up under her chin, like a child, while Susan kissed her forehead and turned out the light. "I'm not ready," she said. "Actually, Susan, I'm not going."

When she couldn't say why, Susan got mad. "This is no time to be impossible, Louisa," she'd said, in the voice she sometimes used in a store to put an uppity clerk back in her place. But she kept on saying no until Susan started to cry and hung up, and then she sat there with her hand on the phone and couldn't believe what she'd done. To keep herself from calling Susan and telling her to come right over and pick her up, she filled the bathtubs with water, got out flashlights, batteries, and candles and lined them up on the kitchen counter, connected a new propane canister to the camp stove, dragged furniture off the first-floor piazza. When she called Susan to apologize, no one answered. That's when she knew she was staying.

Storms were forever heading their way, then blowing themselves out in the Atlantic or veering off and crashing into the coast of North Carolina or Virginia. Even when they swooped down and hit the city, the city rode it out. How many hurricanes had this house survived? Had she? In a hurricane, the family had shut themselves up in the back bedroom on the second floor, Hugh's room. Their house had creaked like a ship, but it had held. Sometimes ocean water had swirled through the first-floor rooms, and her father had gone out to report on its progress up the stairs, but they'd never believed that the water would reach them. She'd always thought it was a fine thing to sit with her family in that upper room with the kerosene lanterns burning, the shutters nailed shut across the windows, while the storm smashed and roared outside and her mother read to them from the Bible or the poetry of Alfred, Lord Tennyson and Mamie rocked and prayed. It might even be finer to ride it out alone, to see the palmettos bent double, the world disappear behind sheets of blowing rain, because you wanted to know if you had the courage left. Because courage was among the things you'd packed up and put away and you wanted to know if it still worked, after all this time.

At ten o'clock, she'd folded her bathrobe and laid it across the foot of the bed, set her slippers under the bed with the toes just showing from underneath the bed skirt. Then she sat on the edge of the bed and washed down ten milligrams of Valium with a shot of bourbon drunk all at once with a quick backward toss of her head. No other living soul had ever seen her drink her nightcap and take her pill, that quick throwing down of the bourbon and the pill, efficient and meant to get the job done, the job being sleep: no dreams, no restless waking. Then she sat for a minute, feeling the bourbon spread its warm and loosening weight all through her body. Her shoulders slumped, her knees spread, and her feet swung free; she rocked the empty glass on her palm.

By noon the next day, she was the only person left on her block. Her neighbors' houses were locked; heavy shutters latched across all the windows; plywood nailed across the doors. The streets were empty. In the harbor, the chop had stiffened; the sailboats were gone. Every one of her neighbors had tried to take her with them and she was worn-out from saying no to them all, and from dragging furniture inside off the piazzas and porches, from reassuring them that she'd watch all their houses. At one o'clock, she was lying down when someone knocked on her door, and she opened it, to find a young black man with a thin mustache, dressed in a yellow slicker and a deputy's hat, carrying a clipboard. Behind him, the palmettos that lined the sidewalk in front of her house rustled in the wind, and in the sky above the harbor, clouds were closing over a silver strip of light. "Ma'am," he said, "I have an order here that says everyone must evacuate the peninsula."

"I've been through a dozen hurricanes in my lifetime," she said. "I'm going to stay and sleep in my own bed. Come back in the morning and check on me if you like. I'll be right here."

In the act of closing the front door, she caught his answer at the same time his hand stopped the door. "No, ma'am," he said. "You'll have to evacuate. I'll arrange for you to be taken to a shelter if you haven't made other plans."

And that's how she came to be jolting along in a crowded school bus toward Goose Creek instead of safely tucked between clean sheets in the little single bed in the guest room over Wesley's garage. And wasn't sorry for it, either, no matter what Susan or her mother said.

That's how she came to be standing in line outside the gym in Goose Creek, waiting to be checked into the shelter. The line stretched halfway around the building and she'd been standing on line for close to an hour, moving forward when the line moved. The sky was gray overall by then, and low, with a strange silvery light running along the undersides of the clouds, and the wind blew steadily, hard enough to send papers flying and whirl up dust devils all over the parking lot. She'd packed in her portmanteau the small pillow she was cross-stitching, her sketchbook, and several charcoal drawing pencils. She'd packed a plastic bag filled with packets of sugar and tea bags, also her satin sleep mask, her nightgown and bathrobe and slippers. As soon as she stepped through the gymnasium's double doors, she saw why she'd packed those things and, at the same moment, why it had been foolish. What had she expected? A private room? A special area set aside for members of the old families? A reserved space, as though this were Henry's Restaurant in Charleston and she and her mother had showed up for their Tuesday lunch at their usual table? *Right this way, Miss Marion.* Well, yes. People like herself, that is what she'd expected. "Our circle," her mother had called the little group behind the high wall that they'd been members of all their lives. Here, though, the walls had fallen. She'd never seen so many black people in one place, not since the civil rights disturbances; certainly, she'd never been in a crowd of Negroes this large. Negroes and poor whites and feeble old people with no one to take care of them and no place to go. Next to the folded bleachers, a group of Mexicans had congregated, migrant workers, no doubt. Their tape player blasted music that was all blaring, jittery trumpets sliding over slick floors of sound. One little girl in the group was wearing a white organdy dress and a purple sweater, holding out the skirt, dancing alone.

Finally, the Red Cross worker at the door added her name to a long list of names and another woman handed her a brown blanket and directed her to the far end of the floor. "Excuse me," Louisa said, "where did you say I should go?"

"Just anywhere you can find," the volunteer said, already turning away.

At the far end of the gym floor, under the basketball goal, she spread out her blanket and smoothed it flat. Her closest neighbors, four middle-aged black men in blue jeans and T-shirts, played cards on their blanket. Beside them, a girl in a halter top lay between the legs of a man in a sleeveless black leather vest. A tall, skinny black woman dressed in shorts and a red T-shirt with JESUS! printed in huge gold letters sat on a blanket next to hers, reading from the Bible to four children, all of them surrounded by a collection of Kentucky Fried Chicken bags, a confusion of bright plastic toys. When Louisa sat down, the woman leaned over and held out her hand. It was so loud in the gym, with the tinny echoes of voices and radios, all tuned to different stations, she had to say, "Excuse me?" twice before she caught the woman's name, Charlene, and answered, "Louisa Marion."

Then the children: La Tonya, Noble, Mervin, and Quishana, the baby, a bright-faced little girl with two tiny gold ball earrings in her ears. "How do you do?" she said to each of them, offering her hand.

As night fell, the wind picked up and it blew with a steady moaning sound that rose to a shriek, then subsided. She hung her magnifying glass on a cord around her neck, braced it against her chest, and worked on her pillow. Humming and sewing and smiling at whoever caught her eye (I am here to help. I am here to set a good example), she watched the magnified stitches cross the cloth. It was an intricate geometric design she was stitching, a tapestry pattern of linked diamonds, burgundy and cream, and she was grateful for it, suddenly, for the way sewing had carried her through her life. When she thought about important times in her life, it was what her hands had been doing that she remembered—the movement of needle and thread through cloth, the growth of a design—and when she saw these needlework projects, even now, the weather and light and the feeling of those times came back to her, as though the colors of the times themselves had been stitched into the cloth. When Hugh died, she had been making a pillow top covered with grapevines and purple grapes; when Henry left, a white-on-white altar cloth; when Mamie died, a Christmas wall hanging, bright holly and candles; and last spring, during her mother's final decline, the Paschal Lamb. It was the grass under his feet that she remembered most, the stitch that formed it moving round and round. And this pillow, no doubt, would bring her darkening windows, the changing pitch of the rising wind, and Charlene's frightened eyes. After one strong gust, when Charlene had covered her ears and closed her eyes, she set her needlework down in her lap and asked, "Have you ever been through a hurricane before?"

Charlene shook her head, biting her lip. "We only just came down here from New York," she said. Her husband was in the navy and he was at sea, over in Hawaii, about to lose his mind worrying about them.

Louisa went back to her sewing. "Well," she said—in her element now, sewing, lecturing—"I wish you could call him up right now and tell him that you'll be just fine. I've lived through half a dozen of them and I'm still here." The children looked up at her when she said that, and they kept looking, as though they expected her to disappear. "The city has survived many more," she went on. "There were terrible hurricanes in 1752 and 1813, as well as 1885. I, personally, have survived the 1940 storm and also Hurricane Gracie in 1959 — that was a bad one — and Donna and David, which were lesser storms, in 1960 and 1978. Not to mention Camille and Agnes. We'll all get through this one, too, you'll see."

When the Red Cross workers came around with sandwiches and cartons of milk, she refused supper but helped them hand out the food. She felt better then, going through the familiar motions of charity, her good leather purse over her shoulder and a kind word and an extra carton of milk dispensed to her ancient bus seatmate, a hand laid on a child's head.

By eleven o'clock, Charlene had closed her Bible and gathered her children close, and everyone, it seemed, was keeping an eye on the ceiling girders, where the noise was loudest. Most of the time, the sound of the storm was a moaning roar and a hectic drumming of rain on the gym's metal roof, the occasional thud of a falling tree, the buzz of weather stripping around the doors. But when a gust hit the building, it trembled and above their heads the girders hummed. When the noise of the wind rose, the voices rose, too, as if competing with the wind to be heard. "It's all right," Louisa mouthed, during one loud gust, as Charlene tugged her children closer, then got Charlene's nervous smile for an answer. She pointed to pictures in the Bible now, since it was impossible to be heard over the noise of the wind, while Quishana slept, draped over her mother's shoulder in openmouthed oblivion.

After that gust, Louisa folded up her sewing and tucked it into her portmanteau, got out sketchbook and charcoal. The gritty sweep of pencil over paper was comforting, and the lines piled up faster on the blank page than the tiny stitches had filled the pillow top. That was comforting, too. On the book's first page, she found a charcoal sketch of a narrow sand road lined with moss-draped oaks and splashed with sunlight: a stretch of the old King's Highway down on Edisto Island, a picture from another world. She turned to a blank page, began to sketch Quishana's sleeping face. Then, as the sound of the wind rose again, she turned the page, tried to sketch the reception room in her house. Chair, lamp, and footstool, sewing box beside the chair. Her charcoal stick stopped. Where was her sewing box? The deputy had been waiting; she hadn't had much time; surely, though, she'd remembered to carry it upstairs and set it on a high shelf in her bedroom closet. As the wind hit the building and it trembled, she pictured the box there, then tried to think of other high places: the steps to the Fireproof Building, where water had never risen, and the museum with Eliza Hilliard's gown surrounded by the pictures of the Hilliard babies in the tall glass case on the pedestal. All safe. She thought of Susan and her family in Columbia; of Susan in her pink chenille bathrobe, her feet propped up, watching the storm on TV.

But the later it got, the harder it became to keep those places and people safe. With every gust, water seeped through the mortar between the bricks in the walls; it came in around the door frames and poured in around the windows high up in the walls. Even the floor hummed, as if the wind were tunneling under the building, too. But it was the sound that was so terrifying it froze her senses. With each gust, a whistle began inside the continuous booming surf of wind that rolled and rolled against them, and that shriek rose until it overpowered the roar, until it seemed that the world outside the walls of the gym was made of nothing but wind.

A portfolio of quick sketches, four, five, six to a page: Charlene kneeling with the baby in her arms and her children kneeling around her, all of them with their eyes squeezed shut and hands folded, praying. A teenaged girl in hysterics and Red Cross volunteers holding her. Fear on every face. The cardplayers hunched over their cards. Her seatmate from the bus with her eyes shut tight, her hands over her ears. Mouths opened to scream, pantomimes of fear. Finally, when it seemed that the wind was making the charcoal skitter over the page, warping her lines, Louisa closed her sketchbook, put it back in her portmanteau, then sat up straight with the bag on her lap, as though she were waiting for a ride. The cardplayers had stopped playing; their cards still dealt on the blanket; the tattooed man and his girlfriend had rolled together on their blanket and were holding each other tightly.

Just after midnight, water started in under the gymnasium doors, a wide, shallow river, pushed by the wind. As it spread across the floor, the people nearest the door jumped up, grabbed their blankets, and looked around angrily, as if someone had to answer for this. A man was running; she saw him stumble over legs, knock a woman down. A man from the Red Cross ran after him. Panic came over her like cold liquid thrown suddenly in her face, and she wanted to get up and run, too. The name of Jesus rushed up her throat and filled her mouth, and she hadn't been thinking of him. Then the next gust began, a howling shriek that spiraled higher, then higher, as though it would never stop until it had reached the sound that was the key to the lock of the door into the place where destruction had been kept since the beginning of time. Now the whole building hummed; the walls bowed in, and the roof lifted. She could feel it tug, feel the bricks of the walls pulling up from the ground with a subtle ripping sound, like a tooth coming out, as though the pull of the wind were irresistible; it had filled the bricks with a mania to fly. Soon, Louisa thought, soon. The roof will be torn off and the wind will come down and scoop us up and fling us away, like scraps of paper thrown up into the roaring darkness. *This is the end of my life.* She felt calm, peaceful, and for a moment she thought she was dying right then, drowning, because this peace was what was supposed to come with drowning. When Charlene looked at her, wild-eyed, she smiled gently and nodded.

Then the lights flickered and went out, and she wasn't drowning anymore. A scream with her voice in it fought its way up through the sound of the wind. In the dark, she reached over, found Charlene's arm, and patted it. Then she felt in her bag for her flashlight and, by its light, looked at her watch: 12:30. The watch had been a present from her parents on her thirteenth birthday, and ever since, the same small face had measured time's steady progress, wherever she'd been. She tried to picture the upstairs room in their house and all of them gathered there; she closed her eyes and listened for her mother's voice, but there was only the wind. She tried to picture her house, her chair, the light of the lamp beside her chair, to picture the banister rail, worn smooth by all the hands that had followed it, but the wind had filled up the universe now; it had swept her house away. She tried to picture the three brick Hilliard tombs beside the brick walkway in the back corner of St. Philip's churchyard, but all she saw was water pouring over the Battery wall, washing through the streets, smashing tombs, uprooting graves. They couldn't bury deep, and after other hurricanes, it had happened: coffins bumping around the flooded streets, washed out to sea and never found, or found overturned and empty.

Someone nearby switched on a lantern. It threw a small circle of bright light and a wider pool of dimmer glow. By its light, she saw Charlene's children swarming over her, trying to claw their way into their mother's lap. When one scrambled on, another fell off; they were hurting the baby, her face screamed, and Charlene was frantic, too, trying to hold on to them all and protect the baby from their scrabbling. That is when it came over Louisa, another wave, like panic: She had to get to Charlene, and it wasn't charity this time, charity had unraveled and blown away hours ago. It wasn't Charlene who needed comforting this time; that's not why she was crawling or why her heart was pounding until she thought it might rip through her chest. Then she was sitting next to Charlene on her blanket, each of them grabbing for the other's hand. Holding on to Charlene with one hand, Louisa grabbed one of the boys with the other and pulled him into her lap. He huddled against her, panting. He clung to her by two tight handfuls of jacket, as though she were the edge of a cliff he was about to fall off of. She stroked his stiff short hair, laid her cheek on top of his head, and this wasn't charity, either; this was touch — it was to be two instead of one in the wind that was about to smash this building, come in among them and smash them, too. "Noble? Mervin?" She said the names into the child's ear, but he trembled, clung harder, his heart beating so hard, she could feel it thud against her chest where her own heart hammered. She wrapped her arms around him, and still he was rigid, buzzing with fear. She rocked him and told him that it was going to be all right, all right, over and over, and then she realized, amazed, that he believed her, because she felt his heartbeat slow and his grip loosen.

Evelyn Pope
1989
Edisto Island, South Carolina

She worked for Rembert Eubanks, managing his tomato-packing operation out on Edisto Island. Had worked for him close to twenty-five years now, since right after Cassandra, her youngest, was born. Her husband, Albert Pope, had been a smart man, a kind and generous man, but he never was a very ambitious man. They'd met at South Carolina State, both business majors, but when his father died the summer between his sophomore and junior years, he'd dropped out of school and gone back to Edisto to take over the family shrimp boat; she'd stayed to graduate, then followed him home.

Once they were married, he'd renamed their boat the *Lady Evelyn*, after her. Every day for the first year they were married, she'd go down to the dock on Big Bay Creek and watch him back the *Lady E.*, with her complicated racks of net rigging jutting out, into the short slip between two other boats, as nimbly as if he were parallel parking their Oldsmobile in downtown Charleston. Sitting on the dock every day, watching Albert handle the boat, she'd wondered and dreamed how their lives might be if her husband ever turned the skill and energy with which he parked the big boat to buying a second boat and hiring another crew, investing in a refrigerated truck and selling his shrimp directly to the Charleston restaurants. More than once—not so he'd think she didn't believe in him, but casually, as though it were a new idea each time—she'd offered to call on the restaurants, try and put them under contract for their shrimp, guaranteed fresh off the boat, four times a week.

All during their married life, though, Albert was content to work his one boat and sell his catch right there at the dock to people who turned around and upped the price by a third before they sold it. They'd built a nice brick home in a pretty stand of oaks back on St. Pierre Creek where Albert could pull his oyster boat right out of the water and up into the yard. When he wasn't shrimping, he was out in the creeks harvesting oysters, and when he wasn't oystering, he was fishing or putting on oyster roasts and fish fries at the church anytime anybody so much as mentioned the words, because Albert loved being out on the water, eating what he pulled out of the water and feeding people, more than he cared about making money or getting ahead. That was the truth about Albert; she'd realized early on that it was what she'd loved about him in the first place, and she'd made her peace with it.

So, right after Cassandra was born, she'd gone out and gotten a job at Eubanks's packing shed. Mr. Eubanks's operation was the biggest one on the island, spread over the old Toogadoo Plantation land: one hundred acres of tomato fields and a packing shed—an open pavilion, the tin roof held up by thick posts over a concrete slab; inside, a long conveyor belt and heavy wooden crates, stacked high—set in the middle of the field next to the highway and shaded by an enormous oak. She'd started out working on the grading line, and within six months she was handling the payroll; within a year she was running the place for Mr. Eubanks. Now Albert was dead and buried these seven years; the house on St. Pierre Creek was paid for; Cassandra was grown and off in the army, with children of her own; Albert junior, the one everybody called Son, was standing on his own two feet at last;

and here she still sat in her little office at the back of the packing shed, where the adding machine whirred and the air conditioner labored and dripped water into a pie plate on the floor, because there were always people in her church who needed work and because there was still more to learn about the tomato-packing business. No one knew it yet, but she had her eye on one of the smaller operations on the island that she'd heard might be coming up for sale, something for her daughter to come back to after her tour of duty was over.

From late June into September, the shed was lit up round the clock; the tomatoes flowed by, an endless rumbling stream of them. They always needed more hands to pick the crop or unload the boxes of tomatoes off the wagons coming in from the fields and start them along the conveyor belt; to cull and sort and hold the boxes at the end of the line; finally, to lift the heavy boxes onto the trucks that backed up to the loading dock at the rear of the shed. Plenty of work for all. When he'd started his climb up from the bottom of his life, Son had worked there for almost a year. He'd hosed off conveyor belts, carried out buckets of bruised and rotten fruit, stacked boxes, anything she told him to do without getting loud or arrogant. That's how she'd known he was serious this time. It had been while he worked there, too, that he'd turned his life over to God and set his foot back on the pilgrim's way that he'd been raised to walk. Cassandra had worked there, too, culling and grading every summer from the year she'd turned thirteen straight on through high school, until the day after graduation, when she'd driven to Charleston and joined the army.

Most days, even in fall, Evelyn came in early to open up, and this was one of those mornings. Earlier, the hurricane had passed over them like one of the plagues over Egypt. Boiling darkness and wind that had split old trees and sent them crashing and driven water up out of the creeks to flood the roads. This morning as she drove into the lot, the eastern sky was lightening, fog draped the long straight furrows in the field, the shed seemed to float, an island on a cloud, surrounded by the dozing shapes of tractors and combines. As her headlights swept across the field nearest the shed, a great blue heron lifted out of the fog and rowed slowly away toward the treeline. She watched until it disappeared into the dark, massed trees at the field's edge, then she sat in the car with the engine off and the windows rolled down, listening. Listening to the quiet move out and out, pushing trouble in front of it the way the big brooms swept trash out of the shed, until whatever she'd been twisting and worrying in her mind as she drove to work had been pushed into the trees and she sat at the middle of a wide, clean space full of silence and morning light.

Then she went inside, switched on her coffeepot, tidied her office, dusted and straightened the pictures on her desk. Cassandra and the babies; Son in a white shirt and a red tie, looking straight into the camera, his Bible open on the table in front of him. There was Albert, throwing his cast net out in the creek behind their house. And there was Grandmother Mamie down at Edisto Beach, holding a fishing pole and sitting on a yellow lawn chair in the edge of the ocean, little white pigtails all over her head and her bare feet in a swirl of ocean water. The picture had been made in August of her last year; by Christmastime, she was gone, her grandmother, who'd raised her in the Marions' kitchen house in Charleston, then sent her out to Edisto to live when the time came for her to go. In the picture, her face was the weariest face that Evelyn had ever seen this side of the undertaker's front parlor, and yet, shining out through the weariness was a peace you could lean against. *My soul is rested*, that picture said. *My work is done*.

She'd just settled down with the invoice for the repair of the John Deere disk harrow. It had looked high to her, so she'd had the repair shop itemize the charges, and she was combing through them, line by line, when the phone rang. "Evelyn Pope, please," a voice said, a quiet, familiar voice, and even though those three words weren't enough to place it, her heart startled at the sound.

"Speaking."

"Evelyn, this is Louisa Marion calling. I hope you're well."

She put her hand to her chest and patted the spot where her heart pounded. That explained it, then, the sudden fright at the sound of Miss Louisa's voice. It had been Miss Louisa who'd called one evening years earlier and said, "Evelyn, I'm afraid I have bad news for us all." She'd known, of course she'd known, what the bad news would be. During her grandmother's last months, Evelyn had driven to Charleston almost every day after work to see her, and every day the old woman had looked smaller in the bed; every day, she'd been weaker, until Evelyn had had to support her head just to bump a glass of water against her grandmother's lips. She'd known the end was near, but that hadn't made it easier when it came. Now she said, "Very well, thank you. And yourself? That storm didn't bring you too much grief, did it?" as her heart fell back into its normal rhythm and she resumed ticking off her numbers, holding the phone between cheek and shoulder to leave her hands free.

"Oh, my house was just a mess. Glass everywhere and water and mud. I'm still digging out from under it, to tell you the truth. But it wasn't as bad as some. How did you all fare out there?"

"Tree fell and crushed my carport, and I had to tear up the carpet where the water ruined it. Out here at the shed, we lost some roof and the packing boxes got scattered clear out to the road, but, all in all, it wasn't too bad. At least we didn't lose any*body*."

"I'm glad to hear that," she said, and then she got to the point. "Evelyn," she said, "I was wondering if you might come help me finish putting my house back in order. That mold and mud are getting the best of me, I'm afraid. I'd pay you, of course," she said quickly, "whatever you think it's worth."

Evelyn put the invoice down on her desk, took off her glasses, laid them on top of the paper and folded the stems, heard Son's voice answering for her: *Like money's the point, Mama.* For once, she agreed: No amount of money anyone could offer would make her set foot in that house again, but to Louisa Marion she said, "Miss Marion, I have a job, you know," in the voice that she was going to use later, when she called that man who'd clearly over-charged them for repairing the disk harrow.

"Oh, I know that," Miss Marion said. Her voice was still soft but there was no give to it now. "Of course I know that, Evelyn. I just thought if you had some time to spare over the weekend you could come help me out." Miss Louisa Marion had spoken. Evelyn would help her; the only decision left to be made was when. Evelyn sat very still. This was the voice that had pushed and pulled and moved her around for much of her young life. Now it had found her again and started the memories flowing.

The three of them—Mother Mamie, Granddaddy King, and Evelyn—had lived together in one of the two big rooms that made up the kitchen house. Right after she'd come back to Charleston with her mother, there'd been four of them: she and her mother slept in one bed, Mother Mamie and Granddaddy in another. That wasn't supposed to last long—the Marions wouldn't allow it—and it hadn't lasted, but not because of any-thing the Marions had allowed or forbidden. She and her mother were going to move out, but her mother was so sick; she didn't re-member much about her except how tall she'd looked, lying on the bed with a sheet pulled up to her chin and her feet hanging off the end of the bed; that and the way she'd turned on her side and dangled a key chain over the side of the bed for Evelyn to play with. But what she remembered most about her mother was the way her breathing had filled the room; night and day it had raked the air. Then one morning she'd been sitting on the brick floor beside her mother's bed, following an ant as it wound its way be-tween bricks, when the house had gone quiet. She'd watched the ant and the house had stayed quiet until Mother Mamie came out to check on her. Then there was a sharp single clap, the sound

Mother Mamie made in church sometimes when the Holy Ghost came to her, then a rising wail: *"Oh my Jesus. Oh my Jesus Lord."*

After that, it was the three of them, and the brick wall beside her bed had been her room. As a child, she'd studied the crushed shells in the tabby mortar between the old soft bricks. Older, she needed someplace to hang her things. Granddaddy King had scrounged some old wooden shutters from the house and leaned them against the wall beside her bed. He'd tacked small nails along the tops of the shutters and she'd hung a mirror there, a necklace of green beads, two dresses, and a coat. During the day, she worked alongside Mother Mamie in the house, and at night she lay on her bed and studied her things. When she'd turned thirteen, Mother Mamie had pushed a bureau between Evelyn's bed and their own, hung an old blue calico curtain printed with sprigs of tiny yellow flowers above the bureau. From her bed behind the curtain, she could hear her grandmother and grandfather rustle and groan on their straw tick mattress.

As she grew, it had seemed to her that she couldn't move or look around without bumping into another person or their possessions. Granddaddy King was so tall, he stooped when he came through the door. He fished for a living, and in hot weather his smell filled up the place. In her prime, Mother Mamie was tall, like her daughter, Evelyn's mother, with big feet and wide, flat hands. Over time, Evelyn had learned to lie on her bed and read with her back to the room. In winter, she sat quietly and looked into the fire, her knees drawn up to her chin, pretending that there was a circle drawn around her and inside this circle, she was invisible.

Her grandparents had set two straight chairs with caned seats in front of the fireplace, with a table in between where Mother Mamie kept her Bible. In cold weather they sat there every evening. One winter night, they were sitting in their chairs in front of the fire while Evelyn sat on the floor between the chairs, wrapped in a blanket. Mother Mamie was sewing buttons on the Marions' shirts while Granddaddy King mended his shrimp net, and as he held it up to inspect it, he'd said that another fisherman had seen a mermaid in the harbor that day. She'd come swimming right up beside his boat and asked his name, but he'd told her "Cooch"; he knew not to give his real name, else she might call him by it and he'd have to go with her.

"Remember it been over there to Dr. Trott house on Tradd Street time the big fever going round and the rain won't stop?" Mamie said. Granddaddy nodded, bent over his net. "Word come back that rain and that fever was account of the mermaid been snatch out of the ocean and lock up in a jar down there in Dr. Trott cellar. Awful smell like fish and old butter all over town. Everybody been clamor to turn her loose so the rain stop and the sickness go away. Somebody been heard her tell how that's what would stop it if she was toss back where she come from. That's how people come to be mingling round Dr. Trott house trying to look in see the jar where she been kep."

A stick snapped in the fire; the chair cracked as Mother Mamie shifted in it. Evelyn looked up; Mother Mamie's stories always stopped before they were done. "What happened?" she said.

Her grandmother shrugged. "White folks got mad finally, ran peoples off from around that house."

"Did the rain stop? Did people stop dying?"

"Look like they must've," Mother Mamie said, "sooner or later."

By the time Evelyn left the kitchen house for Edisto Island, Miss Louisa was the boss. Her mother was forever out and about, and Miss Louisa made up the menus, supervised the cooking, assigned the housecleaning chores and saw that they got done. It had been her voice that had come through the screen door at Mother Mamie's: "Evelyn, we need you in the house, please," though there was nothing polite about that *please*; it was the period at the end of the sentence, nothing more. As a girl, living in her grandmother's room, Evelyn had tried to hide when Miss

Louisa came to the door, hoping she'd go away. But Miss Louisa would shade her eyes, her hand pressed against the screen; Evelyn remembered the dark, blurred bulk of her at the door and herself with no place to hide. Even now, in her nightmares, which didn't come often but lingered when they came, she was always crouched in the corner of an empty box while a big face stared down, looking for her.

All that from a voice, a simple request, and no one the boss of anyone anymore, at least not in the old way. Evelyn took a deep breath; her heart was starting up on her again. Then, as usual when she got scared, she got mad right behind it. She could feel it flooding up inside her chest, like hot water rising. "Well, no," she said. "I wouldn't be able to do that, Miss Louisa."

For a moment, there was silence, then: "Well, all right, Evelyn, but would you know anybody who might?"

She didn't know that, either, she said. She didn't know anybody who did that kind of work any longer.

"Nobody in your church?"

"Not that I can think of right offhand."

There was a silence; then Miss Marion said, "Well, if you think of anybody, please give me a call. You have my number, don't you?"

"I'll do that," Evelyn said; "I surely will."

She hung up the phone, snugged it down good in the cradle. Then she went back to the invoice, and she didn't think about the call any more that day. At home later that evening, though, cleaning up the kitchen after supper, as she draped the dish towel on the edge of the sink to dry, the thoughts rolled and rolled. You go along and you go along *lippity-clippity*—Mother Mamie's words for the pace that would carry you most reliably through life— pulling steadily away from things you wanted to forget, keeping your face always turned toward the rising sun of the next day that the Lord had prepared for you to live in, when all of a sudden, a voice came over the telephone line, called you by name, and yanked you back. And just like that, she was a child again, standing in the Marions' kitchen with Mother Mamie, beating biscuit dough a hundred, two hundred strokes, snapping warm biscuits into the bread basket liner, a loose linen flower, with petals to tuck the biscuits into. She was standing next to the sideboard in the Marions' dining room at Christmastime, dressed in a black taffeta uniform, an organdy apron, and a stiff white cap, holding a silver tray on which the party guests placed their empty champagne glasses. The bobby pins that held the cap in place had pressed into her scalp and made it itch, but she knew better than to scratch her head when she was serving a party. The one time she'd tried it, Mother Mamie, dressed in her own apron and uniform and cap, had snatched her hand down, nearly upset her tray. "Scratch yourself on your own time, girl," she'd hissed into her ear. As she was falling asleep, she remembered the angelabra in the middle of the Marions' dining room table and how she'd watched it go round and round, the tiny chimes ringing as the small dangling rod on the foot of each trumpeting angel struck a bell.

Next morning when the alarm went off, it was light outside; she sat up in a panic. *Late, I'm late.* She'd been dreaming that she was back in Mother Mamie's house after she'd failed all but one of her courses her first semester at South Carolina State and dropped out. Too much loafing and partying—she'd been a good-time girl. Mother Mamie hadn't batted an eye ("Too many stars been cloud the girl eyes," she told her churchwomen friends); then she informed Evelyn that her lazy behind wasn't going to be lying around *her* house all day long. Either work for the Marions or Mamie would find work for her to do. Evelyn said she'd rather do anything than work for the Marions again. Granddaddy King was dead by then; it was just the two of them, but being back in that place in her bed in the corner with the green shutters leaned up against the wall had made her feel crumpled up and small again, like a piece of tinfoil mashed into a ball. Mamie had gotten her hired onto a crew that one of her friends ran, cleaning rental houses over on the Isle of Palms. The van would come around before daylight and the driver would tap the horn once and wait, but not for long, motor idling, mosquitoes dancing thick in the headlight beams. And Evelyn would stumble out of the kitchen house and climb onto the van, lunch in a paper sack that Mother Mamie had packed for her.

When she went back to school, she settled down and studied hard; she made the dean's list every semester until she graduated. She'd met Albert at South Carolina State, and they'd had a good life. All that had happened to her, and yet Louisa Marion's phone call lingered like the flu, dragging at her all the next day. And on the evening of that day, she was sitting in her own living room after supper, reading the paper and drinking a glass of tea, when some leaves rustled suddenly outside, as though someone were walking through them, and she shot out of her chair and stood there with the paper in her hand and her hair prickling up on the back of her neck. "Who's there?" she said, half-expecting to find someone standing on the stoop of her house, looking in through her front door.

Welcome Home
(Louisa Marion, 1989)

Evelyn or no Evelyn, the work got done. It wasn't the heavy, grinding labor that she'd needed Evelyn for in the first place; crews of men had already replaced the Sheetrock in the downstairs room and refinished the floors. All she'd needed had been an extra pair of helpful hands to roll some paint on a wall, to wax a few pieces of furniture and polish the silver, but Evelyn couldn't even spare the time to do that. Well, fine. But just to show that God was in His heaven and all was right with the world: She'd been in the middle of her fifth walk up and down the first-floor piazza, breathing deeply and calming down after the phone call, when there'd come a knock at the door that opened onto the sidewalk from the piazza, and she'd opened it, to find two Mormon boys standing beside their bicycles in their bright white shirts and black trousers, offering help. They'd meant it, too, rolled up the sleeves of those clean white shirts and worked all morning without even stopping to drink a glass of water. One painted the walls in the downstairs reception room; the other hung the door of the kitchen house back on its hinges, then trued and oiled it so that it swung open and closed without squeaking. When they were done, they wouldn't take more than a peanut butter sandwich and a glass of milk each in payment. They ate at her kitchen table as diligently as they'd worked, and when they'd finished eating, they'd lined up at the sink and taken turns washing their plates and glasses, setting them on the drain board. "God bless you," they said as they rolled their bicycles back onto the sidewalk. Watching them ride away, she knew He had.

Then Susan had found a woman, a quiet, hardworking young woman who didn't consider housework beneath her. Two weeks later, the pictures were back on the walls of both their houses and the silver was polished. After that, Susan left on a trip: a cruise through the Caribbean first, with two granddaughters for company, then on to Europe, where her whole family would meet her in London for Christmas. Then Susan would go on to Greece until spring. It was just like Susan to take a trip like that. As long as Louisa had known her, her friend had lived by this law: If something terrible happens, something equally wonderful must follow, for balance, as compensation. After her husband died on his sailboat off Sullivan's Island of an aneurysm in the brain, she'd had their beach house there torn down and a larger one built, four stories tall, with room for all the children and grandchildren, and the children and grandchildren to come. In the hurricane, Susan's house had lost its roof and the rain had poured in. Now she would travel around the world.

It was late November when Susan left. That morning, Louisa had driven Susan and her granddaughters to the airport. Susan and the little girls had worn matching dresses with sunflowers on them. That had been the last she'd seen of them: a flash of bright sunflowers moving down the walkway to the plane. Now she was home, sitting on a lounge chair in her garden, a cup of coffee on a small table beside her, steaming in the cool air.

The day was clear, the light of the sun thinning; the dew on the grass was cold. A hundred years earlier, she thought, it might have been on a day just like this one that a person might have let out the breath she'd been holding all summer as she waited to be struck down by whatever fever was circulating through the city during the hot months, the sickly season, and let herself believe that she might live another year. She felt the sun warm her face, the cool air all around. She watched the light on the old bricks of the wall, the shifting, patchy sunshine filtering through the leaves of the water oak that spread over the corner of the yard, the stir of the moss that hung from the tree. Looking up, she noticed that the blue plastic was gone; the roofs of her neighbors' houses were coming back, and the walls. New glass shone in her own windows and doors; the young tea olive tree she'd bought to replace the old one, which the saltwater had killed, had just this week put out its first tiny sweet flowers. Hard to believe after what the hurricane had done.

She remembered coming home three days after the storm. The National Guard had been patrolling her street and the power was out. The street had been wet and coated thickly with mud, a chaos of limbs, bricks, shingles. It had been late afternoon when she'd pushed open the street door and stepped onto the piazza of her house, seen twisted hinges, broken glass on the sills. Silver, china from the sideboard, pictures—all lay in the salty gray mud in the yard. In the side yard, her flowers and ferns were plastered to the ground. An uprooted palmetto had smashed the railing of the first-floor piazza. A drowned cat lay curled around the trunk of the tea olive tree. Sparrows, gulls, terns with claws still curled as if they gripped an invisible branch littered the piazza. And the smells! After the storm, the weather had been cool for two days, but then the heat returned, and the city smelled of mold and sulfur. Of rotting fish and rotting greenery and spoiled food and dead animals. How long she'd wandered in the yard, she could not remember, only that when she'd begun picking up silver and wiping it on her jacket it had been daylight, and when she'd looked up again, it was dark.

Until her dying day, whenever she remembered the hurricane, it would be darkness she would remember first: the dark gymnasium and the wind that had pushed at the walls and pulled at the roof, the darkness she'd walked into inside her own house. Dark-

ness and then the light of the lantern she'd loaded with fresh batteries and left on the counter beside the kitchen sink before the
storm, and how that light had seemed so small, moving through
the larger darkness of the house.

In the reception room, she'd stopped, held the lantern high to
throw a wide circle of light, and saw what she'd dreaded to see.
Her sewing box—which she had not taken upstairs after all—was
turned over and empty, everything washed away. The breakfront
stood swollen and burst open, all the glass knocked out. Her
mother's porcelain shepherds and milkmaids lay smashed and
chipped in the mud on the floor. A magnificent piece, the furniture expert who'd come from the Charleston Museum to appraise
the breakfront had said. Charleston-built, of black cypress, of all
woods most impervious to heat and damp and insects. But not to
floods. When the ocean comes into your house, your house becomes the shore; your possessions and your treasures are the sand.

Backing out of that room into the entrance hall, she'd stumbled, and by the light of the lantern, she'd seen her mother's
shoes, which had overflowed the upstairs bedroom closet and
been stored in the closet under the stairs, lying in a jumble, along
with an old leather suitcase, lying on its side in the thin layer of
mud that covered the floors. Her mother's suitcase, with her initials stamped in gold beside the handle. She set the lantern on the
floor and squatted beside it, flipped the latches. Inside were damp
manila folders, typescripts on onionskin paper, transcripts of some
of her mother's famous talks on Charleston style, on antebellum
manners and customs, on Eliza Hilliard's christening gown. The
last of the Hilliard family things. Receipts, daybooks, a ledger. All
of them damp but none soaked, none ruined. She'd found at the
bottom of the suitcase a bulky package wrapped in plastic and
crisscrossed with several thick rubber bands. She'd stripped off the
rubber bands, found Eliza Hilliard's diary in her hands.

She hadn't seen it in at least ten years. Every time Louisa had
gone to the home to see her mother in her last month of life, she'd

made a mental note, then half a dozen *written* reminders: *Ask Mother where Eliza Hilliard's diary is*. The three times she'd asked, the answer was always the same: Eliza Hilliard's diary had been given to the Historical Society years earlier. It wasn't true, but finally she'd stopped asking; she knew better than to butt against the wall of her mother's stubborn confusion, because whenever she did, it just got harder and higher. Now here it was, and it had been here all along, as though this house were some ancient landscape—or time itself, with its layers of years and centuries—in which lost things appeared when the surface was broken, the way arrowheads, bullets, and bones turn up in plowed fields. Since the storm, she'd felt far away, as though the wind had blown her high up into the air and she were looking down on the wreckage of her house, her city below, but finding the diary had brought her back to earth. That night, it had seemed as though she could feel the old pages dissolving in her hands, and she'd run with her lantern through the house, gathering towels to spread on the dining room table, where she laid the diary out to dry.

Now the work was done and today, for the first time since the hurricane, she was doing nothing more than sitting in her chair in the garden with her hands folded, enjoying the pleasing confusion of warm sun coming through cool air that signaled the arrival of fall. It was at that moment of deepest peace when a strong breeze rattled the fronds of the palmetto near the front wall and lifted the leaves of the hostas off the brick path across from which she sat, and something flashed at her from under the plants. She got up from her chair and lifted the hosta leaves, found Eliza Hilliard's crane-billed scissors. At first, she just held them on her open palm, enjoying the familiar weight, and stared at the curve of the crane's neck that formed the bow handle, the outstretched beak that formed the blades. Then, she snipped the air; the blades moved as easily as though the pivot had been recently oiled, and the blades closed with a small, clean snap, the way they'd always done. That sound made her happy, and she stayed happy until she slipped the scissors into the pocket of her slacks, and that is when it came over her: *My mother is dead.* And she sat back in her chair, put her face in her hands. She hadn't cried at her mother's funeral or after the hurricane; at Hugh's funeral, maybe, but not at her father's, and every day for a month after Henry had left, but she hadn't forgotten how. She sat with her hands over her face, her elbows on her knees and her knees spread wide, and cried until it seemed that she'd emptied a place inside her that had been full so long, she didn't notice anymore, as though it were just another discomfort she'd learned to live with, like an aching shoulder or a stiff ankle.

After that, the restlessness began. Roaming the house at 3:00 or 4:00 A.M., unsoothed by five, then ten milligrams of Valium, she would watch the sunrise over the harbor from a chair on the second-floor piazza. If she did sleep, dreams woke her or, worse, sounds, or the lingering echoes of sounds. The roar of the wind, and other sounds, too. When the seasons turned or the weather changed, the wood in the house shrank or swelled. For two centuries, sleepers had been waked by the shiftings in the old house's joints. She'd lived in this noisy place for sixty-five years; she'd heard every kind of creak and groan. But these latest noises didn't come from wood; they came from life, from time, as though the wind and water had gotten in and let loose whatever had been sealed away behind plaster and lathe, set it free to swirl and wash through the house.

Once, it was a heavy shower of ashes down the capped chimney of her bedroom fireplace, a medicinal bitterness in the air. Another morning, she woke in her cold bedroom, in clean autumn sunlight, to a familiar jingling sound. Mamie had owned a dozen narrow silver-plated bracelets, costume jewelry that everyone gave her for Christmas and birthdays, and she wore them all on one arm. Without opening her eyes, Louisa knew it was Mamie by the sound of those bracelets, the smell of sweet soap, and by the rough skin of the palm that smoothed back her hair. "Get up, Miss," she said. "Schooltime now."

"All right, Mamie," Louisa answered, and swung her feet over the side of the bed, held out her hand. Most troubling of all, she began to sleepwalk. One night, she heard a woman crying and went to help. She woke up halfway down the back stairs. The sight of her own bare right foot lit up by the stairwell night-light made her grab the handrail to keep from falling. Another time, she woke up at the long oval table in the dark dining room with her glasses on, holding a page from Eliza Hilliard's diary. "Turn on the light, Louisa," her mother's disapproving voice said. "Even you can't read in the dark."

The next night, she woke up in the dining room doorway (or maybe she didn't wake up, because what happened then, the swirl of time and the woozy shift of image, shape, color, and character, happens only in a dream), just as a page from Eliza Hilliard's diary fell back onto the towel, as though, startled by her approach, someone had dropped it. At first, she was frightened; then she got very still, listening, and she knew by the way the hair stood up along her arms, her eyesight sharpened, that someone was in the room, standing behind the dark the way Mamie used to stand behind her mother's chair while they ate a meal, ready to be sent on her next errand. "Mother?" she said quietly. (It would be just like her mother to come back to check up on her this way: bossy and invisible, untouchable, completely out of reach.)

Silence. "Hugh? Papa?"

"I thought you couldn't read," someone said. And she heard, from the room's far corner, near the fireplace, the rustle of cloth and then a sizzle, as though someone had spit into a fire. "Mamie?" she said.

Once in broad daylight, she heard her mother humming in the

kitchen. Once, the springtime smell of jasmine, tea olive, wisteria, and basil came in through the locked window and filled her room. Another time, it was the late-night slide of the cut-glass stopper in and out of the bottle of port, Hugh's careful footsteps on the stairs. Once it was the sound of keys, the hiss of her mother's oxygen. Then it was herself at nine, embroidering her first sampler, the tree of life, and her mother's voice: "That row of stitching is crooked, Louisa. You'll have to tear it out and start over." This last made her clench her fist and swallow hard in anger, a long, banked anger, stirred up. There was always *something* more that needed doing, always more effort to be made; the most she'd learned to expect from her mother was permission to go on to the next thing and try to get *that* right, knowing as she did that it would never be. Sometimes it was only drifting strands of talk. "We always had linen napkins at our table," her own voice spoke once from somewhere behind her as she stood at the sink, rinsing her supper dishes. "My mother liked a formal table."

Then one morning, her mother called, "Mamie?" and she woke to the smell of hot cloth. Downstairs, she walked into the pantry off the kitchen, where Mamie had always ironed; the room was bright with sun and the smell was strongest there, the way it had been when Mamie ironed and blouses, shirts, dresses swung from every door and cabinet knob.

Sometimes, it was Eliza Hilliard's baby gown that Mamie ironed. Her mother was always giving talks about their seamstress ancestor, and before every talk, Mamie washed and starched the gown by hand, then ironed it until it hung stiff as thin cardboard. Passing by the room where Mamie ironed, Louisa had watched the gown turn in the breeze. Sometimes, if Mamie wasn't around to fuss at her for touching it, she'd run her hand down the dress; she could almost feel a shine coming from inside it, out through the threads. She could look at it every day and notice something new about it; it was as dense as a tapestry with needlework. One time, it would be the French knots that dotted the bodice and sprinkled down the skirt and hem that she noticed; the next time she saw it, the openwork around the hem would draw her eye; another time, it would be the vines or the leaves with their smooth tight edges. Or she would stand back and take it all in, the way the designs poured down the dress and swirled around the hem.

The morning that the smell of ironing was in the house, she was on her way past the dining room door, following the smell, when she saw a piece of paper lying in the middle of the circle of diary pages that she'd laid out on the table to dry. A yellowed scrap of paper with letters printed on it. A note. "COME FOR MY THINGS," inside a lopsided circle. She stopped, then went into the dining room and picked up the note. Had it slipped from the diary pages, been overlooked in the suitcase? She picked up the paper, held it close to her eyes. Who had written this? It didn't take long to tell. She would have known that printing anywhere. Thick, childish, labored. An image came into her mind that was as vivid as the recent dreams: Mamie licking the point of a pencil, frowning, shaking the bracelets down her arm, holding down the top of the paper with her left hand, bending low over the paper and, with the tip of her tongue between her teeth, cobbling her letters together into words. Then it made sense. Evelyn wouldn't come, so her grandmother had. "Of course you have, Mamie," she said. "Welcome home."

But if this were Mamie, she was behaving in a most un-Mamielike way. Their Mamie had been humble, God-fearing, trustworthy, and steady. You could set your clock by Mamie, her mother had always said. You could leave your jewelry out in plain sight and never worry. Their Mamie was expert at all domestic chores. She could pick a bushel of crab in half an hour; her chicken salad had been the wonder of many luncheons. Before the fall candlelight tour, it was Mamie who'd made their woodwork gleam.

Her mother always said that Mamie was the best silver polisher in the city. Around holidays and before big parties, Mamie made extra money, polishing silver for all their friends. She knew better than to touch anyone's silver until she'd put on cotton gloves. She would never have handled their silver with her bare hands, and yet, every morning Louisa found fingerprints all over their famous trade winds pitcher.

Likewise, their Mamie would not have plundered the sugar caddy, a tall mahogany box with a brass lock. She would never have taken the key ring down from the hook in the pantry, where it had always hung—only the mistress of the house ever touched those keys—found the tiny brass key to the sugar caddy, then rummaged in the sideboard drawers and helped herself to a teaspoon. Their Mamie would never have left a mess like the one Louisa found every morning: sugar scattered all over the table and the teaspoon dropped carelessly in the middle of the mess, a line of black ants trekking back and forth across the tabletop.

All these things this Mamie had done, but the most un-Mamie-like thing of all was the greed. "COME FOR MY THINGS." Mamie had not asked for a thing her entire life. What could she possibly want? The day after the note arrived, Louisa went out to the kitchen house to find what she might offer. The herb garden around the sundial in the garden behind the kitchen house was full of spindly yellow stalks of four-o'clocks; a few crickets sang their thin songs. The saltwater had killed everything. Inside, Mamie's things were heaped on the floor, where they'd been dumped after the storm. Of course. Mamie didn't like coming back and finding her house torn apart. "Neat as a pin," her mother always said. Mamie wanted her house back. Not that Mamie *herself* or even her spirit would ever *occupy* the place—it was frivolous; it was dangerous to think that way—but maybe what she wanted was the dignity of *having* a place and having that place respected, set to rights. She'd learned that much during the civil rights movement. Mamie was always touchy about her house. Careful about the spirits of the dead. They were touchy, she said, they had to be appeased or they'd get you. Now she knew what to do. For Mamie, in memory of Mamie, she could put the house back in order. Maybe then her own house would settle down to its usual rhythms; her own life go back to being the life it had been.

She built a fire in the small fireplace on Mamie's side of the kitchen house. In Mamie's time, there had been a gas space heater and Mamie had kept the jets turned on full; even in winter, the room had felt so stuffed with heat, it was hard to breathe in there. Now, as the fire caught, she spread the old patch quilt on the bed, placed the white chamber pot with its chipped lid beside it, straightened the green shutters beside the bed where Evelyn had slept. She found a nail on the wall and hung the triptych, painted on velvet, of Abraham Lincoln, Robert Kennedy, and Martin Luther King, Jr., set the two straight-back chairs in front of the fireplace, and placed the footstool covered with red velvet in front of Mamie's chair. She set the blue metal teakettle, mended on the bottom with a screw and a washer, on the small gas stove. Finally, Louisa picked up the photograph of Maum Harriette. A wide, unsmiling black face under a white turban looked up at her. The woman wore a shoulder cloth, a dark skirt. She held Louisa's mother on her lap, a small girl in high-button shoes, her hair done in ringlets and bows, who sat up very straight, with her feet crossed at the ankles, already looking on at life as if it were a pageant being performed in her honor. She hung the picture over the mantel, where it looked down on the room. She warmed her hands while the fire caught and burned higher, and still the room stayed cold. "There you are, Mamie," she said to the room, and saw her breath in the air. "Are these the things you want?"

In the morning, she went out to the kitchen house in her nightgown and found the answer. Everything she'd placed so carefully the day before had been picked up, handled, dropped, and left where it had fallen. What Mamie was looking for, she hadn't found yet. Then she saw that Maum Harriette's photograph was missing. A thief, she thought, Mamie has turned into a thief. She stalked back into the house, into the dining room, and found sugar all over the table again and Maum Harriette's picture leaning against the wall as though someone had carried it into the room, gotten distracted, and set it down.

All that week, no matter where she put that picture, it ended up back in the dining room. No matter what she offered, it was refused. The speech she gave when invited to speak about the Hilliard family, for instance. She'd found it among the papers in her mother's suitcase after the storm and laid it out to dry on the dining room table. This, then? She read aloud: "We must never think that the planters were an idle or an indolent people, living off the labor of others." The speech went on to talk of the idea of labor. How in the past there had never been a point where work stopped. Hard to understand in our time of cheap mass-produced materials and overwhelming glut, but true. "Work was an endless weaving. Even the beginning was not something you could easily find. Traced back far enough, even the starting point disappeared into more labor. Bricks, for instance. To make bricks, you needed sand and clay. To dig the sand and clay, you had to make a shovel. To shape the bricks, you had to build a form; to build the form, you had to cut a tree and plane it. To cut a tree, you had to make an ax, a plane. To make an ax, you needed a metal ax head, which a blacksmith had to fashion or which you had to order from England, where they were forged."

Next morning, the pages were scattered on the floor, flung aside. No.

This?

Her report on Eliza Hilliard. In her junior year at Ashley Hall, Louisa had written and then read a report on Eliza for the declamation project in her English class. All the girls in her class had written reports on their families and brought in family heirlooms and made presentations. The Middleton girls, the De Sassures, the Simmonses. She'd taken one of Eliza's samplers, her scissors (made of fine English steel, not the inferior product of a northern factory—that had gotten an appreciative laugh), a lace collar, and the baby gown that Eliza had sewed and they'd all been christened in. She hadn't actually *read* the diary to do her report; her mother had summarized it for her and she'd written from her mother's synopsis. *Eliza Hilliard was one of our most fascinating ancestors. She was an exquisite seamstress (show baby gown). Come with me now to her time.*

No.

Surely this is what you want, then, your grandmother's story?

Maum Harriette
Age: 80, b. circa 1850
Edisto Island, South Carolina
Interviewer: Miss Julia Murray

Written in Louisa's mother's hand: "This was our Maum Harriette, who raised me on Fairview Plantation on the Edisto River (also known as the Pon-Pon) in Charleston County, South Carolina, and in our house in town. Interview was conducted for the Federal Writers' Project in 1930s."

Maum Harriette lives in a tidy frame house near Store Creek on Edisto Island. A newly painted picket fence surrounds a neatly swept dirt yard, and a chinaberry tree shades one corner of the yard. Maum Harriette is well known in the Negro community for her work as a Sunday school teacher at Mt. Zion AME Church, where, until his death ten years ago, her husband, James Matthews ("a good ole man, for true"), also served as an elder. A tall, light-skinned woman, she speaks well, as befits a teacher and former house servant, in the Gullah patois that is prevalent on these Sea Islands. The interior of her house is neat and clean and shows the obvious marks of deep religious faith: a well-worn Bible and several pictures of Jesus that hang near her bed and above her fireplace. A basket of wood sits within easy reach of the ancient rocking chair in front of the small fireplace where she spends the cool autumn days. A cheerful fire burned in the fireplace on the morning of our visit and the mantel over the fireplace was crowded with curling photographs of some of her Sunday school classes as well as pictures of the Hilliards, the "gran fambly" of her affectionate memory. A rough-hewn low stool serves as a resting place for her feet. During our talk, she rocked constantly and smoked a pipe. Her mind is clear, though she is crippled with "the misery in all two both" her knees. During the course of the interview, she was visited by a constant procession of well-wishers: once by an old man bringing her a croaker sack of pecans; another time by a young local fisherman who presented her with a fresh mullet; the last by a neighbor woman bearing greens from her garden. Each caller was greeted with enthusiastic warmth, introduced to the visitor, and asked to sit down and join the talk. Though none accepted the invitation, it is clear that Maum Harriette is held in high regard in the community of which she has been a member for over fifty years.

"Before Freedom came, us been Hilliard labor. Worked for Mr. Francis Hilliard out to Fairview Plantation, Pon-Pon River. That been where I first seen light. Our white folks all been big buckra, had dem dat Fairview house and dat house in Charleston and us travel back and forth with them. When the mothers be for go to the fields or up to the big house in the morning, children stay behind. Old lady been watch the children time they mothers work. I remembers that old lady clear as if she been sitting here in the room right now. Little bitty dried-up thing, look like a wasp. Mean as a wasp, too. Used to carry a switch, her tell us say, 'Pick up dat trash, fetch dat water.' Didn't do it, her gone and put a switch to both we legs. Had a big wooden trough up near the kitchen house and when it be come time to eat, ole woman mix up grits and whatnot, pour 'em into that trough. Us each had a wooden spoon, gather round that trough fuh eat. Time come for me for go to work, I go in the house. Lay out the missis clothes, brush hair, all that kinda work. Big, fine house, hadda porch out back, grapevines go clear up 'em. Us be sit out there, clean fish, all kinda work.

"I remember clear as day when Freedom come, end of the Rebble time. I been ten years old. Sunday morning, so nobody been in the fields. My mother work in the big house and she already been up there, see about breakfast, come back down. My father been driver on the place. Us been gone to church and back. Ma'am? . . . Yes'm, us had our own chapel there on the place, Marse Francis built 'em, and us all go there of a Sabbath Day morning. Afterward, people be clean, wash, cook, all dat Sunday work. Us look and see Mr. Francis walking down from the big house, hands clas behind he back, studying the ground. Everybody stir round, tell 'em say, 'What he come here for today, enty?' Us seen him walk that way many and manys of a time, coming down on New Year Day to tell who been sold. One woman husband been carried off the year before. She cry and snatch at she hair, say, 'Do he got the paper? Do he got the paper?' Some tell they children say, 'Go hide to the cabin.' Not do any good. If Marse Francis put your title to that paper, you been gone. That been the way in those slavery times. Come a bad year for the rice, us'd know that sorrow be walking out 'mong us come the New Year Day, for true. My own mother, Abby, been sold one year, come a bad crop, and to this day I can close these old eyes and see her back moving off in the herd they driving down the road. That been the last I ever seen of my mother. Mr. Francis didn't permit no good-byes.

"That Freedom day, though, Mr. Francis walk up the street that run 'tween we houses and when he seen we all be cluster round, he said, 'Well, y'all is free, not a thing I can do 'bout it. Don't know what you gonna do now, but that not my business anymore. Stay here, work for me, I treat you same as always.' Then him turn, walk back up to the big house. Us wait till him be good away, bust out shouting. Old ones been say, 'What gonna be happen to we, enty?' Young ones been sing and shout, glad for freedom till they fool.

"One day after freedom when us still live to Fairview Plantation, my mistress, Marse Francis's wife, us call her Miss Polly, tell me say, 'Harriette, go up to Miss Eliza's old room and fetch me down that blue shawl been lying there.' Now us all been heard 'bout Miss Eliza. She been gone these many years by that time but the colored people scared to go up to her room. Say you could hear a spinnin' wheel there, just spinnin' and spinnin'. Say it spinnin' still. I been nothing but a girl, but I been know what it mean that we been free. I speak plain to my mistress, say, 'No, ma'am, Miss Polly, I not going up in that room.' She turn on her heel and walk away. Been in the ground 'fore two more summers been pass.

"My mother been name Abby and she say my grandmother been call Diana. Run away, is all I know. Don't know my grandfather name, but my own father title been Prince. Live over there to Saint Helena, carpenter work to the school there. [Ed. note: "The school" to which Maum Harriette refers is the Penn School on Saint Helena Island, first established as a school for colored freedmen just after the War Between the States.] We been always told our grandfather been a sailor. In slavery time, any colored sailor come into Charleston harbor on a ship, the buckra been snatch 'im off, put 'im in the Workhouse, what you call the jail. He hafta stay there till time come to sail out again. Buckra be frightened, you see, of strange colored people mixing round.

"Up there in Charleston, I usta been hear 'bout Haiti, where the slaves rose up, threw off the yoke. Used to hear talk in town all the time about Haiti and such. Ma'am? . . . Just whensomever the mistress send we on errands, market, dock, anywhere really. Used to send me out into the street to catch the shrimp man when he go by. Say, 'Take this letter to so and so over to Meeting Street.' Look like there'd be somebody there had some news to tell about the doings of colored people in other parts of the world. So us always hear that our grandfather been a sailor, got together with Grandmother Diana in the Workhouse. Ma'am? . . . Don't know, Miss, no'm sure don't. See, the buckra didn't do the whipping when they stay to town. Back home at Fairview, them be haul off and whip a nigger for whatever he done whensomever he done it. Miss Polly, she fit her hand to the whip, time or two in my remembrance. Yes'm, I seen it with my own two eyes. Lord God! My Jesus put words to my mouth to speak. Lord, Lord, must be the tribulations drawing close, for true! In town I guess they figure it cause too much fuss to have niggers bawling and crying, so send 'em to the Workhouse, whip 'em there. Called it 'the sugarhouse' where they sent 'em. Somebody get sent there us call it 'giving him sugar,' course that's not what he got there, sugar, surely wasn't. Sometimes, if what the nigger done been specially bad, they take 'im down to the market, whip 'im there, say it been a lesson for all the niggers.

"My mother say her mother run off when she been a girl. Some say she land in Philadelphia, Pennsylvania. Some say no, she been gone west, marry a red man. All kinda stories. I got a scrap of old cloth my mother give me before she been gone away. It been kindly golden yellow. Say Grandmother Diana used to wrap up her head in it, sit down to the market, sell sweet potatoes for the missis. Say she been smoke a pipe. Say she been tall.

"I been had six children myself, and two grans. Yes'm, for true. Five in the earth now. Only my oldest gran, Mamie, still living. We sure did hear lots of stories about my grandmother, though. Shut my eyes up tight, sometimes look like she about to appear before me, like I can almost make her up out of everything I heard. [At this, the old woman closed her eyes and began to rock.] Only thing I study over is this. Did my mother know the Savior 'fore she reach to the end of her days? If she did, then I have my

Savior's assurances that we will meet in His kingdom not made by humble hand. If not, then I will never no more know my mother in this or in my blessed Jesus kingdom. [At this, the old woman paused, sang a garbled verse from a hymn, punctuated by emphatic nods and gestures and stampings of her feet. "Oh, my mother done move! / My mother done move. / She done move her campin' groun! / Oh Lord, Lord, have mercy!"]

"You mighty good come see old Harriette and I hope you'll be for to look 'bout that pension. Ma'am? . . . Yes, I been heard about Lincoln, say it's his plan for every man to worship under his own vine. You want I should say some more 'bout slavery times? Those been some times, slavery days. Old Master treat us mighty good at Christmastime, give us jelly biscuits. Alla girl be for get a hand-kerchief, the boy a length of string and a hook. Frolic? Yes, Lord. Go to a frolic or a cornhusking, us girl crush up honeysuckle and rose petal, wear it in we bosom. Make necklace out of chainy-berry. Us take dirt from the smokehouse floor, run water through it to make salt for bread. Our white folks all been big buckra, so many carriage in front of they house in town, line stretch clear round the corner. I never had no quarrel with them. Come back some other time, maybe I remember more."

Over this, Mamie brooded for three days. Brooded, ate sugar, and waited. The air in the house stayed cold and damp, no matter how high Louisa turned up the heat. On the morning of the fourth day, Louisa walked into the dining room, found sugar all over the table. "You poor thing," she said out loud. What else but suffering, she asked herself, would cause someone as neat and tidy as Mamie to make trouble this way, to leave these messes every-where? She said it again: "You poor thing." The air in the room warmed by a few degrees. Who would not lean into pity and let herself be wrapped and comforted in that softness? Then the chill came back. Mamie had not come for the easy comfort of pity.

The next morning, the pages of Eliza Hilliard's diary had been stacked at her place at the table. "Well, thank you, Mamie," she said out loud, in the same voice her mother had used when someone finally had done what she'd asked them to do. So it was the diary she was interested in.

Mamie could read, but reading was work for her, and she loved being read to more than almost anything else. When Louisa was a child, whenever a book was being read, Mamie would appear, carrying her mending or a bowl of potatoes to peel, a basket of laundry to fold, and work so quietly, listening, that the clothes hardly made a sound when she shook them, and the peel curled silently off the potato. Every evening during the last month of Mamie's life, when Evelyn had gone back to Edisto or the women from Mamie's church had washed up the soup bowls and cups they'd used to nurse her and gone home, Louisa would walk out to Mamie's room and find the old woman restless and mumbling, picking at her white cotton bedspread. Louisa would pull the rocking chair close to the bed and read to her until the mumbling and fussing stopped and she lay still. Her skin was the gray of wood ash then, and she did not breathe so much as she sipped the air, a sound so small that Louisa had to put her finger in the book to mark her place, lean close, and listen and watch for the next rise of Mamie's chest to show her that the old woman was still alive.

What did she read? The Bible, of course, and the newspaper, Tennyson from the hurricane times. As long as Louisa read, Mamie was quiet, and sometimes, she smiled, but it was the poems of Robert Frost that brought the deepest rest. Sometimes she would open her eyes then and watch Louisa as she read, her eyes growing darker and darker, as if the old woman were drawing in the words, melting them there. "Tree at My Window" seemed to be her favorite poem, and "After Apple-Picking." As the month went on, Mamie got quieter, took smaller sips of air, and did not open her eyes even to hear Robert Frost. One day, Louisa had just started reading "The Oven Bird"—"There is a singer everyone has heard, / Loud, a mid-summer and a mid-wood bird"—when Mamie died. But the dead were hungry, so Mamie had always said. Homesick and hungry for life and its stories. They gobbled it up wherever they could find it, stuffed it in their mouths like sugar. So it was words that Mamie had come for, Louisa thought, and she had more of those to give.

Eliza Seabrook Hilliard
May 25, 1837
Charleston, South Carolina

We have not been a week in residence here and the rhythms of
city life have again impressed themselves upon my country senses
with the same jarring shocks and dislocations as ever beset me on
coming to town. This morning, I woke to the sound of Mrs.
Legare reproaching her servants from the second-story window of
the next house. It appears that the morning's crime had to do with
broken eggs and the scorched edges of breakfast waffles. She continued her tirade for upward of ten minutes, calling this one
black-hearted, that one a lazy scoundrel, threatening to send
Tenah, her cook, to the Workhouse, to sell their coachman,
Daniel, to the sugarcane fields, remonstrating them all in the
most dire and terrible language—which I shall *not* repeat—and
she a Christian woman, the first into St. Philip's when the doors
open on a Sunday morning. When the Legares are in residence,
the Workhouse treadmill is assured of a constant supply of Negroes to keep it humming. Meanwhile the servants, as is their
habit, languished and drooped and sighed in abject and mournful
misery until Mrs. L. withdrew and all returned to their noisy wash
pots and the boisterous grooming of horses.

I have received so many visits, I do not know when I will have time to return them all. At least I am brought up-to-date on the latest scandals and current news: who is to marry, who in decline, who brought low by the dismal financial state of our city. As my brother has explained to me, our current distress began when a period of intense speculation in western lands caused anxiety among European lenders; then the collapse of I & L Joseph provoked a European rush to call in American loans, which they have done, to the detriment of our economies. Now the banks hoard specie and everyone is short of coin and some much worse and failing. The men go about the streets with worried faces and hands clasped behind their backs, their eyes cast down to the pavement, worry etched on every countenance. Only yesterday, my own brother, sunk deep in thought, bypassed our door and would have wandered on to the end of the street had I not called out to him from the second-floor piazza and roused him from his gloomy musings. Cotton and rice lie wasting on our wharves. The Simmonses, it is said, sold five Negroes last week. And I must resign myself to a longer stay in town (when I had hoped for a brief stopover en route to the Pendleton District).

Mrs. Petigru was my cake and wine guest this afternoon, and later, Mrs. Manigault called, and after that, Mrs. M.'s boy brought cards announcing her daughter's upcoming nuptials to Edward Pringle. Tonight, Thomas is absent from the house for the third time this week. Once to the Agricultural Society dinner and again to a meeting of the Association. Tonight, I know not where he has gone, but he must be about this business of mending the rupture in his relationships with others of our circle caused by his recent stand as a unionist among the nullifiers, of which number the latter outnumber the former, it seems, by several hundreds to one — a mending which, he gave me to understand, was much aided by his contribution to the Agricultural Society dinner of several bottles of our good Madeira. Tonight, when he set out, he looked fatigued, but I could not persuade him to stay home, as he will hear no objection from me concerning his nightly errands. This city has ever worked a transformation in him, and made restless and nocturnal he who at Fairview is the most sanguine and constant of men. When I saw the carriage brought up and Ned standing at the horse's head, I brought my brother his gloves and inquired as to his destination and the likely time of his return. He made no answer, only looked at me fondly and said that I must not add to the store of my worries by troubling myself with his whereabouts. He and Ned drove off in a great boisterous clamor. I pray daily to God that Thomas may yet find a wife and marry again. Since the death of his good wife, Susan, and our beloved mother's passing these two winters past, my burden is increased by the need to create the stabilizing and uplifting feminine sphere of influence in his life. God in His Wisdom has not chosen for me the comforts of the married state; therefore, I rest at peace in His Will and bring what comfort I am able to bring to my brother.

Read the Bible to the household and then retired, refreshed in spirit, to renew my correspondence and to enter this record of the day. Wrote a letter, long overdue, to our brother, George, at Belle Isle Plantation and hope to receive swift assurances that Mary's late infirmities are resolved favorably. Were it not for the difficulties attendant upon traveling up the coast to the Beaufort District, I should go myself to see to my sister-in-law's comfort, but as I am needed here, these slow missives hither and yon must suffice. Afterward, I took up a volume of great interest to me, recommended with much enthusiasm by Mrs. Petrigru, entitled *Letters on Female Character,* by Mrs. Cary of Virginia, in whose wise remonstrance on women's duties, I find my task set clearly before me. "The obligations of charity, coextensive as the benevolence of their hearts— the sweet courtesies of social life—the gentle interference with angry spirits for the purposes of peace-making—the secret prayer— the deep and faithful self-inspection—the meek surrender of all contested privileges—the single-hearted efforts to promote the glory of God, and cultivate good will among men. These indeed are feminine pursuits, and their sweet incense rises to heaven."

So I have again taken up my Charleston journal, wherein I resolve to record the fruits of this "deep and faithful self-inspection" as well as God's dealings with me, His mercies and the necessary trials with which He chastens us in order to elevate our natures. I have further resolved to chronicle in these pages the progress I have made from last year to this in the matter of conquering my besetting sins. All last winter at Fairview, I labored diligently to subdue the twin serpents of willfulness and curiosity that slumber in my bosom. This season in town will prove if I have subdued my will to the will of the Almighty sufficiently to have earned the title of mistress of the household by virtue of having achieved mistressship of myself. To this end, I resolve to pray and read the Bible daily—and to seek to know *His* Will in all things. Lastly, I resolve to question myself regularly on the performance of these duties and to record my findings herein for the good of my soul and the enlightenment and edification of those who come after.

After the time spent in prayer and reflection, I see that Thomas was right about the store of my worries, as they seem greater this year than before. This year, our city household consists of Thomas and myself and the following Negroes: Ned, the porter and coachman; Chloe, the washer; Nancy, the cook; Lucy, Nancy's daughter and cook's helper and market girl; Caesar and Abraham, who tend the fires and run and fetch and carry and see to the yard and stables; and Diana, the new girl. Each year since our mother died, it seems, we require more servants. Our beloved mother ran this household with Nancy and Ned, a washer and a maid, efficiently governed, but I have neither her gift for organization nor her serene forbearance with Negroes. And too, Thomas is much given to sending our servants on errands about the city, and to hiring out Ned and Caesar for various and sundry tasks, and so we must have three where one would suffice, and my powers as mistress are tested daily.

At a quarter past ten, the tattoo sounds, a welcome series of tolling bells and drum taps ordering the Negroes back to their quarters and domiciles. The sound of them hurrying through the streets to reach their appointed dwellings before the drumbeats cease and the watch is mounted is, of all the sounds of this noisy city, the most unsettling to me. Already, our laws forbid them to carry canes, smoke segars, dress above their stations, or congregate in the streets, and yet, it seems, we have not yet found words sufficiently broad to encompass all the prohibitions that must be laid against them. Last week, the council passed an ordinance that forbids the Negroes—slave or free—from raising their voices in the streets. And yet every night when the tattoo sounds, they create such a clamor and din with their running feet, their loud talk and brazen laughter that should every man set out to seize a raucous Negro and bring him into compliance with the law, our houses should be emptied of all able-bodied men, and still the numbers would be insufficient to the task.

Sometimes I walk to the end of our street in search of a freshening breeze off the water, a view out over the ocean to a far horizon, but the glare that rises at midday from these streets of sand and crushed shell blocks sight. How I grieved when the river curved and we lost sight of the Fairview landing and the little Negroes who were all lined up along the riverbank, waving good-bye to their missis and master. From the deck of our sloop, Thomas called to them to mind his shoats and to raise them big and fat and help him win the Agricultural Society prize this year. Last year, we raised five hundred pounds of sweet potatoes! What a comfort it will be to see those small ebony faithfuls waiting for us when we return in the fall and to note how they have grown and prospered. But I could not grieve overlong, for Thomas is so lighthearted on the river and on the ocean going to town, laughing and pointing

out familiar trees and bird life and delighting in the sight of white
sails before the wind that it would be hard-hearted not to share in
his happiness.

We came into town early this year because Thomas was determined to move us out of danger before the miasma rose from the
swamps. No doubt my brother's haste in conveying us so soon to
town this year was occasioned by the deaths last year of our good
neighbors upriver at Willtown Bluff. That unfortunate family, de-
layed by the need for repairs to their sloop and taken with the
sight of their rice lands bedecked in their fine June green, lingered into the sickly season and were struck down. To drive away
the miasma, so we have heard, they shut doors and windows, and
kept indoors, where they built fires and sat close by them, and yet,
before the month was out, the parents were dead of the country
fever and the children sickening, who died before July was half
done. A whole family taken in the twinkling of any eye, a household emptied and a graveyard filled. Now the house lies silent,
the once-thriving lands untended, the Negroes idle or vanished,
though we hear that the place is soon to be occupied by a physician and planter from Savannah.

Once again, I must bow to Thomas's judgment in these matters. He is cautious and thorough, perhaps conscious that of all
our family, only we two, our brother, George, and his wife, Mary,
are left, and these latter are far from us. No doubt he is conscious,
too, of his own reprieve from Death. He has gone through life
much marked by the smallpox he suffered as a child and by the
loss of his gentle wife, our Susan, to the country fever two years
past. Susan placed all her confidence in my brother, and he lives
in torment still that he betrayed that confidence by lingering too
long at Fairview when the heat had increased and the water in the
rice fields and ditches had turned a thick and unwholesome green
and the miasma was clearly rising, because he wanted to oversee
the end of the sprout flow and the beginning of the long water.

That fateful year, I questioned Thomas daily and urged him to set a date for our departure for town, while Susan, as was her habit, showed no anxiety. The sight of her walking serenely about the place, ministering to sick Negroes and overseeing the weaving while the rest of the household kept fearfully indoors, was testament to her faith in her husband. When she fell ill, how often did I pray during the two weeks in which she lingered in great suffering that God would take me in her place. During those two weeks, my brother had to be forced to leave her bedside, even to sleep. In the extremes of her suffering, she was never ill-tempered, and when she came at last to meet the King of Terrors, she cast fond and loving looks upon we who attended her, folded her hands upon her breast, and answered the Dread Summons. I never heard an unkind word pass her lips, and the week before she breathed her last, I vowed to look after Thomas and to see that he did not go astray.

While the Negro gale was blowing full force through the streets, I came into the downstairs parlor and found the new girl leaning out of an open window, conversing with a member of the mob and laughing. I spoke to her forcefully about opening windows at night and exposing the household to the night air, since even in the city we must be vigilant. Here, we are surrounded by swamps; the city itself rests on low, boggy ground. We are never far from the reach of the miasma and all its attendant fatal outcomes. Even the breeze from the sea cannot sufficiently disperse the unhealthy emanations from the soil. When I had finished speaking, she closed the window, dropped a curtsy, and left the parlor, but she seemed not at all chastened.

She is a likely girl, a bright mulatto, eager, it seems, to please, quick and clean, and yet there is something about the set of her head that gives me cause to question the suitability of bringing her so soon to town. She was bought, along with her girl child, Abby, from Mr. Alonzo White in March and warranted sound and free of vices, as testimony to which, she bears no marks of correction. She wears on one finger what appears to be a whalebone button smoothed and thinned into a crude ring, but when questioned about its origins, she looks down at the floor and offers an obscure, confused report of a husband, a boatman on the Waccamaw. She was Thomas's gift to me on the occasion of my thirty-fifth birthday, bought to replace old Lucy, who died last spring. According to Mr. White, she came from a large Virginia plantation, where she had often been afflicted with female maladies and unable to work. From thence, she was sold to Mr. Pierce Butler at Butler's Island, where the afflictions and complaints continued, though, according to her former master's description as conveyed to us by Mr. White, it was believed that a strict master or mistress could cure her of her complaints. Daily I pray to God that I shall prove worthy of that task.

At one of our conferences in preparation for coming to town this year, I spoke to Thomas of my misgivings about bringing a new, unseasoned servant to the city, where temptations and distractions importune them far more urgently than they do at home. How pleasant it was to sit on the porch and to watch the river, which flowed as it has flowed forever through our property, sipping the coffee that Nancy brought and talking over our affairs. That world now seems as far from this one as the East is from the West. I raised with my brother the possibility of Diana's proving to be a burden to me, who must see to the smooth running of the household and attend to all its wants as well as to the health and discipline of its inhabitants without our dear mother's guidance. At Fairview, as part of her seasoning, this Diana was put to work in the field closest to the public road and ordered to keep the crows away from the new rice shoots after the sprout flow had been drained and the Negroes were at their hoeing. She discharged her task well enough, though within a month she had secured Thomas's permission to tend a flock of English ducks and had set up a stand on the road there where she sold duck eggs to travelers as well as the ducks themselves, with their necks deftly wrung if fresh duck was her buyer's fancy. I fear the result of such license was to make her impudent, though Thomas takes delight in Negro initiative. "If she carries her head high in the country," said I, "what will become of her in town?"

"She must be taught to lower it," my brother answered, indicating with a sweep of his hand our fields full of Negroes diligently hoeing, and with those words, the matter was laid to rest, and I submitted myself to my brother's will, and thus it came to pass that Diana was brought with us into the city and the child, Abby, left behind at Fairview.

But I am the most ungrateful of sinners. I have dwelt too long on troubling subjects and forgotten my debt to Almighty God for all His blessings. From year to year, I forget how beautiful this city is. The harbor bristles with the masts of ships. The house is filled with friends and activity to chase away the hours when melancholy thoughts might interpose themselves between one's mind and its proper habits of happiness, serenity, and gratitude. I have taken to my needle again and while away many pleasant hours at my sewing. The pages of the *Courier*—the only newspaper my brother will allow in our house because its unionist sentiments lately matched his own, while the *Mercury* was aflame with nullifier sentiment—are filled with notices of the arrival of the most exotic goods and pleasures to our port. It is dizzying just to scan the list of books arriving daily on the English ships. Today alone brought notice of a new edition of the works of John Milton and several fascinating new botanical texts, though I am determined to resist the temptations attendant upon such desires and strive to carry out my plan for spiritual advancement. And there is ink in bottles! And paper, of which I have covered a sufficient number of sheets for one day! And when the Negro din has subsided and order is restored to our streets, when the lamplighter makes his rounds and the sound of the horses of the watch passing through the streets begins its comforting tattoo, then I am grateful once more to God, who in His infinite Goodness and Mercy has given us this world in which to live out our mortal destinies, and I ask His blessings on us all. "God, grant me a double portion of the grace of Thy Spirit that I may learn to do Thy Will." Amen.

June 12, 1837

Good news has reached us over the din next door. (For all Mrs. L.'s vigilance, her yard is the noisiest on the street, loud with constant Negro comings and goings, quarrels and outbursts.) After dinner this afternoon I went to return Mrs. L.'s visit of two days ago and found her cutting out a suit of curtains for the servants to make up, her face wreathed in smiles at the glad happiness of her news. Her oldest daughter, Rachel Hayne, will travel here from the Waccamaw to undergo her first confinement in her mother's house. Rachel has asked that her mother travel to Georgetown to attend her in her Trial, but as Mrs. Legare could not be spared, Mr. Legare being at times absent from the family and at other times so much present as to require the full attention of every member of the household, it was judged more desirable for Rachel to travel to her mother's house. She will travel by boat, an easy trip on the outside route if the weather hold fair. Mrs. L. has this day instructed the factor to book passage.

Mrs. L. reports that though R. is healthy, she is much affrighted by her approaching Trial. Hearing this, I promised my friends that I would write to R. and offer reassurances about our city's many excellent physicians and convey to her my wish that she cling fast to her faith in God's Will, for she has ever been a favorite of mine, much like a daughter, who in times past sought my advice on matters for which she feared her formidable mother's response.

We adjourned to the downstairs sitting room for refreshment. Mrs. L. cast her usual baleful glances and sharp words at the girl who brought our tea, then waited until she had left the room and closed the door and my hostess had satisfied herself by listening at the door that the girl had gone away before she turned her attention to the tea. She then poured the tea and examined the liquid in cup and pot, tipping each vessel this way and that, and carrying them to the window for further perusal. Last, she dipped her finger into the liquid and tested it between her fingers, then, cautiously, took a bit upon her tongue, while I, in order to spare her the embarrassment of too-close scrutiny, occupied myself by looking out the front window at a dray hauling casks and up to its axle in sand, all the while watching this peculiar ritual out of the corner of one eye.

This extreme caution about her servants, though unsettling, is understandable given the family's recent harrowing trial. Last winter, so we are told, while the family was in residence at New Hope, Edward Legare had reason to flog his field hand Quash for repeated shirking of a task, but when the moment came for the man to receive his correction, he wrested the cowhide out of Mr. Legare's grip and said that he would "see him in Hell" before he would submit to this flogging. Mr. Legare called for reinforcements from among his other Negroes and together they secured the miscreant to a tree, where he duly received his rightful stripes and more for his insubordination. When his stripes had healed sufficiently for him to return to work, he dutifully completed his tasks, but within a week of his insubordination and correction, several members of the household, including E. Legare himself and the youngest Legare daughter, Amelia, fell ill with an extreme disorder of the bowels, which caused them much anguish and conveyed young Amelia Legare almost to the Dread Threshold. All medical measures had been exhausted and their fates given over to God's Will, when a house servant named Sally came to Mrs. L. in a near-hysterical state and confessed that she had twice seen Minda, the cook, who was the wife of the man who had been flogged, drop powder into the family's soup and once into the soup intended for the invalids. Shortly thereafter, on her way up the stairs, carrying soup to the invalids, this Minda was detained and commanded to drink of the broth herself, whereby it was determined by the extreme terror occasioned by this order that the soup contained poison.

The matter was swiftly resolved by hanging Minda and selling Quash to a sugarcane planter in Louisiana and conveying their children to the factor to be sold at the next opportunity. Amelia and Edward Legare recovered their health by a strict regime of bleeding and purging and dosing with calomel, and have suffered no lingering effects to their persons. Amelia, spared by God's Mercy, will pass the summer with relatives upstate in the Pendleton District. Though she is fully recovered from the effects of the poison, she will take no food that black hands have touched and is still given to unpredictable attacks of disorder in the bowels, which are much relieved by the cooler, drier climate of the uplands. Now I fear that Mrs. Legare's mind—though she herself was not harmed—has indeed been poisoned against her Negroes, and I further fear she will not recover her former benign opinions of the race. If sifted about it, she always returns to this—Minda grew up at New Hope and Mrs. Legare nursed several of her children through severe illness. She had never been ill-treated, nor worked beyond her capacities, nor seen any of her children sold or mistreated, and yet this was how she repaid her master for his benevolence and his care. Now, into every conversation, no matter the subject, Mrs. Legare interjects admonitions to strictness, vigilance, swift justice. Like the Ancient Mariner of old, she holds all with her glittering eye to tell of the treachery of the domestic enemies who shelter under our roofs. She hovers over cooking pots, lingers behind doors, listening, and of course there is the tea ritual, which all who visit must endure for her sake.

Went home with Mrs. L.'s counsels weighing heavily on my mind and looked to discover the location of each of our servants. Nancy and Lucy at the market—Chloe washing—Caesar and Abraham gone about the city on Thomas's various errands—Ned in the stable polishing the carriage brass. Only the new one, Diana, was idle—found her sitting on the hearth in the wash-house, talking to Chloe. Wishing not to fail in my duty, I ordered her to wash the front stoop, which had been fouled with dirt and droppings, and from there to proceed to tidying up the yard, then to assist Chloe with the washing. She performed these tasks quickly and with cheerful alacrity.

Evening soft and fine, with a fresh sea breeze blowing in from harbor. A pair of red cardinals in the Pride of India tree. Walked with T. down to the harbor, where a forest of masts stands off the harbor bar awaiting the tide's turning.

Purchased a length of fine linen at Ketchum's for a good price and, once home, proceeded to cut out a gown for Rachel Hayne's baby. Read the Testament to the household, Paul's letter to the Romans: "Know ye not, that to whom ye yield yourselves servants to obey, his servants ye are to whom ye obey; whether of sin unto death, or of obedience unto righteousness?" As usual, I was touched by their great reverence for the Scriptures and their gratitude. None but do put on clean head coverings and scarves to attend to the Gospel. Even D. listened, instead of slipping her feet in and out from under her skirt, studying her shoes. Afterward, Nancy pressed my hand tearfully and thanked me sincerely. How is it not possible to feel tenderness toward these, the least of God's people, or to feel our burden as their protectors, who must answer for their souls before Almighty God? Before she was carried off, it was Susan's task to provide the household's daily Spiritual Food, a duty she discharged most faithfully. When I think of S., I remember her prayer: "Lord, help me to be at last worthy of the devotion of these wretches, to hold always before them the image of our humble and suffering Lord and Savior, to be for them a beacon in the darkness, for have they not immortal souls that hunger and thirst for God's word like our own?"

After Scriptures, called D. into the front room with the intention of putting her to sewing on T.'s shirt, which I had basted together during the morning. Perhaps her labors can be put to use in these trying financial times. Only this week, Mrs. Prioleau lamented to me the decision to leave her seamstress back at The Oaks when they came to town this year. Said she would look to hire a seamstress's time for five dollars / week. Remembering Mrs. Legare's wise counsel, I had the girl sit on a stool at my feet. D. sewed quickly, and in no time she had joined the garment at shoulders and sides. I held it up for inspection and found the seams admirably tight and firm. When I told her that her work was good, she seemed genuinely grateful and thanked her "mistis" sincerely. Asked where she happened by this skill, she reported that her mother in Virginia had taught her. Much heartened by evening's events, though when I questioned D. about the content of the earlier Scripture passage, she answered without looking up from her sewing that she "disremembered."

T. reports that among his fellows who convene daily at the Library Society for conversation, the subject of the religious instruction of the Negro is as much debated as the miserable state of our finances. Only last week, my brother reports, Mr. Robert Dubose swept the tables clear of the newspapers and journals belonging to Mr. John Porcher when the latter judged that the former was remiss in his Christian duties and had failed to attend to the needs of the immortal souls of his slaves by refusing to provide them with suitable religious instruction. There was some fear among the company, T. reports, that Mr. Dubose would be carried off in a fit of apoplexy.

For good measure, kept D. at her sewing past tattoo while I continued my work on Rachel Hayne's baby gown. When the din and clamor of Negroes hurrying to their houses began, she looked up from her task and, finding me observing her, returned to her work. Ordered her to close the window shutters, and this she did in good order, without distraction or lingering, then returned to work and worked steadily while the din subsided and we were alone again with the ticking of the mantel clock and the sound of the horses of the watch passing through the street.

T. came back in around 10:30 looking haggard and distracted. Dismissed Diana then and listened to his report that the factor has today conveyed to him the news that the last dozen barrels of last year's rice, which remained unsold, have spoiled in the warehouse on Adger's Wharf due to a seepage of salt water during a high spring tide. Calculations of the result of this accident alarming—at current prices, we have lost upward of $2,500. If this draining away of our profits continues, says T., we shall be hardpressed to reduce our indebtedness this year but must instead increase it or sell some of our property. And thus, with those words, was any hope of a trip this year to the pines or the salt entirely extinguished. We are here for the duration and in straitened circumstances.

Around midnight, Diana's loud voice followed by an outburst of hilarity from the kitchen house roused me from sleep. Called Nancy in and questioned her. D. and Chloe laughing over an incident at the market, as best I can gather from Nancy's report. Enjoined her to take back to them the prohibition against such demonstrations. Diana being sent in to me, I ordered her to sleep in the hallway outside my room in case I had need of her during the night.

June 14, 1837

The heat presses down as though the city were a great vessel full of heat with a lid clapped over it—the air thick as smoke from a distant fire and the sun over all, a blazing orb. Fairview boat arrived yesterday, laden with sweet potatoes, along with some fine English peas and a request from the overseer for nails and hoes. A bright bit of greenery in a basket of potatoes caught my eye—peach leaves, from the look of them. The sight brought a flood of memories of my sweet home and of my mother, so lately gone to her rest, who loved the sweetness of summer peaches above all other tastes on earth.

T. at his ledgers all morning. After breakfast, wrote so many passes, my hand was sore. Questioned each of the servants carefully in order to determine the legitimacy of the proposed errand. Nancy and Chloe to market to sell sweet potatoes at the assigned price of ten cents for five. Both admonished strictly to come home straightaway when their errand was done and to deposit into my hands all monies taken in as a result of this endeavor. Diana clamored to be allowed to accompany them, but I denied her request, as she is yet too bold and unseasoned to resist the many temptations of the market. Ned drove me there and I purchased four baskets of figs to make my good preserves. T. urges me to send one of the servants on this errand. It is not fitting, he says, for a lady of our circle to be seen among the crude and commercial trafficking and rude jostling of the wharves and market district. In truth, the scene there is appalling, close with the crush of bodies and loud with Negro voices. The market, as T. maintains, is the seat of the evil that afflicts our Negroes. There, all is clamor, disorder, vultures perched on the market roof ready to swoop down and snap up any scrap of provender that falls to the pavement. Many a traveler has remarked, upon landing at our wharves and traversing the market, that one sees only Negroes in gaudy head scarves and bloodstained aprons, that one hears only Negro voices, and thus believes that he has landed in some country inhabited entirely by Negroes and vultures. Yet, I cannot entrust the choosing of figs for my preserves to Lucy, who, though she can be sent on errands for which she has been given specific and minute instructions, cannot be relied upon to judge fruit or vegetables, a strange deficiency in a country-born Negro. Left to her own devices, she returns with bruised, spoiled, or otherwise-misshapen offerings, and though I have often charged Nancy to look to Lucy's instruction in this matter of choosing fruits and vegetables, she has thus far proved intractable.

Returned exhausted from my morning labors. Those among our northern brethren who call us *idle and dissipated* miss the constant labor of the *mind and will* with which our days are filled. A glimpse of my brother at his ledgers or bent in consultation with the factor, assessing our stores or drawing up his lists of supplies, and the sight of him overseeing the rice planting in spring and the harvest in fall, should suffice to dissolve the shades of indolence with which our neighbors to the north so readily paint us. Likewise the labors of the mind and will required in that assigning of tasks and accounting for the Negroes that are the mark and measure of a well-run household. And so, when we seem to luxuriate in idleness, we are but taking a well-deserved rest from our labors. He who has eyes to see, let him see. Spoke with T. for upward of a half an hour and thus it was decided to hire out Diana's time, as she is a competent-enough everyday seamstress and I am confident in the firmness of my mistressship in directing these labors.

After dinner, I called at Mrs. Prioleau's concerning some Fuel Society business and the hiring out of Diana's time. Then, the week having been dry enough to make the streets passable, I ordered Ned to drive up King Street. A passing glance was enough to reveal to me that Babcock's window held that collection of books just arrived in port whose titles listed in the *Courier* had so recently arrested my eye—the imposing Milton volumes in striking red leather bindings were prominently displayed, accompanied by the complete plays of Shakespeare in a handsome new edition, *The Christian's Defensive Dictionary*, Plutarch's *Lives*, two volumes of botanical engravings, *Plants of the Southern Lowlands, The Oxford Book of Drawing*. Noted down this way, their names reproach me, for what we see, we soon desire. ("If thy right eye offend thee, pluck it out. . . .") And though I ordered Ned to drive on, and despite the fact I have over the course of a year's diligent practice of prayer thought to have snuffed the pernicious flame of appetite in my spirit, I found it instantly sprung into life again when fanned by the merest breath of city life. And now I find that though I seek to discipline my appetites or plug my ears or lash myself to the blessed mast of domestic duty, the sweet siren songs of the books in Babcock's window call out to me and I find myself in a quiet corner of my bedroom reviewing this list of luxuries.

Worked with Nancy cleaning and preparing the figs. T. arrived around six o'clock, much displeased to find me in an apron in the kitchen house, tending a bubbling cauldron of fruit. In his eyes, it is a sign of debasing coarseness to labor this way. I am not delicate, as was our beloved Susan, to whom he oftimes compares me. In truth, I possess not her high degree of virtue or efficiency in any of the domestic realms. Whether through want of inborn grace or through stubborn and willful ignorance of my duties and responsibilities, I fall woefully short of the mark. T. will forget this scene soon enough, however, when my preserves are brought to him on breakfast toast some morning. He often praises them as his favorite delicacy.

Diana did not appear until tattoo, then hurried into the kitchen house and up to her quarters, where a candle still burned in her window alone while all others were dark around midnight when I sought my bed. Tomorrow, I shall review with her once again the requirement of this household that the Negroes are to be in their quarters with their lights extinguished by 11:00 P.M. If the necessary cultivation of the virtue of patience be any measure of spiritual advancement, then we are far advanced indeed by the daily exercise of this and other virtues necessary to the governing of servants, charity and forbearance following close behind patience in this solemn procession.

June 15 and 16, 1837

The air in our city these last several days has been smothering and we move about as though wrapped in thick robes of heat—even the palmettos are becalmed and hang with scarcely a rustle. Flies worry loudly at every window. A glassy shimmer rises from stone and sand alike while a shrill rattling cacaphony of cicadas rises and falls, a maddening hymn to heat and filth, and the smell of cow yard and privy vault, fish and sea engulfs and threatens to drown us. All must sleep under mosquito cloth or risk being devoured. Awakened today at first light by the clatter of a bucket against brick and the sounds of loud Negro voices mingled with the squawking of alarmed fowl. From my window I saw the rooster leaping and flying this way and that and Nancy hauling Diana around the yard by her hair while D. lunged at her with a large iron fork, which sight caused me to cry out to them, much to my chagrin when I heard in my own voice and manner of speaking the tones and manner of my good neighbor Mrs. Legare. (I never heard my mother raise her voice to a servant, and yet she possessed a complete command of her household, which I fall woefully short of mastering.) The riot had awakened Thomas (who had only just retired the hour before) and he at once went down into the yard and began laying about him with his cane until at last he had separated the two combatants, each of whom spat on the ground at the other's feet, then as quickly rubbed out the spat-upon spot with her own foot.

Thomas sent Diana to her quarters and brought Nancy in and ordered her to give a full report to the both of us concerning her conduct and the incident that provoked it. She produced the usual Negro version of events, full of cries, lamentations, and confused and contradictory protestations, which nonetheless left me no better informed concerning what had occurred than when I first spied them from my window. In any event, it had something to do with money that Nancy and Chloe had gotten from selling our sweet potatoes and eggs at the market, of which venture D. had no part yet she had attempted to claim a share. T. dismissed Nancy, then turned on me a stern and solemn face. "Was this money stolen?" he asked. I reviewed with him the long-standing household marketing arrangement our mother had begun and that I had carried forward: To wit, of the profit from the sale of our produce, Nancy and Chloe may each keep two dimes and turn the rest over to me. Thomas questioned me closely, especially as to the wisdom of letting the servants handle and account for money. Meanwhile, as we talked, Nancy found occasion to pass in and out of the room. They see through walls; they hear around corners.

Finally, he sent her downstairs and delivered his final word on the matter: Our financial practices where Negroes are concerned must be handled with strict control and care must be taken to account for all monies and to the orderly handing over of said monies to T., their proper and intended recipient. The fiend Denmark Vesey, he reminded me, bought his freedom with lottery winnings and stayed in our city to work his evil plot against us, *all as a result of having gotten his hands on some money*. We who avail ourselves of the benefits of the practice of hiring out our servants must ourselves practice vigilance, restraint, and sound judgment.

He delivered, then, a disquisition on the character of Negroes, touching especially upon their weaknesses and how we must not place temptation in their way, as their natures make them vulnerable to all vice, nor encourage them in pursuit of money, the acquiring of which will surely persuade them to think of themselves as managers of their own destinies. He ended by recommending that I might visit the women of our circle to whom we have hired out our servants' time in order to *collect their fees.* I meekly surrendered this "contested privilege," as the wise Mrs. Cary advises, but all that day I found my brother staring at me with the most curious and appraising glances, as if he knew not the face he looked into.

After our talk was concluded, I sought my bedroom. I will not provoke my good brother, yet I believe our Negroes trustworthy. Besides, if my brother finds it unseemly for me to shop for figs at the market, is it not the height of unseemliness for me to drive about the city collecting slave-earned coin from the ladies of our circle? Perhaps in the next crumbling of order I shall take up the reins and drive myself, as we have heard Sarah Grimké drives her carriage and team around Philadelphia, calling on the abolitionists with whom she has cast her lot.

This turbulence and disorder put me into a state of agitation. Took valerian tea with twenty drops of LD to quiet my spirit and sat for upward of half an hour in the second-floor drawing room, above the noise and dust and dirt of the street, which commands a view of the harbor, the gray-green sea on which one can imagine sailing far away to more peaceful shores. While thus engaged in contemplation, I did for a moment imagine I felt the grass of Fairview under my feet and smelled its sweet air and heard the songs of our boatmen plying the river's waters. Thus quieted, I took up my own sewing and called Diana to me and attempted to question her about the incident in the yard. Her version as confused and incomprehensible as Nancy's, but by all perceptible signs, she is repentant. Put her to work hanging gauze over the mirrors, as the flies are worse this year than I can ever remember and already every mirror glass is specked with their filth.

Diana has sewed *four shirts* this week and *two more* close to completion—my work goes forward steadily on the baby gown. Called the girl to me and informed her that Mrs. Prioleau has requested her services and that she is to be hired out to sew for her one day a week. She listened carefully as I paused—grappling with my conscience, which cried out to me to honor my brother's wishes and heed his warnings concerning trusting the servants with money—but I was then overcome by a proud and willful spirit, which possessed and convinced me that I should continue along the path to which I had already set my feet. Informed her that all monies were to come directly to me, and she rose and left the room *without being dismissed*! But even as I spoke to her, I saw my brother's face before my mind's eye, reproaching me for my flagrant disregard of his wishes.

Summoned next door by Mrs. L., who had heard the commotion in our yard and wished to sift me about it—guardian of our street, she is ever watchful after our welfare. She implored me to be stricter with the Negroes, never to let them know by word or any outward sign of the slightest doubt or faltering of will. Two remonstrances today, from wiser hearts than mine, about correct relations with our domestics—I cannot ignore either, yet I find her sternness at odds with my temperament. We must show Christian kindness to the wretches in our charge in order that the domestic sphere remain unpolluted.

Poor Mrs. Legare, working to make preparations for R.'s arrival and confinement, and now Mr. Legare has become embroiled in a dispute with William Ravenel concerning the boundary of some adjoining properties on Meeting Street, with the result that each has threatened to *kill* the other should they encounter each other again. And yet, how can they not meet? Mrs. Manigault remarked to me on hearing the same news, living as neighbors as they do, moving in the same circles in society, both prominent members of the Association and officers of the Agricultural Society. It is feared by many that the Society's customary pistol shooting at the Edisto property will take on disastrous coloration for the two combatants. I suggested to Mrs. Legare that she might look to her husband's diet, as I have noted in my brother an increased tendency to inflammatory temper when he is costive or when his stomach is acid. At those times, a diet of game without butter, tame ducks, hard crackers, and no beef, mutton, or ham has a salutory and calming effect on him.

Walked home from Mrs. L.'s thanking God for His providence and plan for my life in sparing me the burden of the temperament of the men of our circle. Only last fall, my own mild brother responded to an incident in which the patrol apprehended one of our Negroes without a pass on the road *just inside our property* by warning the patrols to keep off Fairview, where he is the master and sole arbiter of law and order. Sometimes all their proud opinions weary me. No doubt I would make a weak and willful wife. Arrived home humbled and brought low by shame at these disloyal thoughts. "The heart is deceitful above all things, and desperately wicked: Who can know it?" Surely, I have sent no sweet incense heavenward today.

Louisa stops reading. She must have water. The words have begun to stick to the roof of her mouth and peel away when she speaks. The water in the glass on the table in front of her is lukewarm now, but she drinks it anyway, the whole glass, without stopping. As she drinks, small sighing breezes touch her face, lift her hair, circle the room. What comes to Louisa then is a memory, a picture of Mamie in a chair at the kitchen table, a basket full of socks and shirts and pants at her feet, sewing. It was nothing fancy, the work Mamie had done, just everyday sewing: buttons, hems, all types of mending. Her stitches were straight and tight enough to hold, but sewing was a chore for her; it was work, and she did it with her tongue bitten between her front teeth and a frown on her face. Which was why her idea of herself as a fine seamstress had been so funny. Hands clasped behind his back, Hugh Marion, Sr., would circle her while Mamie labored at button or hem. Then: "Tell me, Mamie, where'd you learn to sew?" he'd ask. "How'd you come by that skill?"

"Well, suh," Mamie would answer, without looking up, "my grandmother Harriette been for teach me, but mos'ly it been the blood."

"What's that you say?" he'd ask, winking at any other members of his family who'd stopped to witness his performance.

"Yes, suh, for true. One my people way back when uset sew."

Now, Louisa asks quietly, one last time: "Mamie, is that you?" The breezes and the sighing hesitate, then begin again. "I didn't think so," she says.

But if this is not Mamie, then who? The telephone rings and rings and rings then stops in midring. Has she missed an appointment? Is it her morning to work at the Bargain Shop? She can't remember; she doesn't know or care. The mail slides through the front door chute and lies in the sun on the polished floor of the hall. Among the envelopes is a postcard from Susan, a sunny Caribbean scene, a white ship in blue water, a message from another world.

It would not be Eliza here, she thinks, stirring the air, waiting. What misplaced piece of her life would she have come for? This house and everything in it belonged to her. Her portrait on the wall among the other family portraits shows a woman whose narrow face and calm eyes are nothing if not serene. Even so, isn't there always something missing, forgotten, or lost in any life? Wouldn't anyone have something to come back for? "Eliza?" she says. The air chills.

Then she tries the names she's learned, the ones that have come so recently alive and attached themselves to the human beings who once peopled this house. "Nancy?" she says.

Nothing.

"Lucy?" A sigh, a stir of the window curtain, as if brushed in passing.

Worse, then. Now there is a name to match the restless circling that moves around the room, like someone pacing; now there is a name to match the hunger.

"Diana?" she says. There is a sound like the wind in the chimney, a shower of ashes. She picks up the diary pages and continues.

June 17, 1837

R. Hayne will depart Georgetown next week for her mother's house. Mrs. L. expects her to be brought to bed within the month. Upon receiving my letter of encouragement and advice, R. replied with the tenderest expressions of gratitude and brave demonstrations of her readiness to undergo her approaching Trial.

Dr. Joel Wyman, a young physician lately come to town from the Beaufort District, will attend R. He comes well recommended for his training in the north and for the skill with which he carried Lucille Manigault Huger through her own arduous Trial two months past, in which her infant was lost a scant three hours after his birth, when his breathing became labored and strangled and finally ceased, and she herself was carried almost to the Dread Threshold—from which travail (as well as the loss of her beloved husband, who was thrown from a horse and perished a week before her infant's demise) she has not yet fully recovered, but lies all day, sometimes with her face turned to the wall and unable, in spite of numerous visits from Bishop Gadsden, myself, and other like-minded women of her mother's circle, to submit herself to God's Will in carrying off her husband or her child. As my dear friend Mrs. Beach has said so often and so compassionately, it is our fate to mourn and be humbled in the dust—thus are we broken in order that God may mend and persuade us to surrender our will to His and to trust in His love.

On my last visit, Lucille unburdened herself to me—she feels her infant son's death came as the result of her own unhealthy habits during pregnancy. She did not rest and often occupied her mind with novel reading and other frivolities, rather than keeping her thoughts elevated in the higher realms of education and parental duty. I conveyed to her my fervent belief that God chastens whom He loves, the better to cleanse us and prepare us to receive His grace. If we but submit ourselves to God's Will, He will make straight our path, for "Every branch that beareth fruit He purgeth it, that it may bring forth more fruit." Her sorrowful heart could not receive this teaching and she became agitated to a degree that caused her mother to become alarmed and me to make a hasty exit from the house.

Smothering, heavy weather today. Not a breeze to dispel the reek of marsh and privy vault. Took to my perch on the second-floor piazza, from which vantage point I might gaze upon the world of harbor and sea, though, today, even the ships lie becalmed beyond the bar. Diana brought five dollars, deposited it in my hands, then stood waiting. Dismissed, she offered me a sullen look. The principle of our custom of hiring out eludes her still: To wit, we who bear the burden for caring for those in our service are the rightful owners of the fruits of their labor. She may, in future, receive some return for her labors, *when we see fit to reward her*. This is my brother's will, and thus it is mine, as well.

Intended to present my brother with the fruits of Diana's labor, but he returned late from an Association meeting, accompanied by a group of men. He made a great outcry for Caesar, and when he was not to be found (T. proclaiming loudly his intention of sending Caesar to the Workhouse upon his return), my brother ordered Ned to rouse old Abraham from his bed in the stables, then sent him creaking up and down the cellar steps after spirits. They set themselves up in the second-floor drawing room near my bedroom door. T. set to tuning his violin, and they settled into playing games of loo, accompanied by a great cracking of nuts and unstoppering of bottles and frequent calls for more candles. Opening my door a crack, I saw the room ablaze with light and returned to bed, counting over our stores of candles and calculating how long it would be before I would need to replenish our supply.

I perceived among the voices that of Mr. Legare, who discoursed at great length and volume on his dispute with Mr. Ravenel, and then Thomas's voice deploring this rupture and urging Mr. L. to make peace with Mr. R. In return for this advice, T. received a burst of outrage from Mr. Porcher, who demanded to know of my brother how he could offer such advice to a man whose honor had been violated, as Mr. Legare's clearly had by Mr. Ravenel's obdurate stand in the boundary-line dispute, which all clearly seemed to feel should be resolved in Mr. Legare's favor. (Poor Thomas, visited once again by the specter of his conciliatory unionist stance.) Then ensued a discussion conducted in lowered voices of some young man lately come to town and his traffic in "Carolina bright and dark," which at first I took to be a discussion of rice or tobacco. But, by the secretive tones and low laughter, I soon divined that something unchaste and having to do with Negroes was being spoken of. Turned to the wall then and asked my Savior to stop my ears, which He did, mercifully, by causing at that moment a carriage to pass in the street.

Nor was the city quiet, thereafter, but restless, rather, with footsteps, rough, quarrelsome voices, and horses' hooves. The tattoo brings our domestics back to our yards and houses but does not quiet them. As the St. Michael's bell tolled twice, I looked from my window and found our own yard still lively, the fire not banked in the kitchen house, but burning brightly, Diana in the doorway, gnawing a bone, and no sign of Caesar. At such times, I believe that law and reason rule only our daylight hours; the night belongs to Negroes.

At daybreak, the party of men departed and I arose. Smoke rose from the kitchen house fire, where Nancy was already at work, Lucy departed for the market, swinging her basket, Caesar (who had materialized with dawn's light) stood in the yard grooming the horse, Chloe crossed the yard toward the washhouse, carrying a basket of linens. Found my brother asleep in his chair, holding in one hand his violin, which he had been unable to tune after repeated efforts throughout the night—Susan used to perform this task for him, as she had a fine ear, a light hand and musical training—and a segar smoldering in the other. Removed the segar and extinguished it. A haze of smoke hung in the air, the table was strewn with playing cards and empty bottles of spirits, and the shells of almonds were everywhere underfoot. Flows of candle wax covered the tabletop and some had dripped off the table and pooled on the floor.

Sent Ned to summon Diana, and thus transpired this scene. She came slowly from the kitchen house, tying her kerchief and tucking up her hair. A gaudy fringed head scarf of gold marked with some bold paisley design has lately come into her possession, to be tied and retied until it suits her fancy. On several occasions I have discovered her preening before a household mirror! She paused to speak and laugh with Caesar and to stroke the neck of our carriage horse, which C. was grooming, and to study the sky, pointing out this or that feature to Caesar, who also gaped skyward, his brush stalled on the horse's neck for the duration of her discourse. She then drank a dipperful of water that Caesar offered her and then, after another adjustment of her headgear, proceeded on her leisurely amble toward the house, as if *she*, not I, were dictating the time of her arrival in the house.

Nor did her insolence cease once she gained the house, for I heard her voice and Nancy's going on for five minutes by the mantel clock, then her slow progress from the warming pantry up the back stairs and into the room. Yet when I demanded to know what had taken her so long to answer my summons, she replied that she had come as soon as she was called, all the while holding my gaze with her own—*she never once dropped her eyes*—saying, furthermore, that I was mistaken, for *she had not lingered.* This utter and flagrant lie overran entirely the frail, crumbling walls of my patience, and I slapped her. Her ensuing cry woke Thomas, who leapt up with his violin still in hand, looking about himself wildly. When I explained what had transpired, he slapped her as well, so that she fell to the floor, from which station he required her to listen while he informed her that the next time she disobeyed me, was insubordinate, sullen, or otherwise derelict in answering a summons or *promptly* carrying out any order given her by her superiors (and by this—he made plain—he meant *any* white person), he would promptly convey her to the Workhouse for correction. Failing those measures, "I shall have you in my pocket, girl," he said. When she was allowed to rise from the floor, she lowered her eyes, you may be sure, humbled by threat of correction or sale, but the damage had been done to my temper. Mrs. Legare would, no doubt, heartily approve of my action, but I have no stomach for slapping Negroes and lay it all to my besetting sin of ill temper. I am persuaded anew of the rightness of Mrs. Mary Beach's pronouncement at a recent meeting of the Fuel Society that slavery is a hard business, and I share her fear that "we shall have it to our bitter cost some day or other." Perhaps the wholesale destruction and coarsening of female temperaments will be among the chief costs charged to us and we shall become a country of harridans and haughty shrews!

After her chastisement, D. performed passably well the task I assigned her of setting the drawing room to rights, and I conveyed to Thomas the profits of her sewing labors.

These worries with the Negroes had wearied me almost past enduring, and in the afternoon, after dinner, Ned drove me to return the visits I have recently received while Thomas rested in his room. I left orders with Nancy that there was to be no disturbance in the household, as he is much wearied and out of temper and troubled in his bowels. Mrs. Alston sifted me for news of Mr. Legare and Mr. Ravenel. Rumor has it that they passed on Bay Street near the Exchange and traded heated words. Fortunately, no firearms were produced, though it is feared by many that a duel is in the offing. She reports being privy to a long, gloomy discussion of others' financial woes when last her husband was in residence—to which I replied, "At least they were not tuning violins," then instantly reproached myself for this lack of charity toward my own brother. Mr. Alston is much absent in Columbia in the legislature and Mrs. Alston busies herself with her daughter's affairs, membership in a dozen societies, and the Orphan House, and she is ever the first to put on a ball or a dance for the young people. Sara Manigault's trousseau coming along nicely, and though Edward, her fiancé, is troubled with bleeding at the lungs, he is of a noble temperament.

After supper, Thomas arose and took a turn with me along the Battery, where our spirits were lifted by the mild sea breeze and the sight of the tall masts of many ships in the harbor, thick as trees in a forest. Encountered there the Misses Middleton, the elder quite dignified, the younger as lively and impudent as her sister is quiet and serene. "Miss Hilliard," says the younger, dropping a hasty curtsy, "settle a dispute for us. Was it Alexander Seabrook to whom your engagement was broken off?"

Before I could find sufficiently charitable and stringent words with which to reply, she was silenced by her older sister, and Thomas bid them an abrupt good evening and drew me away, but not before there passed between the older Miss Middleton and myself, even as she reproached her impudent sister, a look of sympathetic understanding.

Went home and read the Bible to the household, all except Chloe, about whose whereabouts the Negroes claim to know nothing. The city absorbs them; they appear and disappear, materialize and vanish. Upon our return, Thomas could not be prevailed upon to stay for the reading of Holy Writ but must away to fulfill his duty to the Association. Diana was humble and attentive, sewing on a nightshirt for Thomas. She has mastered the plain binding stitches quickly and sews along smoothly and speedily. Five more shirts completed and the profits handed over to me *without incident* and deposited in the household coffers. But even as I read to them from Scripture—Ephesians 5:3 and 15: "Let there be no filthiness, nor silly talk, nor levity, which are not fitting; but instead let there be thanksgiving. . . . Look carefully then how you walk, not as unwise men but as wise, making the most of the time, because the days are evil"—I felt the coils of the serpent of bitterness tighten around my heart at the memory of Miss M.'s insolence and her sister's compassionate look and the sound of Alexander Seabrook's name.

The elder Miss Middleton reminds me of myself at the fateful juncture of my life when Alexander Seabrook presented himself to my father and asked to marry me. We had been keeping company for upward of six months then, and under the influence I was able to bring to bear on him, he had curbed his appetite for gaming and spirits, with the result that my tender affections had been awakened toward him, as had his for me, for he often swore remorse for his wild and headstrong ways and kissed my hands in gratitude. During our courtship, daily bouquets filled our house, and by fall of the year in which we began keeping company, we were both anxious to marry at the earliest opportunity.

How well do I remember the fateful morning that followed the evening when he asked to marry me. The gray winter look of the ocean and the Battery houses shuttered against the cold wind from the sea. The Christmas gaiety in the streets, the cold, bright air, the picture frames festooned with smilax and a fire blazing in the reception room fireplace as my mother and father discussed my situation and I stood outside the door, feverish with girlish impatience, listening for word of my fate. My father's words echo in my mind and heart to this day: "Catherine, she shall not be made prey to the vices of that unfortunate branch of the Seabrook family."

My mother spoke warmly in defense of Mr. Seabrook (his mother was my mother's second cousin). "As well you may recall," she said gently to my father, "many a man's wild nature has been softened by the steady and beneficent influence of the female character." Whereupon my father, after some moments of silence, admitted in a chastened voice that this was so. How my heart rose when I heard those words. But, he continued, the character of some men is sufficiently hardened in the mold as to resist the fondest blandishments, and such a character did he suspect Mr. Seabrook to possess. And though he had every confidence that if any woman's temperament could effect a beneficent transformation on a man, it would be his beloved Eliza's, still he would not consign his daughter to a life of public humiliation at the hands of a man whose dissolute habits were well known about the city, as it was likewise well known that he must marry in order to receive his patrimony.

"I believe the man to be an opportunist," my father said, "whose fondest affections are reserved for gaming, horse racing, and other, more pernicious vices, which he indulges frequently when the family is in town." Only last fall, he reminded her, after the family had returned to Johns Island, this same Alexander Seabrook absented himself without warning in the midst of the rice harvest and spent three weeks in town before the factor sent urgent word for his father to come collect him. The elder Seabrook was rowed down by his strongest crew of Negroes to recover his son, who had fallen into a shocking state of dissipation and riot.

After this, my mother yielded to my father's wisdom and spoke no more of Mr. Seabrook. Informed by my mother in the gentlest terms of their decision, I strove to emulate her and submitted myself to God's mercy and my father's wisdom. When I saw Mr. Seabrook afterward, it was as though I had never lived. If we passed on the street or on the Battery or happened together at some gathering of our circle, he would speak to all save me. Before too many months had passed, I began to perceive our affections as the disordered elements of a dream I had dreamt while in the grip of a fever, the emanations of a delirium that had possessed me briefly and then passed on.

My father's wisdom was borne out when, two years later, the same Mr. Seabrook, having at last married Juliana DeSassure, was drowned in the Stono River as he traveled home at first light after a night of gaming. It was reported by his wife, whose report was had of the patroon who was in command of the boat that night, that at the fateful moment, Mr. Seabrook stood up for the purpose of singing, in order that the boatmen might row to the rhythm of his song, stumbled, and fell overboard, and, unable to divest himself quickly enough of his coat, whose pockets were heavy with the coins he had lately won at the gaming table, sank and drowned before the Negroes could arrest the boat's forward motion and return to rescue their fallen master.

A decision like the one made for me so long ago has, I understand, recently been made in Miss Middleton's case, whose troth to Mr. Bull was to have been announced at month's end. Did I glimpse in her eyes the same sobriety and dignity with which I greeted my own destiny? It was as if I looked in upon my own soul at the moment of its transformation, that moment at the turning of the year following my father's rejection of Mr. Seabrook's suit when I knew there would be no more marriage proposals for me. After that time, I perceived a subtle change in my parents' attitudes toward me—whereas before they had been willing to indulge an occasional girlish whim or fit of temper or vanity, they now required of me dignity and womanly bearing to compensate for their diminished hopes for my domestic happiness, and I passed from girlhood to womanhood in the space of a few months.

I shall now conclude this gloomy text in abject humility and reliance on the Savior, who knows our frames and remembers we are dust, and in humble thanksgiving that my mother is sleeping in the earth and thus not a witness to my self-indulgence, as she might fault herself for having failed as my teacher, when, truly, it is the pupil who has failed to learn the teacher's greatest lesson of silent forbearance.

Diana returned from Mrs. Prioleau's and went to her quarters, where her light was promptly extinguished, in compliance with my wishes.

June 25, 1837

Sunday. The heat has at last subsided. A pleasant, light, breezy day with fleecy clouds mounting high above the harbor, flower petals blown about the streets and sunlight slanting down. In the churchyard, a red cardinal sits in a moss-hung oak, a cheerful picture among the silent graves. The Reverend Alexander Glennie from All Saints Parish on the Waccamaw conducted services in place of Bishop Gadsden, who has traveled to the pines. With his great red whiskers, long, pious face, and piercing bright blue eyes, he looks every inch the man of God and able soldier in the army of the Lord. Much in demand for his instructive texts for Negroes. Preached to us a most valuable commentary on the character of Eve, in which he praised modesty, retirement, meekness, and purity as the peculiar ornaments of woman. Had our innocent Mother been *content* with them, he suggested in a commanding voice, the subtlety of the Serpent would have made no impression on her mind, nor would her senses have been enthralled by the charms of the Forbidden Fruit. Instantly humbled on hearing these words, which strike at the heart of every woman's earthly dilemma and which could have been written expressly to *me*. How many of our sex remain true to God's commandments and expectations for their lives, or seek tirelessly to discern the Divine Order to which our lives are meant to conform? It was the fruit of the tree of *knowledge* that was forbidden to our first parents. Looking round that eminent congregation, each safe within its own pew, I spied the haughty Miss Middleton, who attended the Reverend Glennie's sermon by glancing round at other members of the congregation, particularly the young male members, unchecked by her mother, while her humbler sister devoted pious attention to the Reverend Glennie's words. (Only weak women are self-willed, young Miss Middleton. Oh, shun the forbidden fruit of willfulness. I hope the lesson prove not unduly painful for you when it come your time to learn it.)

Our lesson concluded, the Reverend Glennie then preached briefly to our Negroes on the subject of Saint Paul in prison: "Wheresoever I find myself, there I am content." The Reverend Glennie admonished them fondly, saying, "Be good children, and rest content in the Lord, for have not your masters a greater Master, in whose vineyards they labor and whose charge they must obey?"

Diana slept through services, as usual. At the start of services, her bowed head and clasped hands suggest piety, but when the conclusion of Divine Office finds her in the same attitude, her head nodding on her breast, one can not but surmise that she has seized the opportunity of this church service to sleep. Place her, however, in a crowd of boisterous Negroes and she would revive soon enough.

His lesson concluded, the Reverend Glennie descended the pulpit and strode before them with hands clasped behind his back and a kind smile upon his face. He questioned the Negroes thusly: "What was the text?" asked he, to which our Lucy quickly replied, "Massa Paul, him be happy in the Workhouse," to the warm laughter of our circle.

"How do we pray?" the Reverend Glennie inquired of his congregation of ebony theologians.

"In faith," answered one.

"In charity," proclaimed another.

"In the name of Jesus Christ," declared Nancy's Lucy. The Reverend Glennie commended her gravely.

After services, Thomas and Cousin Whitemarsh conversed with the Reverend Glennie at some length. His two little daughters curtsied prettily to all who inquired after their well-being or commented upon their beauty. The younger Miss Middleton conversed idly with several young men. Thomas made the rounds of the male members of the congregation as if he had announced for office, his demeanor so somber, dignified, and solicitous. Indeed, it is a task worthy a statesman to restore himself to the good graces of the nullifiers, for no one has a longer memory than a man of our circle who feels he has been betrayed by one of his own kind. Our world is of a piece; we fall or rise together—this wisdom has been long impressed upon me.

Mrs. Manigault, resplendent in an exquisite gown of palest green watered silk, which color flattered the deep chestnut of her hair, her fair skin, and fine gray eyes, drew me aside to remark with enthusiasm on D.'s needlework and to ask that I hire her out to work on Sara's trousseau. When I expressed surprise on hearing of her familiarity with D.'s handiwork, Mrs. M. said that one day last week—she believes it must have been Wednesday—she came to pay a visit and, finding me not at home, was conducted by Nancy into the reception room, where, it seems, Diana was sewing and availed herself of the opportunity to display her work. Mrs. M. was much impressed, whereupon Diana stated boldly that she was available to be hired out as a seamstress. Thus did Mrs. M. feel encouraged to make her request.

Amelia Seabrook has been called away to Columbia to attend an ailing cousin, so Cousin Whitemarsh came home with us to dinner. Truth to tell, the great "Lion of the Low Country" looks somewhat subdued in his wife's absence, as does my poor brother every day since Susan's death: more stooped and insubstantial, the haggard lines etched ever more deeply in his face—only his eyes retain the kind warmth that has ever marked him as the gentlest of men. Would that I could ease his burden, lighten his load, and bring to him the comfort and companionship he so richly deserves.

City thronged, as it is every Sunday. Free Negroes parading the streets in their finery, along with the Irish and French tradesmen. Plantation Negroes thronging the city's lower reaches. T. directed Ned to drive past the pernicious impromptu market that springs up on South Bay Street every Sabbath, in order that he might discuss the situation with Cousin Whitemarsh. He, Thomas, and several other members of the Association are drafting a memorial, calling on the legislature to outlaw this African market, which violates our Sabbath and contributes to our city's instability by reducing our waterfront to the state of an African village. On reaching our destination, we beheld a clutter of rude canoes and bateaux pulled up in disorderly array upon the gleaming white shells of the bank and Negroes lounging everywhere. Great fish laid out on beds of seaweed in the shade of an oak, gaudy roosters bedecked in bronze, black, and red picking their way along the refuse-strewn ground, a brazier on which fish was cooking, baskets of sweet potatoes, piles of melons, and baskets of yellow roots, a bird of exotic plumage perched upon a wooden stave—these were the sights and sounds that affronted our senses as we passed. The Christian soul recoils at the barbarous assembly in our midst. No doubt the marshal will visit later and disperse the mob. This flow of commerce among Negroes is dangerous, my brother and Cousin Whitemarsh agreed. I thought that among the squabbling mob of Negroes milling about the waterfront I caught sight of D.'s gaudy kerchief and heard her unbridled voice quarreling above the din, though I had ordered her expressly to go home at the conclusion of Divine Office and help to lay the dinner.

It was the fire under a brazier that incensed Cousin Whitemarsh and my brother. Cousin W. stopped the carriage and loudly ordered it extinguished, and the lounging Negroes leapt up to comply. Back in the carriage, Cousin Whitemarsh asserted that we had here witnessed *two fires*: the fire under the brazier and the more pernicious fire of Negro enterprise. No sooner has one been kindled than the other ignites, he declared. Such is the state of our city, Cousin Whitemarsh proclaimed as we drove home through the crowded streets with the smells of the Negro market still wafting about our carriage, where well-meaning clergy and free Negroes excite our Africans. It is not our *blacks* who are the problem. When *governed well*, with equal measures of benevolence and firmness, they prove manageable enough; rather, it is the *whites* who allow breaches of law to go unpunished and who permit laxity in small matters to creep in who undermine our foundations. For it is by the punishment of small faults that large ones are prevented. This principle has been impressed upon me since my tenderest years.

Listening, I rode along, watching out the window and feeling ever more gloomy and troubled by the memory of my earlier conversation with Mrs. M. and my woeful lack of discipline. That Diana should presume to take this liberty with Mrs. M. indicates a dangerous instability. Thus this truth is once again borne out: Good turns to evil in our sinful natures, as my intention to be a good mistress to our household has turned to evil by the action of deceit on my weak-willed character. Deceit, and pride as well, for I have presumed to know better than my brother how to handle the hiring out of our slaves. Better that I should make my way from house to house like a tradesman collecting debts than contribute to the unstable climate by my disobedience. Am I one of Cousin Whitemarsh's despised and misguided sinners because I seek to better the lot of the poor wretches whom God has consigned to our keeping? As a Christian, I hold that I can do nothing less; and as a sister, I can do no less than endeavor to help my brother in these trying financial times.

Dined at home on good ham, biscuits, and our English peas, followed by a tasty pudding. T., troubled in his bowels, ate lightly.

Dr. Wyman has purged him repeatedly, yet his condition remains troublesome. After Cousin Whitemarsh departed and T. retired to his room to rest, I called Nancy to me and questioned her closely about the matter with Mrs. M. She seemed so genuinely hurt by the implication that she would have been so bold as to be part of a financial arrangement with a superior that I felt ashamed for questioning her at all. N.'s story was that she had not shown Mrs. M. into any room, knowing I was not at home, but had come in from the kitchen house, to find Mrs. M. and Diana already in conversation, and thinking it necessary to listen in order that she might convey to me a true account of the talk, she stayed in the room—all this spoken with much knitting of her heavy brow, plucking at her garments, and twisting of her hands as she struggled to find words to convey her sincerity.

How could I have misjudged our Nancy? Has she not served our family faithfully since childhood, showing us nothing but a willing and humble spirit, a loyalty to our family unmatched by all but old Lucy, her mother? I remember the day she was given to me, a birthday gift in my ninth year, and how she became from that day forward my companion. When not in the kitchen learning her skills, or laying out my clothes and attending to me, she accompanied me on my childhood rounds. At Fairview, she held the pony while I picked flowers, scrambled up a woodland oak at my direction to gather holiday smilax or mistletoe, fanned the flies and mosquitoes through the stifling nights that descend upon us in this city. Most trusted of servants at home or in town, she has served us faithfully and never given cause for any mistrust in our arrangement whereby a few pennies fall into her hands, reward for her faithful service, until this year, when, under Diana's sway, she has begun to be restless, devious, and cunning. How to halt what I have set in motion? That is the thought that will not let me rest, that shadows me by day and descends at night like the heat. Surely I am one of Cousin Whitemarsh's despised sinners, kindling the flame of Negro enterprise. So Nancy swears that she never spoke to Mrs. M. but that it was Diana who conducted my friend into the house and pressed her handiwork upon her.

When I summoned D., she came quickly into the room, as though she had been waiting nearby, and deposited the week's sewing money into my hands, a large sum, though I did not stop to count it, then sat down at once and took up R. Hayne's baby gown. When I questioned her under threat of being sent to the Workhouse if it should be discovered that she was lying, she answered me without looking up from her needle that N. was getting old and forgetful. The house was very busy that day, said she, and N. was confused about who she had let in and where she had conducted them. Mrs. M., she maintained, being unfamiliar with our servants, mistook the one who had admitted her for the one at work at her needle. She did not deny that she showed Mrs. M. her sewing, but she declares that it was *Nancy* who had procured the shirts and gowns and spread them on the couch in the reception room, as though she were displaying wares at the market. Why, I asked myself, would Nancy do that, unless *she* have an interest herself in D.'s handiwork? And that is a prospect too dark to contemplate.

Mrs. M., it seems, remembers the presence, but not the individual faces, of Negroes. So there we have the usual conundrum that results from questioning one Negro about another. The upshot is, of course, that I made the pact with Mrs. M. to hire out D.'s time to sew her daughter's trousseau for the sum of five dollars a week. I could not deny my friend, a woman of our circle, in such a request. Nancy came to me later to lay out my nightclothes and brush my hair, brought word from the kitchen house that the arrangement with Mrs. M. will "bring plenty much trouble to this house," as D. believes she has been deprived of *her share* of the profits from her sewing and bitterly accosts Nancy at every opportunity concerning this matter. Where was this idea of a *fair share* kindled among them? I bow my head in anticipation of God's just judgment when I humbly confess that I do not like this girl with her ready answers and her shawls and scarves tastily tied, the shoes with the silver buckles (where came she by these?) that she sometimes slips out from under her skirt in church in order to admire. After my talk with Nancy was concluded, summoned Diana and informed her of my decision to allow her to keep one dollar of the money Mrs. Manigault is to pay for her services each week.

June 28, 1837

❧

Neglected to let down my bar last night and woke to a host of feasting mosquitoes. Rose before first light to smothering air and set Nancy to work making up biscuits. All morning, thunderheads mounted over the harbor. The horse stood in the yard, tethered to the iron ring on the stable wall, his rope hanging slack. He stood with one hoof cocked, dozing; only his tail moved, switching flies. Put up ten jars of fig preserves and cut out a waistcoat for T. In the past while we were in town, my brother often importuned me to set aside country habits, but I could not divest myself—nor would I wish to divest myself—of the twin country habits of thrift and conservation when we come to this city where idleness is the mark of one's rank in society—I believe that our Lord values consistency. This year, however, I have heard no such urging.

Rachel Hayne arrived today from Georgetown aboard the *Lily*. Brought home by Mrs. L. with much tearful rejoicing—"Here is my Rachel," and "My darling girl has come home"—and outcry from the Negroes. When I heard the carriage pull into the yard and the clamor of Negroes begin—much weeping and wailing for joy at the return of their "young miss"—I was lying down, weary from the morning's labors and from the heat that presses down upon man and beast alike. I got up and called to R. from the window. She looked up, tired from travel but radiant with approaching motherhood, and greeted me fondly. It appears that my needle will need to fly to keep ahead of her infant. My brother returns from every meeting with the factor weighted down more heavily with care. Sometimes he spends upward of four hours at his papers and ledger books, striving to reconcile debit and credit. Tenant in the Wentworth Street house is two months in arrears and no sign of payment forthcoming. And yet, as in years past, on coming to town, my brother abandons many country habits, restraint and early rising chief among them. The forenoon ofttimes finds him still abed, while the depths of night discover him absent from the house. Often, an entire week passes in which his daily routine begins long past noon and carries him only as far as the Library Society and the factor's office. Evenings are spent riding with the Association, keeping order. My sleep is often interrupted at 1:00 or 2:00 A.M. by the sound of the carriage arriving home and T., the soul of merriment, alighting from it. He succumbs too easily, I fear, to the temptations to indolence, idleness, and luxury that this city places in his path.

Mrs. Porcher came to visit, quite bedecked in the latest silk fashion, and laughed at me for my "country habits," which merriment I endured in silence, knowing that she is of a gay, flighty, and generous temperament. Though resources are scarce, she wishes to hire out Diana's time to sew table linens for the family, as she has recently purchased a length of fine linen from a shipment lately arrived on an English ship. Agreed upon price and time, then set D. to work on a new counterpane for my brother's bed, his own being much worn and the threads loosening throughout. He has complained of extreme vexation on numerous occasions, for if by chance he fall into bed at night still clad in boots or shoes, his buckles or spurs catch the loose threads of his coverlet and entangle him. What is needed is something tightly woven.

The counterpane pattern was gotten from the latest number of *The Ladies' Companion*. It is an elaborate and beautiful bedcovering constructed of many close-worked rows of stuffed work and a center medallion, likewise channeled and stuffed. Complicated but not, I believe, beyond my skill or D.'s. She is a quick study, too quick, it seems to me at times, unlike Nancy or Chloe, to whom I must repeat instructions many times before they fully grasp the required concept or duty. This girl becomes impatient if detained overlong with instructions. D. sewed all morning on T.'s coverlet, then departed for Mrs. Prioleau's. About midmorning, I divested myself of keys—a cumbersome ring that weighs heavier on me than its corresponding number at Fairview—and went out to return my calls. Mrs. Manigault all scandal, scandal, and more scandal: The Reverend McDowell composes his sermons at the widow Gilland's house; the Prioleaus sold two Negroes last week and more to come if financial times do not improve. And yet Mrs. P. finds resources to hire D. to sew table linens, so their situation may not be as dire as cruel rumor would have it. The Huger sisters have petitioned for an uncle to act as their guardian in their dealings with their brother, whom they reportedly fear will *murder them* in a fit of drunken rage. Mrs. M. well satisfied with D.'s needlework, which is of superior quality and evenness, though less so with her temperament, which she finds disruptive of her household. Her old cook, Lidia, will not remain in the same room with the girl, and her other domestics likewise regard Diana fearfully—she possesses some mysterious sway over them.

T. returned from his time patrolling the waterfront with other members of the Association flushed with the success of their endeavor—four Negro seamen removed from a New York ship and conveyed to the Workhouse. He is more energetic than he has been in recent weeks, although he reports the dispiriting sight of cotton on the wharves and shuttered banks, everyone clutching coins against the return of a time when the banks will again release specie payments. I sewed a new apron and listened to his discourse on economics.

Afterward, we reviewed my household accounts and receipts for recent purchases. As he studied the items listed in my small ledger, he questioned me closely: Why four gallons lamp oil? Ten pounds coffee? How long do I intend to make same last? Two pounds sugar? Did we not only last month purchase a like amount? Why must we have more toweling for the house, when every line in the yard flutters with toweling on wash day? I was flooded with gratitude that, though I have no husband, I am blessed with a brother who has assumed a host of husbandly duties. Thus the pleasure that I feel at being watched over by my fond overseer of economics far outweighs the discomfort of being so closely questioned. I well remember my mother's regular petitions to my father for money, his small leather-covered account book, in which he kept a record of the money allotted her for the running of the household. Since my brother's training was had of our father, he is no less thorough in his reckoning and carries his own small book, in which the record of my petitions and his disbursements is scrupulously kept.

Lingering over the ten dollars paid to the city treasurer for a badge for Diana, he questioned me closely to determine if the procedure that he had earlier set forth was being followed. "Is it wise, given the girl's unseasoned status, to send her freely about the city?" he questioned sternly, glancing over the tops of his small glasses with a look so like our father's, my heart began to pound as it did whenever I was closely questioned by my father in this same room over some youthful impudence or act of willfulness. Now my brother stands in the place of both father and husband, and I answered him by reporting that though he was right to question my judgment in this matter, I had renewed faith in my ability to manage Diana. Indeed, I said, I *had* managed her recent activities without mishap. T. was satisfied with this answer, but I went to bed tormented and lay long restless upon my bed, at the mercy of the noise from the street, the mosquitoes, the heat, and the proddings of my own conscience.

At first light, I rose and witnessed this scene between Mr. and Mrs. Legare, the former returned for a day or two from Columbia to welcome his daughter to his house. Mrs. L. clutched her dressing gown about her and talked urgently while he moved through their yard toward the waiting carriage, all elegance in waistcoat and vest, scattering chickens and Negroes with his cane, whistling the while.

June 30, 1837

A pleasant, near-perfect summer day, such as are rare here. After early rain, the heat abated and the sky cleared and filled with high, clean, fleecy clouds. A light breeze blew across the water, carrying the mingled odors of flowers through the streets. I saw an unfamiliar Negro girl in the yard around first light, conversing with Diana at the door to the kitchen house, but she was gone before I could dress and go out to discover her identity. Diana claims she was one of Mrs. Prioleau's Negroes, come with a message from Mrs. P. about her hiring out. Such messages are to be directed only to me, I reminded D., then reprimanded her for the impropriety of speaking with the girl. "Yes, Mistis" was her lackadaisical reply, all the while going on with her work of helping Nancy to assemble the breakfast. After this incident was resolved, all worked cheerfully. Nancy in kitchen house, making up bread and biscuits—Lucy gone to the market to sell surplus sweet potatoes and eggs that came in yesterday on the Fairview boat—Ned to wharf—Abraham cleaning stalls—D. sewing in the downstairs parlor, making good progress on T.'s counterpane while I smocked the bodice of R.'s baby gown. Mrs. Fraser and Mrs. Alston added to my list of households to which Diana is hired out.

Then, after dinner, my calm was shattered—D.'s trip to Mrs. Manigault's to work on Sara's trousseau canceled by a note from Mrs. M., its tone very formal and severe, without salutation or closing: "Miss Hilliard, This will serve as notice that the servant Diana should not be sent to my house again. E. Manigault." Found Diana in the kitchen house at her needle and laughing loudly with Chloe. Demanded to know what action on her part had prompted Mrs. M.'s note. Her answer consisted of a heated complaint about one of Mrs. M.'s "ignorant niggers," who had provoked a quarrel with her by "always be for brag about the buckra." Her tirade would have gone on had I not ordered her to be silent. What would my mother do, faced with such a circumstance?

All morning, I put up more figs, an occupation particularly well suited to thought. T. on hand for breakfast this morning, and in good spirits due, I believe, to the restoration of order to his bowels. Excellent breakfast of creek shrimp and grits, waffles and toast with my fig preserves, prepared by Nancy and served with proper quiet and order by D., received my brother's highest praise. How blessed I am with family. He was full of good spirits over the reception of his talk to the Agricultural Society on increasing rice production and the duties of the trunk minder and the arrival of a letter from our overseer detailing the successful progress of the rice crop, which is presently under the long water. It seems that T.'s ideas concerning advantageous types of soil and methods that foster increased productivity have garnered wide and approving notice among the agriculturalists of our circle. He does not believe in breaking up land too fine, as it becomes so consolidated and encrusted as to prevent the tender fibers of the young plant from pushing through, but, rather, will plant rice in any land, no matter how rough, if it be well broken as to allow for germination of the seed. He has applied for the Agricultural Society's premium this year, as he believes our fall crop will be the finest ever.

After dinner, I read the Testament to the household. All listened and received the Lord's word with gratitude. "He that hath ears to hear, let him hear." The story of Lazarus's raising from the dead, which is a favorite among them. At the moment of Lazarus's resurrection, Nancy threw up her hands with an exclamation of joy. And yet (it seems there must always be this *and yet* in our characters, room aplenty for God to work), as I was putting up the Bible, D. arrived, curtsying and protesting loudly that she had been hard at work and had forgotten the hour for the reading of Holy Writ. Handed over to me thirty dollars in cash and coin, a sum far exceeding the expected one, then stood waiting for what she now boldly calls "her share." Should have questioned her but lacked the *will*, and so stood there like Judas Iscariot with the traitor's silver weighing down my hand, then ordered her back to her needle. By 10:00 P.M., the kitchen house and stable alike were dark and quiet save for the glow of the banked fire in the kitchen hearth. I could just glimpse said fire from my window, which glimpse, along with the stars overhead, led me to thank God again for His Divine Plan and the order with which He invests His universe. (Oh, God, let the fire of Your love and mercy never be banked in my soul, but blaze freely and bring light to the darkness.) Roused from sleep by the image of my mother standing beside each of three small graves—a brother and two sisters—in the cemetery at Fairview, holding a lamp aloft as each was opened to receive its precious weight. The quiet faith with which she bore her grief, the calm authority with which she conducted her affairs—her life a lamp unto my feet and a rebuke for all its failings.

Awakened again, late, by Diana's loud voice and lay long awake, troubled by Mrs. M.'s note and my own failings. Why are our natures sinful? Was it the sin of our first parents, or God's plan that we should be stained in order that the action of Divine Grace may be made more visible in our lives? What is this wickedness that rekindles in our natures no matter how vigorously it is snuffed out? T. returned close to five o'clock from some nocturnal errand. Lit my candle and went down to meet him. His clothing smelled strongly of segar smoke, cooking fires, and spirits. He brushed my hand aside when I attempted to straighten his shirt collar, and he then reported disturbing rumors of a ship lately come from Baltimore and presently standing off Folly Island, on which five victims of the stranger's fever lie ill—island and ship under quarantine, as are the doctors sent to attend them. I hope Dr. Wyman is not among their number, as R. Hayne's lying-in draws near. Further, my brother reports rumors of three cases up on the Neck and one case among the tenements near Adger's Wharf, where the Irish and Acadian wretches crowd together in appalling squalor. Once I visited one such hovel on an errand from the Fuel Society to determine the worthiness of the household to receive our society's charity and found it crowded, smoky, and reeking with the scent of the calamitous lives of the wretches confined therein. The object of my visit, a girl of nineteen beset with the cares of squalor and poverty, had nonetheless kept clean linen over her babe, and flowers bloomed at her doorstep. Thereafter I was appointed to convey our charity and receive her thanks, which she gave profusely and with many tears.

July 7, 1837

Woke today to smothering weather. Sunrise brings the onset of heat, as if the heat of the preceding day had lingered through the night, only to be added to the next day's oppressiveness. Cases of stranger's fever on the Neck increased to six; on Folly Island, all five afflicted have died. The *Courier* daily carries messages from the Board of Health warning against the accumulation of decaying refuse in the streets, as the stranger's fever is due to moisture in the earth, the exhalation of which bears with it the poison and mingles it with the humid atmosphere, until all who inhale it, if not acclimated, take in the deadly portion at every breath.

We are asked to whitewash walls, pump water out of our cellars and allow cellar doors to stand open for some time each day, keep putrifying matter off the streets, and to sweep and clean the sidewalks in front of our houses, allowing nothing to stand that would impede the flow of water. Directed Ned and Caesar to whitewash the walls of the kitchen house and stable. Around ten o'clock, the militia rolled out a cannon onto Bay Street and let fly a salvo (which shook our window glass and brought down a fine dust from the ceiling) to disperse the miasma. Masters of ships coming into port are urged to keep all seamen on board. People hurry through the streets with lowered heads and handkerchiefs pressed to their faces. The Negroes are draped with bits of tarred rope and bags of camphor; black and white alike keep garlic in their shoes.

Our fires stay lit all day in spite of the heat—such is the state of our city, besieged again by deadly pestilence. This time, it is the yellow fever that invades our homes and churches, a sinister interloper that thrusts himself into our midst, threatening the orderly procession of our days and hours.

The cannon's salvo put me into state of agitation. Took valerian tea with twenty-five drops of LD and determined myself to attempt to right any wrongs charged against my soul in case I should be carried off by the pestilence. Directed Ned to drive me to Mrs. Manigault's and passed a most distressing sight in the market: A Negro woman was being secured by ropes to the pillar there in order to receive a flogging, crying and screeching most horribly and begging for mercy before the lash was applied to her back. A small crowd of Negroes and whites had gathered to witness her punishment, and when at length the chastening instrument was applied, the sight and sound of it were enough to cause all but the most callous among the crowd to flinch and turn away. Ordered Ned to drive quickly away from that place, but for a block or more I could hear the fall of the lash and the screams of the wretched woman who received them. Surely slavery is a stain upon our land.

At Mrs. M.'s house, she being slow to receive me, I mounted the stairs to Lucille's room—found it darkened, stifling, shutters closed across the windows, and L. herself still in a despondent state, her face turned to the wall and attended by a servant whose fan weakly stirred the thick air. She will take no food nor drink, and it is much to be feared that in her weakened state the fever will overtake and carry her off. Dr. Wyman, I understand, will bleed her tomorrow if her condition remains unchanged. Spoke to her plainly on the dangers of indulging in despair and urged her to seek peace by surrendering her will to the Divine Will. At last, I lifted her Bible from a stand beside her bed and read to her from the Lord's Word: "Peace I leave with you, my peace I give unto you: not as the world giveth, give I unto you." She lay like one of the dead and could not be persuaded to stir, even to attend to the Word of God.

Descending the stairs, to find Mrs. M. at last "at home" to me, though she remained standing, nor invited me to sit. Our talk ranged over the desolate landscape that we at present traverse — Sarah Huger carried off last night; Rebecca Henry at first light this morning; two of the Porcher children lie at the Dread Threshold. At last, I gathered my resolve and inquired of her whether my servant, Diana, had completed her work on Sara's trousseau. "Not at all," she answered stiffly.

Then, what, I asked, had prompted her dismissal from Mrs. M.'s service with her daughter's trousseau incomplete and the wedding three weeks away? At first, she would only reply that it was D.'s *impudence* that had caused her to take this action. "How impudence?" I inquired. It seems she holds her head too high, speaks plainly to Mrs. M. or anyone in the household, stirs up trouble among Mrs. M.'s servants — Mrs. M. has noted an increase in insolence and quarreling among the blacks of her own household after D. has been among them. Then, at last, she came out with it and solved for me the mystery of her late coolness. "I must tell you," she said, "that I am much put out over the increase in the fee for Diana's services. In this time of straitened financial circumstances, for one member of our circle to attempt to profit unduly at the expense of another member seems an unsupportable outrage."

"How increased?" asked I with great agitation. "I have asked for no increase in Diana's fee, nor would ever ask such of a friend, even in prosperous times."

She then produced from her writing desk a note written in a hand very like my own and on *my paper.* "Mrs. Manigault," it read. "Commencing with this week and on all following weeks, I am to be paid seven dollars for Diana's work, such sum to be paid on Fridays into Diana's hands and conveyed to me. I remain your admiring friend, E.H."

When I assured her that I had never written such a note—in truth, I was wounded that my friend so little observes my writing as to mistake the crude replica she showed to me for my own hand—she urged me to look to my household. Soon afterward, I seized the opportunity to take my leave of Mrs. M. and hurried home in a state of extreme agitation. As the carriage drove past the market, the earlier scene of suffering that had excited such sympathies in my breast, I saw that the Negro woman was gone, the ropes that were used to bind her arms around the column were piled in a heap at its base, a splash of blood remained on the column. Whereas before my heart had been moved by the sight of the wretch's suffering, now it felt cold within my breast and all my sympathies lay with the master or mistress who had sent her hence to receive her punishment. Indignation at the repeated acts of ingratitude that daily test our souls struggled within my breast with sympathy for the ignorant wretches who thought to ape the tone and feeling of our correspondence. Mrs. M. was convinced that I had succumbed to brain fever to write such a letter. Though our friendship was restored, my temper had been sorely tested.

Took up my station in the second-floor drawing room and sent for Nancy, who came into the room, weeping and wringing her hands until ordered to stop, as though she knew the import of my summons before a word had left my lips. She confessed knowledge of the note but insisted she had been forced into stealing my paper by Diana, who threatened to conjure her if she would not do it. All the Negroes are frightened of D., so Nancy says, because she tells them that her father was Gullah Jack, one of the nefarious Vesey plotters, who thought to protect the conspirators with crab claws he had mumbled over and invested with the power to stop bullets. Poor superstitious wretches, they have no defenses against the likes of conjurers among them. She hints that the net of D.'s commerce is thrown wider than her sewing, that she talks among them with certainty of *buying her freedom.*

Dismissed N. then and spent some time looking out over the

ocean, contemplating these events and my response to them, my heart lying cold within my breast with the weight of what Nancy had revealed to me and the knowledge that I, I alone, through my own best intentions, have provoked in this servant a desire for things beyond those naturally accruing to her state, which is ever the cause of evil among them. Summoned Diana, who came quickly enough this time, having, no doubt, learned of my visit to Mrs. M.'s house and the discovery of her deceit. She came quickly into the room with downcast eyes, the picture of humility, dropped a low curtsy, and deposited six coins into my palm. Would to God that I had flung them back into her face; instead, I told her that to touch pen and paper, to *write*, much less to forge her mistress's name and to attempt to deceive her, was a grievous crime and that I might yet send her to the Workhouse. Informed her further that the law in our state forbids the freeing of slaves and that since she will, therefore, never be free, she must cease at once to hope to be able to purchase her freedom or otherwise obtain it. Henceforth, I informed her, her conduct will be regulated by the following rules: Commencing with today, she will no longer be allowed to leave these premises without an explicit and verifiable destination. Second, when at home, she is to remain at all times within reach of my voice. Third, she is hereby forbidden from going to the market, or near the wharves, and likewise forbidden congress with any fisherman, and she is further forbidden to handle money or to keep any for herself. Fourth, she is to keep her eyes lowered when speaking to any white person and is to show *at all times* the humility that befits her station. Fifth, she is forbidden to dress in shawls and scarves, but must wear *plain slave cloth* garments and head coverings at all times. Sixth, she is forbidden to loiter about in the yard, but must always be occupied at some useful task, to be assigned by me or, in my absence, by Nancy. Seventh, she is forbidden congress with any free Negro. Eighth, on Sundays when not attending Divine Office, she is to be engaged in useful activity, as shall be determined by myself, my brother, or, in our absence, Nancy. Under no circumstances is she to mingle with the plantation Negroes who come to the city to defile our holy day. As I spoke, I perceived a faint yet definite trembling of her person, and when she raised her head, the familiar wide smile had been replaced by a look so black, it seemed as if I looked into the very depths of hell, in which dark confines some fiend was crouched to leap at me.

Dismissed D. and sat for a long time looking out over the harbor — today, the sight of the ceaseless ocean, the ever-changing play of light, the bristle of mast and sail and the stately passing ships, the merry tossing of palmetto in the sea breeze, and the white of the seabirds brought no comfort to me. Usually from my perch on high, the street below disappears and I imagine myself sailing out over the water to a better place. Today, however, I found none of the serenity of former times.

Just after dark, a Negro burial party passed, lit by flambeaux, a crush of weeping, swaying bodies, a mournful dirge such as never rises from the throats of civilized men — a scene from Dante's *Inferno*, and I one of the inhabitants of hell.

July 15, 1837

❧

The smothering weather continues unabated—air so thick, it drapes like gauze between trees. Even the shade in the yard is so close and hot, one thinks to stretch out a hand and tear it away. Where are the breezes of Fairview? The cool of evening? Far from us, I fear, perhaps never to be felt again. The clatter of a water bucket in the yard, the stench of fish and worse, the sound of Negro voices, the whine of mosquitoes, the heavy burden of sorrow under which we walk—all these increase the oppressiveness of the atmosphere. Funeral processions increasing daily. S. Manigault much confounded that St. Philip's cannot be promised for her wedding, due to the number of funerals anticipated. She is determined to be married at home if need be, in spite of the pestilence. More cannons fired in the streets. Crews of scavengers working overtime. Port to be closed soon if fever continues. Yesterday when I unlocked the sugar caddy, black ants scattered in every direction. Cockroaches sip at pools of spilled liquid all over the house. Mold grows thickly on cracked plates in the sideboard. Thomas did not arise until nearly noon, and when at last he did appear, he sat speechless before a cup of coffee. I inquired after his bowels, only to be rebuffed with an abrupt retort. Oh, demon idleness.

Spent the rest of the morning sewing in the second-floor parlor with D. at my feet. No matter the heat, we must have fire to keep the pestilent air at bay. Room insufferably hot and reeking; even Lucy's fan only dragged the heat around us. Now, Diana goes no longer out into the city to sew for others, but remains indoors, hung with camphor and reeking bags, sitting so close to the fire that I often have occasion to order her to move away for fear that her clothing will ignite. What my mistressship has failed to accomplish, God has achieved by sending this pestilence. At the mention of going out into the streets, her eyes show white as the eyes of a frightened horse. Mrs. Manigault and Mrs. Porcher's Negroes deliver the work to our house, their eyes likewise rolling, thick cloths pressed to their faces. Took up Thomas's counterpane and studied Diana's needlework for flaw or error. Stitches firm and remarkably even—no give or tear when tested. In addition, she has sewed this week two petticoats for S. Manigault's trousseau and I have taken in the five-dollar payment in full, without her complaint—indeed, with such cheerfulness as to give me pause.

T. at work tonight on a piece for the *Southern Agriculturalist* on the culture of rice at Fairview. It seems we have won the premium for rice production for last year's crop—120 bushels of good rice our yield per acre. This year, he says, reports received from our overseer promise a more bountiful harvest. Assisted my brother by reviewing with him the notes I had taken while serving as his amanuensis throughout last winter and spring.

As we sat perusing the records, another tumultuous Negro funeral procession passed by in the street, attended by members of the City Guard, and I wondered anew at this curious scene laid out before our Maker's eye. We hear the death toll among the Acadian and Irish wretches is rising daily; twelve members of our circle have succumbed in the past week; among the Negroes, the pestilence is likewise laying waste, and yet might Our Savior not find, in the sight of us sitting thus, reviewing our planting schedule and planning the next year's crop in this besieged and sorrowing city, evidence of our abiding faith in His tender mercies?

"On what day did we first turn the soil?" asked Thomas.

"On May twenty-ninth," I read, "with two oxen and one boy each, turning the land with stubble on and four women turning up the sides of the ditches, drains, and headlands."

"Soil condition?" he inquired.

"The field part clay, the remainder light, husky black land with several salty lowlands in process of reclamation by applications of lime."

"How much was planted?"

"Six pecks of seed to each acre, broadcast in furrows fifteen inches apart, center to center."

"We must do better," said he. "Our profits must increase this year."

Oh, what I would give to ease his burden, to lighten his steps, to erase the haggard lines of care from his dear face.

Thus is the somber state of our city—without coin, our products spoiling on wharves or sold for pottage, our city visited by deadly pestilence, besieged from within by domestic enemies. The theft of the paper and the forging of my name, Diana's insolence and careless disregard for all our institutions—so disorder spreads in ever widening circles, like ripples spread from around a stone dropped into water. So wickedness rekindles in our natures, no matter how often it is snuffed out. Took my candle up to bed—how frail its light in the darkness. Amen.

August 1, 1837

How quickly we are pitched from happiness to sorrow in this world—Rachel Hayne's baby, a son, was born yesterday morning at first light, after two days of the most terrible travail, during the course of which her life and the life of her unborn child hung in the balance. Throughout that last terrible night, I assisted Dr. Wyman by bathing her face and holding a basin and by trying to comfort her distraught mother, but still, her case proved intractable. After bleeding her and dosing her with calomel to no avail, the desperate doctor, who had come to attend her after a day and a night spent ceaselessly attending fever victims, cast about the bedchamber with a wild look and asked if there were known to be among our servants any woman with skill in midwifery. Upon hearing this, Mrs. L. jumped up and ran from the room. From the bedchamber window, I saw her in the yard, shaking Tenah, and she came back to report that Tenah had disclosed that *Diana* was rumored among them to have such skill. Sent for her immediately. Upon coming into the room, she sniffed the air, then gave R.H. a bottle to blow into. She carried with her a long strip of red cloth, which she knotted. Meanwhile, Rachel's husband, lately arrived from Georgetown (against Mrs. L.'s strongest admonitions) and distracted with worry, paced through the downstairs rooms, his restless footsteps an accompaniment to his wife's agony. Upon hearing his name, Diana inquired as to his relation to the suffering woman and, learning it was her husband, called for *his vest* to be procured and brought to her. I was dispatched to carry out this curious errand by my distraught friend, and, having persuaded him to give me the garment, brought it up to her. Diana then fitted the garment backward upon his suffering wife. After this episode, he threatened again to flee the house to escape his wife's pleadings for God's mercy and the unsettling atmosphere that attended her agony. Only the day before her Trial began, she had conveyed to me her determination to undergo her travail in meek silence. I cautioned her then not to make promises that it would cause her anguish to break. Even Our Lord, I reminded her, cried out in His agony. I offered this advice while remembering our sister Mary's childbed travail, when she nearly rent the rooftop with her cries, then fell into despondency and could not be persuaded to suckle her daughter for three days and nights, that duty finally falling to a Negro woman until Mary was restored to herself. Detained R.H.'s husband at the door and sought to convince him that it was less dangerous here, where he must endure the sounds of his wife's anguish, than in the streets, where a more sinister fate perhaps awaited him. As he waited downstairs, we heard his footsteps continuing restlessly up and down, then, at last, the crash of a door as he made his escape.

Diana labored beside the doctor while I stood, holding tightly to Mrs. L.'s hand, though my friend twice swooned, watching the agony her child endured. Around midnight, D. insisted that Rachel get up and *walk*. Astonished and angered, Dr. Wyman and her mother at first insisted she remain prone, until they were persuaded by Diana's vehemence and agreed. D. walked Rachel about the chamber, supporting her the while, though R. cried out in sharp agony at every step, but when Diana sought to persuade Rachel to *squat in a corner*, Dr. Wyman, with the adamant support of Mrs. L., ordered her back to bed. In truth, after this incident of walking, her travail seemed to gather speed and strength and was finally brought to its blessed conclusion just at daybreak.

Early today, Mrs. Manigault's boy arrived with a note: Lucille got up from her bed and dressed herself this morning, a small light in the deepening gloom that engulfs their household and our city. It has been raining now for a week, without promise of stopping, and the heat and the fever deaths continue unabated. Yesterday, I left R.H.'s bedside to attend six funerals, and today four. Everywhere one sees carriages and carts mired in mud and abandoned. Today on Meeting Street, I saw a dray horse receive a terrible whipping as it struggled in vain to pull the dray free of the mud. This morning, the militia fired the cannon again to disperse the miasma, and the smell of gunpowder hangs thickly in the wet air, mingled with odors of fish and privy vault. Streets almost deserted except for slaves on errands, funeral processions, doctors' carriages, and undertakers' carts. On every street one sees the baskets loaded with the dead carried out of houses. At the cemeteries, the dripping carriage horses stand with lowered heads. The graveyard oaks stream. The graves fill with water, so that the coffins float horribly until the earth weighs them down.

The saddest funeral I have yet attended was Edward Pringle's, two days past, who was to have married Sara Manigault on Saturday next. Much weakened by bleeding at the lungs, he sickened with the fever early one morning and answered the Dread Summons by nightfall of the next day. As his coffin was lowered, water splashed up and covered Sara Manigault, who was led away by her mother, ghastly pale and spotted with mud from her intended's grave. Mrs. William Ravenel has also died this week. It seems E. Legare was not her husband's worst enemy after all. Mr. Ravenel turned from his wife's grave, leaning heavily upon his erstwhile enemy. Before the Reverend Glennie could gather himself and flee with his family back to the Waccamaw, his wife succumbed to the pestilence and one of his beautiful daughters lies at the Dread Threshold.

After today's sad duties, I sat with Rachel Hayne until late afternoon, while her exhausted mother slept. Carried the infant boy

around the bedchamber. He appears healthy and strong, a welcome reminder of life in this city of Death. Returned home to
find that the sugar caddy had been opened and upward of half the
sugar disappeared. Called in each servant and questioned them,
but, of course, all knew naught of it, though each produced
enough lamentation to fill two churches, with the exception of
Diana, who had to be sent for and, when she appeared, could not
trouble herself to answer my questions about the sugar caddy, but
instead held out to me some cloth that she was holding in her
hands. "I been for finish it for you, mistis," she said, and I unfolded the garment in my hands and discovered it was Rachel
Hayne's baby gown, put aside and forgotten in the turmoil of
these last weeks, now returned to me, though the garment I unfolded bore scant relation to the gown that had last passed under
my hands. The neckline was skillfully outlined in French knots
and flowering vines that cascaded down the length of the gown
and ended in a hem filled with openwork bound into delicate
sheaves, and another vine worked around the hem in exceedingly
delicate stem stitch. As I stood, confounded, testing the garment,
Diana availed herself of my astonishment by suggesting that she
could produce two or three like garments each week *if she were to
be allowed to live outside our household*, returning to the house
once a week to turn over the profits of her labors. She was halfway
into the particulars of her proposition when I recovered my
senses, which had been jolted by this request, made, it appears, in
perfect confidence of a favorable reply, and informed her that our
family had never allowed any servant to live outside our yard and
I saw no reason to breach custom for her and that, furthermore,
we would have no cause to speak of it again. Yet when I dismissed
her, she stood waiting, her eye on the baby gown. I sent her away
empty-handed (and received a sullen look in reply); then exhaus-
tion and dizziness overtook me and I retreated to my bedroom,
where I sat studying the gown and musing.

Where is it in the African that such a gift for beauty resides?

When first she began to sew, I feared she would prove useless as a seamstress, as her hands were so rough as to pick the cloth when she handled it. Now she has created this. How came this gift into the barbarous and unlettered soul? Cousin Whitemarsh would no doubt hold that the civilizing influence of our society, within whose confines they labor, has refined their native sensibilities and that it has largely been our tutelage that has created these capacities in them, and yet, in order for the flower to bloom, must not the seed already reside in the ground of the immortal soul? This is the question that troubled my rest.

Late evening—now, there is more urgent business than missing sugar or baby gowns. Thomas returned from the Glennie funeral much subdued, sank into a chair in the dining room in a melancholy state, and refused my offers of assistance and admonitions that he go straight up to bed with an impatience entirely out of character for my mild brother. When I returned from nursing Rachel Hayne three hours later I found him in the same chair, looking about him with a vacant, staring expression and beset by chills and pains in the back. Oh, God, if it be Your Will, let this cup pass from us.

August 3, 1837

May He alone who ruleth and governs all pestilence stay the scourge and restore our brother to returning health.

In fear, we will retreat to old habits, burrow into old safeties; old loyalties will return. Outrage builds in Louisa the way it has always grown: spreading cold, not heat. A cold like the cold of her mother's voice heard through the closed doors of this room, speaking to Mamie about a rule that had been broken, an order ignored. The cold of heights. Even though they'd lived their entire lives at sea level, they'd always found heights to climb. They were one of the city's earliest families, their history so tightly woven into the city's, they'd felt every shift, every tremor. A British general had chosen their house for his headquarters when the British occupied the city during the Revolution. Their wall was marked with a star where a Union cannonball had struck it during the siege of the city; a crack in their foundation was noted with a plaque: CAUSED BY THE EARTHQUAKE OF 1886.

And so it is out of history that Louisa's anger begins and builds. "COME FOR MY THINGS." The arrogance of it. The gall of thinking that she had things to claim. Diana's willfulness has come to her out of the diary, and those dried and curling pages have also warned her that this girl is cunning, capable of extortion, not above stealing or lying, anything to get what she believes she is entitled to. Likewise, Eliza's anger has drifted up off the page, acrid as smoke, and mixed and mingled with her own anger, the old, stubborn, buckra anger at having to face it at all, at not having the story come out their way.

So she assumes the royal posture: back straight and not quite *touching the back of the chair, chin lifted, fingers curled around the polished curved arms of the chair where she sits. "Well, Diana," she says, "let's see about your things." She rises from her chair then, moves around the room like a docent. "Is this yours?" A nod to the Colonial Hilliards, who stare out of their dark oil portraits, their gilt frames. "Or this?" She opens the corner cabinet and removes the pitcher where the pursed silver lips and the fat silver cheeks of the trade winds perpetually blow. "This?" The blue-and-white china of Oriental design? The fine French walnut sideboard? Finally, her tour ends at the exact spot where her mother always stood to end an unpleasant interview with a servant: at the door, which she holds open, an invitation for the wrongdoer to slink away, and she says, all fine cool politeness, "I don't see anything of yours here, but please, feel free to take what belongs to you and get out of my house."*

All that day, she patrols reception room, dining room, upstairs and down. In every room, she stands and listens, counts plates and silverware, counts iced-tea spoons and gravy boats, then counts them again. The girl is not trustworthy—she knows that from the diary; she must be watched. Each time she returns to the heirlooms, they've moved: cruet stand a quarter turn to the left; trade winds pitcher an inch to the right, as though someone had picked up each one and then taken pains to set it down where it belonged.

All day it's quiet, but something quietly awful is happening. When she turns on a burner on the stove to poach an egg for breakfast, the flame blows out; the pilot flame snuffs itself, too, and won't be relit. She can't cook all day, is forced to spread peanut butter on saltine crackers for lunch and again for dinner. All day, the shine on the floorboards fades; by late afternoon, they look worn and scratched. In the dining room sideboard, the silver tarnishes. The color thins on the walls. Hurrying through the dining room at dusk, hurrying as if she can catch this solvent that's dissolving her house, bottle and cork it, and throw it into the ocean, she notices light coming through the closed curtains on the windows there. The tight weave of the cloth is stripping down to warp and woof.

By nightfall, the fading and thinning and tarnishing have stopped. Everything that has been turned over, picked up, and considered has been put down again. Nothing is missing, nothing except luster, color, heat, and light. The house is quiet and Louisa exhausted from running from room to room, up the stairs, then down to the cellar all day. She has to lie down, to sleep.

A few hours later, she gets up, stiff, and sees from her window that the door to the kitchen house is standing ajar, goes out to close it. What she finds there makes her sit down hard on the old straight chair against the wall just inside the door, and for the first time since this all started, she feels afraid, a cold, stunned, shriveling inside. The old cooking tools are scattered all over the floor. She rises slowly, pushing herself up with both hands on her knees, and goes from tool to tool, studying the damage.

Iron tongs with the hinges sprung, so that the gripper ends no longer meet. The arm on the heavy iron stand in the fireplace from which pots had hung is bent at such a devilishly precise angle, you might not notice it was bent until you hung a heavy pot of soup or grits there, watched it slide and spill into the fire. The hinges of the bread oven's door are sprung, so the door will not close tight, and every other tool is likewise made useless in a way so intimate and particular to its workings that only a person for whom those tools had been like the extension of a hand could have done this. Only a person who had lived every day with the swing of hinges and the grip of tongs could have carried out destruction this precise. Standing there with the tongs in her hand, Louisa knows that she is not done after all; the things that were come for have not been found. She feels that fact sink into her bones the way she'd felt her age come over her the night she'd sat and held her mother on the bathroom floor and waited for the ambulance to come. There is more to find here, more to tell, and she is the one who can tell it. But tell what? *she asks herself. And how?*

August 7, 1837

My brother, my beloved brother, died this morning after two days worsening illness, one day of acute agony while Dr. Wyman, Nancy, and I stood helplessly by, and a final night of intense and unrelieved suffering, during which he cried out constantly for water and drank it through a quill, only to vomit it up immediately upon drinking. Neither calomel or jalap, bleeding nor prayer could save him. Around 3:00 A.M. on his last night, hope revived briefly, for he sat up then, threw off the bedclothes, and asked urgently and with eyes full of exceeding brightness for a taste of my fig preserves. These being hastily spread on some leftover biscuit and brought in to him, he took one bite, then turned on me a most terrible look of sorrow and reproach and cried out that I had deceived him, for these were not my own preserves, but the fruit of another's tree. "Betrayer, deceiver," he cried. No words from the doctor could comfort or assure me that this tirade was caused by inflammation of the brain due to the effects of the fever.

Soon after that incident, the black vomit began, and after feeling his pulse, Dr. Wyman declared that his hour was almost upon him. At this, the Negroes who had crowded into the room—Nancy and Ned chief among them—began to lament so loudly, they had to be sent away. Even Diana wept in a corner, with her apron over her face. I sat and held my brother's hand in his agony, which at times was so extreme as to lift him from the bed, until at last, as the mantel clock struck four, he became peaceful. His eyes searched the ceiling of the room and his free hand picked incessantly at the bedclothes. At last, he held up his arms to heaven, called out for Susan, fell back upon the pillow, and expired, though not before he turned on me a look full of sorrow and reproach, a look that burned into my soul. I could not surrender his hand, though it cooled in my grip, but sat and held it until first light, committing to memory the stern set of mouth and chin, the fine, strong nose, the noble brow, the lines of care deeply etched into his face, re-membering the feel of his small hand clasped in my own on our childhood wanderings. He was ever my protector until he drew his last earthly breath. Shortly after first light, I sent Ned for the un-dertaker's men. Why have I been spared when so many others, more worthy, have been taken? Why am I left alone? How many deathwatches have I kept? How many fevered brows soothed, last words received, pale hands arranged on quiet breasts? My God, my God, why has Thou forsaken me?

August 9, 1837

Thomas was buried yesterday morning. Stayed all day alone in my room, with little care for the household. The Negroes came and went, Nancy weeping, the others moving silently with lowered heads. Diana nowhere to be found. Mary and George arrived on the afternoon boat from Beaufort. Wind and tide conspired to prevent their timely arrival, and in these days of pestilence, committals must be hasty. Mary read the Testament to the household last night. "And the light shineth in darkness; and the darkness comprehended it not. . . . Let not your heart be troubled, neither let it be afraid. . . . I am the resurrection, and the life." All attended to these words with rapt and solemn faces, save Diana, who was nowhere within reach of my voice, even though I had so recently ordered her to be.

This morning, I was unable to sleep for the oppressive drumming of the rain (three weeks now, and no sign of cessation), the stifling heat, the smell of spoilage and offal. At daylight, I called for Diana for help with dressing; no answer. Dressed myself and called for Ned, then found George at Thomas's desk, going over our brother's ledgers. Indeed, on coming into the room, I was given a start by the sight of my good brother in Thomas's chair, bent, as T. was wont to bend over his books, his head tilted at the same angle. We drove together to St. Philip's churchyard, where one funeral was in progress and another waiting to begin. Thomas's grave looked muddy and forlorn. George wept heavily upon my shoulder, though I felt cold and empty as the tomb. Rain lightened to fine sheets of mist as we drove beside the wharves, when my eye was arrested by the sight of a long canoe out in the harbor and rowing for shore through the rain and heavy swell. As the boat came closer, I saw that it was full of Negroes, and I heard their laughter drift across the water. Bade George stop as the boat came closer, for I had heard a familiar tone in the loud Negro laughter. Closer still and I spied a rude umbrella made of palmetto fronds and under it a familiar gaudy head scarf and laughing face, though the laughter ceased soon enough as they drew near enough to the wharf to see who it was who waited for them there. A boatload of Negroes, George reported, after descending to question them, returning from a frolic on Sullivan's Island while our city mourns, most of them free Negroes, and Diana among them, *dressed in a lady's silk dress* and sitting in the boat, coy as a maiden in her finery. And though my brother sought to calm me, and entreated me not to expose myself to the rain, and the wench herself begged for mercy, I dragged her from the boat by her hair and sent Ned for a member of the City Guard and ordered her conveyed to the Workhouse with an order for three days on the treadmill and thirty stripes for correction.

At home again, took valerian tea with twenty drops of LD and sat at the second-floor parlor of the silent house, looking out across the sheets of gray rain that swept and veiled the harbor, remembering Diana's laughing face under the gaudy head scarf and the palm-frond umbrella, the picture of gaiety, when the household and all its members are in mourning. As though the death of my beloved brother, her master, meant nothing to her.

After dinner, the brooch I had commissioned to be woven of my brother's hair arrived. I put it on and walked out alone to the Battery in the rain, where I dropped my store of coin got from Diana's labor into the harbor, but my heart felt no lighter for this unburdening. My God, my God, why has Thou forsaken me?

September 25, 1837
Fairview

❦

I had been so occupied with mourning and with preparations to return to Fairview, I had neglected to write here until we had reached the safety of Fairview once again. Diana returned from the Workhouse much chastened and subdued. Hearing of our brother's death, Cousin Whitemarsh returned to the city, and when he was apprised of the gravity of Diana's disloyalty, he communicated to the master of the Workhouse (with George's assent) our desire that two of the girl's front teeth be pulled from her mouth in order that she might be more easily identified if there should again arise a need to pick her out from among a crowd of Negroes. Once returned, she was confined to house and yard, on my orders, for the duration of our stay, and she made no attempt to leave. Dutiful and subdued, she dressed in slave cloth, kept her eyes cast down, carried out commands promptly—and yet, before our departure for home, I often came upon her sitting idly, her sewing in her lap, gazing out of the window. She will go no more to town. Mrs. Legare fled for the pines, taking Rachel and her infant son with her. Before we departed for Fairview, her yard had become entirely the province of Negroes, her own and numerous unknown Negroes who came and went. The pestilence at last subsided, though close to one hundred in the city died, including our Lucy, who succumbed to the fever the week before we fled to the country.

Conveyed home to Fairview by Simon, my father's patroon, and a silent crew of our boat Negroes. When at last our sloop had left the open ocean and found the river's mouth and turned for home, Simon sought me out. "Mistis want we to sing?" he asked, as it was ever Thomas's pleasure to hear the Negroes singing as we gained the river and made for home. "No, Simon." Along the riverbanks, the woods, from whose low-sweeping branches serpents hung, were shrouded in mist and autumnal rust. Now and again, we heard the harsh cry of some woodland bird, a grim reminder of the pleasure my brother used to take in our yearly voyages to town and back, when every strange birdcall or flash of unfamiliar wing was cause for renewed delight. In our fields, when last we reached them, newly cut rice lay upon the ground, awaiting transport to the barn. A larger harvest, from the looks of it, than last year's. Only the sower is absent from the harvest. Negroes on flats in the rice fields looked up from their work and bowed their heads. Greeted at the house by drooping, weeping Negroes crying, "Massa, oh, Massa."

Discipline has become very lax in our absence. Have found occasion to order three floggings this week. At least I have fulfulled one of God's requirements for my life and restored the servant Diana to her proper place. It is my fervent prayer that God will weigh that act of obedience against all my failings and transgressions. Upon her release from the Workhouse and return to Fairview, I ordered the overseer to place her on the work gang felling trees, repairing our road, and clearing a new field to bring under cultivation. For several weeks, until the first leaves began to turn color and fall from the trees, I observed from my window her gaudy head scarf passing in the road gang, though after a month I saw it no more. I shall go no more to town to be beset by desires that lead to ruin. Better to be set upon by the country fever and be buried in this beloved earth beside my mother and father than to lie, like my brother, far from home in the earth of that city where all is vanity and a striving after wind.

I have taken up now the duties of autumn here. Have put down rugs to keep the chill from the floor. Someone let the pigs out and they have gotten under the house. I must inventory the Negro clothing and prepare their clothes for the coming year. When I ring for Nancy, she comes silently into the room, and utters not a word about our Lucy. This morning was cool and pleasant and I walked out to our family cemetery and stood for a long moment beside my mother's grave, taking a reckoning of my spiritual progress. After standing thus for some minutes I judged myself an utter failure as mistress, as sister, as frail woman, overcome by the sin of our Mother, Eve, whose willful pride led to the downfall of the race. God have mercy upon me, a sinner.

Time Was
(by Louisa Hilliard Marion
April 1990)

What are we to do with what we've learned? This may be the question our lives were given us to answer. Today is Palm Sunday, the celebration of the Lord's entry into Jerusalem and the beginning of His last week on earth. A mark in the turning year, always returned to. Last night it rained, and this morning the city looked washed, as if a film had been stripped away; the light was clean and sharp, a pure spring light that seems to shine out of the new green grass and make the pastel houses glow. Walking up Church Street toward St. Philip's for the ten o'clock service, I saw the flagstones gleam, the steeple of St. Philip's standing out against the blue sky. In the street, puddles of water reflected clouds and blue sky; wisteria and dogwood blossoms floated in the water there.

The tall double doors into the church stood open, and the choir in their red robes was gathered there, carrying palms. I stepped up and found my friends ("Hello," "Good morning," "What a beautiful day") and stood with the other ladies in the Altar Guild to hear compliments on our altar. I could see our work down the central aisle of the church, the white cloth I'd starched and ironed that we'd smoothed over the altar, the white vase of red roses in the center. Very simple. Red and white. That was my idea: white for the spirit and red for the human blood. As the bell tolled, we chose our palms and began our walk around the churchyard, three abreast, holding our palms and following the minister and the choir in their long red cassocks, stooping to duck under the moss that trails from the low oak limbs and the mimosas there. Like marsh grass would look if it could get up and walk, that's how we looked in our procession, our palms held high. The palmettos rustled and the breeze off the water smelled fresh. Once around the churchyard and then we crossed Church Street and went into the larger graveyard there. Passing Isaac and Thomas and Eliza Hilliard's low brick tombs, I stooped to brush off the small sticks and brown crepe myrtle flowers that had collected there. Then we all walked in procession back across the street and into the church, holding our palms high, while the organ thundered and the choir sang "Halleluia!" escorting the Lord into Jerusalem.

Inside the church it was cool, almost chilly. Even on the hottest summer day, the inside of St. Philip's is cool and dim, as though the heat had been stopped at the door and asked to wait outside. I sat down in the Hilliard pew—halfway back on the left side of the aisle—and swung the small door shut at the end of the pew. For a moment before every service, the church is filled with the clicking of latches on the other small doors that make our pews into private places that have been owned by the same families for generations. There was the Alston pew and the Hilliard pew; the Simmons pew—occupied today by two of Susan's daughters, Ann dressed in blue, Amelia in yellow, both wearing wide-brimmed black hats of lacquered straw, and their children, who peeked and smiled at me over the back of the pew.

At the Gospel, the Reverend Bennett climbed the pulpit steps, adjusted the microphone, perched his glasses halfway down the bridge of his nose, and studied the congregation for a moment, smiling the way he does, as if our secrets, which he knew, filled him with affection and amusement. "The Passion of Our Lord,

Jesus Christ," he said in a voice that sounds almost British, though he comes from Columbia, South Carolina, and has never visited England, so far as I know. The Palm Sunday liturgy is a kind of reader's pageant: The minister reads the story of Christ's betrayal and death and also the part of Pontius Pilate, while the congregation answers as the mob. Not as vulgar as the Holy Week pageants at the Baptist churches—those crucifixion dramas, complete with the dragging of the cross, the whip and the crown of thorns, embarrassed men dressed as Roman soldiers in pleated kilts and cardboard helmets—but still strange, a ritual to be gotten through every year. Pages to be turned and lines to be read. That's how I'd always seen it.

But today, I found myself listening to Pilate. He was asking us to choose which of two prisoners he would release: Jesus or Barabbas, the thief? "Whom should I release to you?" he asked three times, and three times we answered, "Give us Barabbas."

"Then what shall I do with this Jesus?"

"Crucify him," we answered, as we did every year.

"But why?" the Reverend Bennett asked, reading Pilate's lines into the microphone. "What has he done?" His amplified voice filled the church.

"Crucify him!" we answered, louder now. Then the Reverend Bennett, as Pilate, had a bowl of water and a tea towel brought to him by a teenage girl in a pale pink dress, her long, crinkled blond hair held back with two silver barrettes. Always, it seems, he picks the prettiest girl in the church to hold his bowl and towel and pour the water over his fingers when, as Pilate, he washes his hands in front of the crowd. "I am innocent of the blood of this man," he said as he turned to face us, drying his hands, one finger at a time, on the towel the girl handed him.

Hearing him call himself innocent that way, watching him dry each finger on the white towel the pretty girl held out to him, that is where it started to be real to me. Something about the way he looked—the satisfied piety of his expression—and the way she looked beside him was so much like Henry and like me (though I was no girl when Henry came along, and had less claim to innocence) that when it was time for us to answer the question about Jesus again, I called out, "Crucify him" louder than I'd intended, and a few people turned around and looked at me, but I didn't care. I meant it, and it frightened me, because as soon as I'd said it, I knew that it was in me, this urge to kill and harm; it had been there all along.

That is when things changed for me. I felt as though I'd just awakened or had my sight restored to me after a long spell of blindness. Always before, this service had been just a reading, words on a page, but this year it was as if we were doing more than playing parts, reading lines; we were doing something real and something necessary. Because it's important to know the part you play. To find the traitorous seam in your seamless makeup, to discover hatred and send Christ to His death. To tell that story and tell it again until you come to the part where you're innocent and then to renounce that claim and find yourself humbler once you know what you're capable of. Once you know that you are human and weak, easily flattered by power; that you wish to avoid pain, and that you will take comfort wherever it is offered. Without all this unmasking, there would be no Solemn Collect on Good Friday to speak and to believe: "Let the whole world see and know that things which were cast down are being raised up and things which had grown old are being made new."

Now I know what I must do. That is why I am here, at Eliza Hilliard's writing desk in this second-floor room. The doors to the piazza are open and the windows all over the house are open, so the wind moves through and this house is like a ship under full sail. That is what I would have had my children imagine with me: this house like a big ship sailing through time. Or time itself like a cloth and our lives flying in and out like needle and thread, leaving a design for others to trace and know. All those images we make in order to bring what is distant close and to make the invisible vivid. My children would have had the imaginations to grasp this. Now it is my turn to trace the design, to tell the story and see where it ends, my turn to gather what I know, to take what I've read, what I've heard, what I've breathed in: to breathe it out, to go on with the story and leave a record for those that come after. I read that diary aloud, and when I came to the end, I said, "The dress is yours, Diana, but what can I do about that now?" This morning, I found the corner cabinet in the dining room unlocked, and the trade winds pitcher thrown so hard on the floor, the handle was nearly buckled. That is the other reason I know that the things come for have not been found, and I am here going on with this story: to save my house and my family's possessions from destruction. There isn't much time.

The house at Fairview was broad and faced with deep porches, front and back. Up the back porch posts, grapevines traveled and the lawn in front sloped down to a sand road that led to the river and the plantation landing. Eliza Hilliard's room was the front room on the corner of the second floor and it looked out across the road and beyond the road to the rice fields that stretched to the far-off silver curve of the Edisto River. Across the river to the west lay more rice fields, and the sun went down into them every day, so that from the house, she saw only Hilliard land and Hilliard water, a line of Hilliard oaks, Hilliard Negroes working in the rice fields, poling flats on the river. The old, blameless watercolor landscape that we love so passionately.

In this room, twice a day, she sat on the necessary chair, moving the stones that her bowels made of the food that passed through them. Since her return from the city, her bowels had become troublesome. Maybe she'd been grazed by yellow fever; perhaps a corner of it had brushed her that summer in town. Or maybe it was the parasites that lived in their guts. Even the richest among them were humming kingdoms of parasites and worms. Every summer when I was a child, all the children were wormed, like puppies.

Every day, Eliza Hilliard wore a brooch, a bracelet, a medallion, a cross, woven of hair from the family dead. The unstiffened cloud hair of children, the white or gray or silver hair of the old, brittle as wire, the brown or bright hair of those who'd died young, snipped from the heads of the corpses she'd sat beside and followed to their graves. And not just a few wisps, but whole hanks scissored off and taken to the jeweler on King Street, who passed the hair through thin mesh tubes, then wove, coiled, braided, and knotted these casings into crosses, into flowers, and brooches, bracelets, necklaces, and wreaths with birds perched in them.

Each day, depending on which of the departed beloved her mind's eye pictured, Eliza pinned one of the memorials to her breast or hung it by a silk cord around her neck and went to work. That fall, as the rice was harvested and the river filled with flats carrying rice to the barn, she pinned the cross woven of Thomas's hair to the neck of her blouse because it was her brother's face that she recalled and missed, as we will miss our loved ones most keenly in the seasons of their deaths or in the seasons in which their lives were lived most vividly upon this earth. Thus, the marsh in winter, red-winged blackbirds clinging to the grasses there, white egrets roosting in a bare gray tree remind me still of Henry, and in the fall, my brother, Hugh, returns.

Mother never really accepted that Hugh killed himself, and so, as October 2, the anniversary of his death, approached, as regularly as some people go to the cemetery to rake and weed and leave fresh flowers on their loved ones' graves, Mother and I had to go through Hugh's death again, to pile up more words around it. How many conversations did Mother and I have about Hugh? Dozens, hundreds. You ask what good were those words then? What good are they now? What do they change? Nothing, of course, but because we walk upright and have souls and brains within whose laps and folds hope constantly seeds itself and grows, we join words together to name what can be known, and for what cannot be known, we also find words and house things there until they come to sound like the truths we need in order to go on living the lives we've built around them.

Every September, a day would come when Mother and I would be sitting in the reception room having a drink before dinner and reading the newspaper, when I'd hear the paper drop into Mother's lap, then a sigh, and, looking up from my own section, I'd find Mother staring out of the window again.

"Poor Hugh," she'd say. "He was wearing his hunting jacket that day, wasn't he? I just know he was on his way bird hunting."

There, right there, I could have stopped the story. Any year, I could have told what I knew, which was plenty. "True, Mother, but there's more," I could have said. That would have been a start. Because it was true that Hugh had worn his hunting jacket that morning—the jacket, an old white sleeveless undershirt, and a pair of khaki shorts—just as it was true that he went dove hunting every fall, that he knew how to handle a gun. All those things were true and not one of them changed the fact that Hugh killed himself. You don't put a pistol in your mouth and blow the top of your head off by accident. That was what the coroner told me in private, because I asked him.

I could have told my mother those things. Instead, every year I'd say, "What exactly was he hunting with a pistol on Sullivan's Island at daybreak, Mother?" or something like it, depending what uncertainty my mother had found. One year, it was the hunting jacket, another, the car's full tank of gas that opened up the question again.

"Well, he must have gotten lost," she'd say. "Or else he was in his cups and ran up on that dune and got stuck. Hugh drank too much. In this day and time, I suppose we are required to call him an *alcoholic*," she'd say angrily, holding on to both arms of her chair, hard, as if a confession had been tortured out of her. "It runs in the family. No sense in prettying that up."

"*Oh, he was most definitely drunk, Mother,*" I would say, speaking loudly, as though she were deaf. That much truth, I insisted on, even then. "We saw the blood alcohol–level report, remember? It was four times higher than the legal limit necessary to establish drunkenness in any court."

"Well, maybe when he realized he was stuck and he'd have to wait until daylight for someone to find him, he thought he'd put his time to good use and clean his gun, the way his daddy had impressed upon him to do."

"There were no swabs or gun oil found in that car, Mother. You know that."

"Well, someone might have stolen them. Maybe the tow truck man, or the policeman, or that colored fisherman who found the car. Oh, yes, it's been known to happen. We have a different class of Negroes these days, a different class of people altogether. And while he was cleaning his gun, he must have looked down the barrel to make sure it was clean. You know how Hugh was about his firearms, always scrupulous with them, and *always cautious*. Your father drummed that into him."

And that's how it went, year after year. And always at some point, I'd realize that I was lost again, that I'd ended up back in my mother's story, when what I'd intended was to tell my own. But I went on being lost. For Mother's sake, I told myself, but now I see it was for my own sake, too, because as long as we argued about that morning, the question of Hugh's suicide had not yet been settled. Arguing with Mother, I always hoped that she would find the detail that would make my brother's death accidental and ourselves no longer witness to and part of the long failure of his life, but bystanders at the scene of a terrible accident. Better bystanders than agents, onlookers than narrators, I suppose you could say. Because, as I can tell you, people will go to any lengths, to any lengths at all, to believe what it comforts them to believe. But I am after something other than comfort here.

Eliza Hilliard inspected curtains and bedcovers for wear. She hated waste, my ancestor; she had a need, I think, to number and to keep. Who was washing? Cooking? Sewing? Answering these questions, and recording the answers, occupied most of Eliza Hilliard's days. She left ten ledger books filled with the details of these hours. "Completed this week," she wrote in her ledger. "Ten shirts; five pair slave cloth trousers." She visited the garden, then the spinning house, where the slave women worked at their wheels and looms. She inspected the cloth, pulled and stressed warp and woof to test its sturdiness. She was the woman who stayed at home and lived her whole life among her family, who had not gone away to make a home or family of her own, the spinster who spun and saw to the spinning in order to do her part, as everyone did his part, in that work in which all were engaged: tending the land, making the rice crop that sustained them all. I know her well. Waste was chaos; it was death disguised. When the curtains or the covers grew worn, she took them down, ripped them into rags. When the rags shredded, they were pulped and made into paper. Candle stubs went into a kettle to be melted into wax to make more candles; slivers of soap back into the kettle of ash and lye. Thrift and conservation were pleasures to her. In this country of smothering heat, where the air was white and thick with haze all summer, where the heat piled deep even in the shade of the trees, and the body and the mind moved slowly, where jars of meat spoiled and there was no time to sit with the beloved summer dead before they began to swell and must be buried, thrift was a cool pleasure, a moment of salvation, a small New England farm in the soul.

In the spring of 1838, Eliza's surviving brother, George, leased his plantation in Prince William Parish in the Beaufort District and moved to Fairview, bringing with him his wife, Mary, their ten-year-old daughter, Alwyn, his slaves and household possessions. His boys, Francis and George, were away during the school year at South Carolina College. One morning in March, George Hilliard's sloop arrived at the Fairview landing, followed by four fine canoes with his Negro boatmen at the oars, all dressed in blue. Eliza heard the Negroes before she saw them round the curve of river, singing as they rowed. What a sight: the sloop under sail and George standing in the prow, a fine, tall man, well formed and stronger than their brother Thomas. The long, heavy canoes tied up one by one at the landing. All that day and the next, more boats and wagons, carriages and carts docked at the landing and pulled up to the house and Mary's silver and plate was unloaded. A line of Negroes trooped up from the river, carrying bundles on their heads, carrying furniture and barrels of books and trunks of clothing. Mary, who was sickly then, struck down by a wasting disease at the end of the terrible summer of 1837, was carried from the landing to the house and installed in a second-floor bedroom, Alwyn skipping beside her mother's litter as it was carried up.

George had come to husband Fairview's rice lands because those five hundred acres were richer than his own, thanks to their late brother's genius for agriculture. Everywhere Thomas's handiwork showed: in the diking systems, the patches of salty ground, reclaimed with lime, the new Negro sick house. He would not soon fade from that place. George had come because Eliza was a woman alone and, with their brother's death, the property had passed to him. He came because, throughout the fall of 1837, the overseer had written to him, had written to him again—a series of letters addressed to G. Hilliard at Belle Isle Plantation—to complain that Eliza was capricious with the people—that is what they called the slaves: "the people," as the oxen were called "the oxen." One week she was strict, then suddenly, unpredictably, lax and indulgent. He could not manage the slaves for her interference, and they *knew* it; a dangerous instability was being created out there on the Edisto; surliness was on the rise, as well as malingering, quarreling, and stealing.

The overseer wrote to George Hilliard of a plantation near Beaufort where mistress and overseer were at odds this way. One gave orders that were contradicted by the orders of the other. They were often overheard arguing over plantation policy. The master, meanwhile, was away much of the year at the legislature in Columbia. One summer day, the overseer was found lying facedown in a rice field ditch with the back of his head split open. No one saw the blow fall; no one knew who had done it. The entire work gang was punished; the floggings went on for days. At Christmastime, the murderer still had not been discovered, and there was no Christmas for any of the Negroes that year. Still, they all swore they had had their eyes on the ground, on their work, when it happened.

He wrote to report that Miss Eliza summoned him to the house every week, into the dining room, where she sat at one end of the long table while he stood at the other, and she demanded an accounting, a report of the work accomplished, which she noted in her ledger. The whereabouts and tasks of the girl named Diana were of particular interest to her, he reported. Early that spring, before George's arrival, on Eliza's orders, the girl was sent to the fields as a hoe hand, but the driver complained that Diana was too small for the heavy work with the iron hoe, that she was slow and careless, as well. In her hands, hoes splintered, rice slips were buried too deep and never sprouted. Hoeing, she chopped the young rice shoots along with the weeds. She might better be put to work spinning or sewing, the overseer said. His wife had seen her needlework and judged it exceedingly fine. Besides, the overseer reported to Miss Eliza, the girl was pregnant, unfit for a hard day's work. Perhaps she could be put to work shooing crows away from the corn seedlings, or working in the house, where she claimed she belonged. But Eliza Hilliard would not listen to the overseer, and her brother, the new master of Fairview, found her adamant as well on his arrival at Fairview in the spring of 1838.

This Diana was insubordinate, Eliza told her brother, and the overseer was too soft: He placed too much emphasis on the comfort of the Negroes. Let the reins go slack on a team of horses and what do you get? she asked George. Runaway horses with the bits between their teeth. Overturned carriages. Mayhem, chaos, disorder, and death.

Eliza reminded her brother that this was the girl they'd dragged out of the boatful of laughing Negroes coming back across Charleston harbor from a frolic on the morning after their brother, her master, had been buried. The one they'd sent to the Workhouse, whose teeth they'd ordered pulled from her head in case she decided to frolic again and needed to be picked out of a crowd of Negroes. Reminded, her brother gave in and ordered the overseer to put her to work clearing the new rice field, the most terrible work of all: out in the sucking mud and the smothering heat, hacking at the underbrush while the overseer, who carried a pistol in his belt when he went out among the knives and hoes and axes, rode his horse among them, watching. One day in late March, the overseer counted *twenty poisonous serpents—ten moccasins, six copperheads, four rattlesnakes*—driven out of the undergrowth in the new ground as the slaves felled cypress trees and dug the stumps—the roots of the cypress go down and down— then cut and buried trunk and limbs because the trees were so waterlogged, they would neither float nor burn and so had to be buried where they fell. That is where Diana worked, knee-deep in the stinking black mud, with her skirt tied up between her legs.

Every night that spring, after the family was all in bed, Eliza stood at her window in her nightdress while Chloe brushed her hair, which was long and streaked with silver, keeping watch until the candles and the pine-knot flambeaux down in the quarters were all snuffed out. She watched, and even as she watched she knew that just because their houses were dark under the night sky, they were not all asleep. One morning, a pig would turn up missing and no one would have seen or heard a thing. Questioned about mischief, the people drooped and wailed; they were outraged along with her. "Lord, Old Miss," Nancy said of a missing ham, pilfered bacon, "catch the scoundrel what for tieff that smokehouse, hope he punish for true." Or "Hope you not too long for trouble yourself bout that tieff, Old Miss. The Lord deal with we in good time."

And yet, where Nancy was concerned, there was also trouble. She could not command her, Be who you were to me before last summer. Since her daughter's death, the woman never spoke about her child. If Eliza tried to speak to her about their Lucy— her sweet singing voice or her piety—while Nancy shucked oysters, cleaned fish, dressed game, made up biscuits, she got a blank look, a mumbled reply, or nothing. Eliza never saw a sign of emotion in the woman over the loss of her only child, and Nancy's husband, their driver, Cato, was likewise mute.

"Have they no feelings for their own flesh and blood?" she asked George at dinner one afternoon soon after her brother's arrival. That morning, she'd tried and failed again to speak with Nancy about her sadness over the loss of their Lucy. "Does barbarism so deeply infect into their natures, it has extinguished the light of family feeling?"

It was early in the planting season then; the sprout flow covered the fields and the tips of new green rice shoots showed above the water. They dined on venison, the first tender English peas, sweet potatoes, pudding, almonds, Madeira. The shutters and the windows were open and the sight of the river came in, brimming from bank to bank, the tide full and turning. The smell of water and new grass and blossoms, and the sound of an oar chocking against a boat, the sound of Negro voices—all of it tumbled into the house. The flames of the candles on sideboard and table were knocked sideways by the breeze and by the air that was stirred by a boy with a feather fan who kept the flies from settling onto their food, the mosquitoes off their arms and necks and faces. On the dark oil portraits of their mother and father, the thick paint glistened.

George answered her by speaking at length on the Negro character, a subject on which he judged himself to be something of an expert. He had recently written an article on the subject for the *Southern Agriculturalist*, and it had attracted such favorable notice among their circle, he'd printed it in a pamphlet that now circulated among his fellow planters the way Cousin Whitemarsh's pamphlets circulated from the Edisto to the Waccamaw. This lack of family feeling in the Negro character, so his argument ran, was not a matter of something that has been mangled or torn from him by his state of bondage, but a sign of an *original* lack of the higher feelings that, among other characteristics, had equipped the African for his state of bondage. He reminded Eliza, again, of their mother's tender care for ailing slave children, her tireless, sleepless vigils in this very house, where she had caused the sickly creatures to be brought to her and placed in her bed while the mothers of the children slept, unconcerned, on the sickroom floor. And when the children died, it was the mistress, *their* mother, who wept, while the impassive mothers of the dead children returned to the fields without letting one tear fall.

Listening to her brother, Eliza's agitation ebbed; her understanding was refreshed. As further comfort and confirmation of the rightness of his thinking, George gave her another treatise to read, and reading it occupied her evenings for several days. It was written by the Reverend James McDowell, a Presbyterian minister and biblical scholar from Georgetown who had closely studied passages of Holy Writ and discerned there confirmation of the rightness of their peculiar institution. There was the Genesis prophecy of Noah to consider: "Cursed be Canaan; a servant of servants shall he be unto his brethren. Blessed be the Lord God of Shem; and Canaan shall be His servant. God shall enlarge Japheth, and He shall dwell in the tents of Shem; and Canaan shall be His servant." The red man, George explained, was generally believed to be descended from Shem, the white man from Japheth, and the black man from Ham, Canaan's father. And so, the prophecy was fulfilled in America: "We dwell in the tents of Shem, and Canaan is our servant."

God's work going forward right here in her own beloved country! Out under the oaks beside the river, in the rice fields, the prophecy was being fulfilled. By the strength of their wills, the Divine Plan unfolded. The earth rolled along its vast and windy path, the tides ebbed and flowed, the seasons advanced around the year as the rice advanced from seed to shoot to plant to full head of grain, and on earth, among men, all was likewise replication and repetition of this ordering of high to low, as though a great chain were stretched between heaven and earth and upon this chain all were hung in their places, highest to lowest, according to God's plan.

At those times, she might have stood at the window and, looking out, found the world lying entirely within the scope of her vision, the reach of her will.

In this way, life went on for two years. In the summer of 1840, the family traveled to the Pendleton District up near the mountains, where cedar trees spiced the air and cool water rushed over stone, because George had managed Fairview well; each year, the rice harvests increased.

In the fall of 1840, George was away in Columbia at the legislature. And Mary Hilliard lay in bed, wasting away from an ulcer in the breast, alternately putrid and inflamed, which caused much anguish. She was bled and purged and cupped and dosed with calomel and jalap, but she grew steadily weaker and more confused. She struck out at Nancy, who hurt her by shifting the sick woman in bed; she raged at Chloe. Only Eliza could handle her, and this she did with firmness, mercy, and patience, habits learned and practiced at all the sickbeds and childbeds and deathbeds beside which she'd watched. Stooping to lift her sister-in-law onto the chamber pot, she caught the sick woman's wrist, and if Mary tried to strike out, she spoke to her quietly.

Sometimes, though, she was not quick enough and Mary's fist caught her in the side of the head, causing her to stagger back. Before she could gather up all her feelings—shock, pain, outrage, fury—tamp them back into their proper places, and call upon the Lord to subdue them; before she could summon meekness and humility, or remind herself of the beauty of uncomplaining suffering, black anger spurted up from her heart. Yes, it might have come then, this blackness that rises when a woman begins to count the ways in which life has hurt or failed her, so that for an instant she saw the room, its furnishings, and Mary's suffering face as though through that biblical sheet of dark glass, and she felt a wild burst of cruelty, an urge to harm, to strike back, to hurt until she'd hurt Mary to the same degree that Mary had hurt her. An ungovernable blackness in the face of injury that must have seemed to her primitive in its strength, its tenacity and resistance to reason. And so, she might have prayed, whispering, "Create in me a clean heart, oh, God, and put a new and right spirit within me," over and over, until God answered her prayer and her heart grew quiet, her spirit serene in its submission to God's Will in sending her these Trials to test and strengthen her. But the black feeling lingered, and it troubled her to find it so deeply rooted in her nature that she could not pluck it out. It might have recalled for her the look Diana had shot her when she'd told her that she was forbidden by law from buying her freedom; she might have felt such a look spread over her own face sometimes, when the blackness came.

To the list of Eliza's duties had been added the education and care of her niece, Alwyn, George and Mary's young daughter. To teach the child needlework, Eliza directed her work on a sampler. Each morning under Eliza's direction, beginning in the fall of 1840, the girl stitched and tore out her crooked stitches. She wailed, drummed her heels against the floor, and went red in the face, unseemly displays of temper, which her aunt would not abide, then formed her stitches again and sat quietly, as her aunt directed her to do. Her aunt, who took pains in order to shape and refine the girl's soul into the serene and meek, forgiving and pliable soul of a woman of her time. That summer, the girl carried the project with her to the Pendleton District, and by the time they returned to Fairview in the fall for the rice harvest, her first sampler was done. Adam and Eve beneath the tree of life and the thick serpent reposed along one flowering branch. *This have I done to Let You see / What care my parents Took of me. / This work in Hand my friends may have / When I am Dead and Laid in Grave. Miss Alwyn Hilliard, aged 12 years in the year of our Lord 1841.*

To teach her mistressship, Eliza took her niece with her as she made her daily rounds. Kitchen house, vegetable garden, weave house, sick house. Sometimes, she allowed the girl to order breakfast for the household or to carry the keys, unlock the smokehouse, and select a ham. She instructed her about the slave Diana: what she was allowed, what forbidden. Sitting beside the bed, with her feet up on a small stool and her back very straight, Alwyn read to her mother from the Bible and the novels of Sir Walter Scott. But even here, there was difficulty, a clash of wills. For her thirteenth birthday, Alwyn asked for her own slave, a girl to brush her long brown hair, to lay out her clothes and run and fetch and hold the pony. The child begged and wheedled until Mary, in her weakness, agreed. But Eliza quarreled with her brother about this, and he, in return, reminded his sister that Nancy had been given to her when she was only a girl. Still Eliza resisted, fearful of the damage that would be done to Alwyn's character, her developing female temperament, to have such power over servants so early in her life. She summoned Mrs. Cary's arguments and offered that lady's opinion that children, especially female children, should not be given dominion over slaves, as it fostered an unhealthy willfulness and coarsening in the child's character to be exposed too early to those of low degree. Her brother listened, smiling fondly, indulgently—as brothers have always smiled at their sisters' passionate opinions—and went ahead with his plans.

Already, there was confirmation of the rightness of Mrs. Cary's views on the subject of children and slaves. One morning just after the new year, Nancy had gone to Alwyn's room to wake the girl before the child was ready to rise. When Nancy insisted that she get up, Alwyn slapped her, called her a "black dog," and Nancy returned the slap and harder, so it stung. The girl ran weeping to her mother's room with her story, and Mary would have ordered Nancy flogged but for Eliza's intervention. She calmed Mary, who wept until her teeth chattered, until she shook all over and vomited on the floor, then went rigid in the bed, her eyes rolled back in her head. Eliza sent Alwyn downstairs, ordered Nancy to clean up the vomit and change the bed linen. She wiped Mary's mouth and stroked her hair, talking quietly as she worked, until Mary fell into a peaceful sleep. Still, George and Mary were determined to give their daughter a slave for her thirteenth birthday in May.

The slapping episode threw Eliza Hilliard into such a state of agitation that she took her valerian tea with twenty drops of LD and went up to lie down in her room. Dozing on her bed, she might have imagined that Mrs. Cary had come to call and that she was talking with the author of that good text, *Letters on Female Character*. She imagined the two of them walking down by the river, the rich odor of sympathy sweetening the air between them, as she discoursed on her problems with Diana, on Alwyn's peevish nature and her fears for the girl. On Mary's neglect of the child's moral education due to her illness and Eliza's own uneasy motherhood: She must guide the girl as a mother might without usurping Mary's role, even when dementia threatened to overrun the frail and crumbling borders of her sister-in-law's reason. Because it was necessary—it was *essential*—that everyone keep to their rightful places in life, for on this fulcrum the entire weight of their civilization balanced.

The rice harvest at Fairview was abundant in the fall of 1842, due to George's canny husbanding of the crop, Thomas's genius for agriculture, and God's great beneficence. One October morning, at winnowing time, the wind began to blow. All day, the slaves worked at top speed to take advantage of the wind: throwing the rice up into the air, where the wind could blow the chaff away, catching the grain again in the wide, shallow fanner baskets that they wove from marsh grass and worked with such skill. By noon, the air was hazy, blurred with rice chaff, and loud with the rasp and scrape of rice thrown into the air, falling back.

Down at the winnowing house, Cato, the driver, was among them, shouting, urging speed; the overseer was among them; sometimes his whip whistled through the air and nipped a back, an arm, a cheek, to remind some Negro to keep up the pace. The overseer's whip was a curiosity among other overseers up and down the river: The lash was made of rolled cowhide, like their own, but, unlike the plain handles of their whips, the oak handle of the Hilliard overseer's whip was carved in the likeness of a black man's agonized face. Sometimes, you would guess—and approach that guessing soberly and with humility at what you're about to acknowledge about your people and their past, about the subtlety, the thoroughness, and the daily inventiveness with which they enforced their wills—it would not have been necessary even to *use* that whip; it would have been enough to shake it loose and to hold up the handle in some erring Negro's face, a threatening mirror. At noon, they stopped for half an hour and ate corn bread under the trees. At moonrise that night—a fat, full moon rippling on the river—the wind still blew, and so they worked until after midnight, when the wind dropped to a breeze, then stopped. The next morning at daybreak, when Cato blew the conch and the slaves lined up to go to the fields and barns, Diana was not in the line.

"Diana, missing Sept. 25, 1842," the overseer entered in the ledger. I imagine that he waited to tell Eliza Hilliard, not wishing, perhaps, to be the one to bring news to Old Miss that was sure to provoke a flare-up of animosity between them. Depending on Mary's condition, Eliza conducted or did not conduct Scripture readings for the people in the house on Sunday evenings. Finally, on the last Sunday in October, when Diana did not come to vespers, Eliza sent a boy to summon the overseer to the house. She called him away from his supper and stood in the doorway, waiting for him, her Bible in her hand. Where is Diana? she demanded to know. Had she not made plain to him on several occasions her requirement that Diana attend these devotions?

"Run away, Miss Eliza," he said. "But she'll be back," he added quickly. "They never go far." He had hoped to keep the news from Old Miss until the patrols caught up with the runaway. The alarm was out, he assured her. *Run away from Fairview Plantation, a mulatto girl.* She would be caught or she would crawl out of the swamp on her own, he told her, sick and frightened and hungry, nearly eaten alive by mosquitoes and ticks, flies and gnats. Once a hound had dragged itself up to the house—he'd seen it with his own eyes—so covered with ticks, there was no way to touch the animal without encountering one of the gray parasites, swollen tight with blood. He'd seen slaves dragged out of the swamps in nearly the same state, eyes swelled shut with insect bites. He'd seen them dead from snakebite. The girl would realize soon enough that she had nowhere to run. Their land was a new moon crescent bowed into the river. River on three sides and tidal creeks behind, and one road, a causeway, leading out and in, and beyond the creeks on the back side of their land, miles and miles and miles and miles of cypress swamp. Lastly, he reminded Eliza, she was too visible to disappear. She was marked as clearly as if she'd been branded, and he had circulated the description of her missing front teeth and her scars to the patrol and to the overseers of plantations nearby. Finding her on the road, any white man could order, "Open your mouth, girl." Any white man could grab her jaw and force it open; he could pull her dress down from her shoulders, note the marks of correction across her back and shoulders, the scar on her face. *"This is that Hilliard nigger, for sure."* Even with a forged pass or papers, those marks would reveal her true identity.

Charleston Mercury, November 1842

$50 Reward. Run away from Fairview Plantation, Edisto District, September past, my Negro girl, DIANA. About twenty-five years old, of light complexion, tall and spare. She has a sullen countenance and a downcast look. She was last seen wearing a dark blue slave cloth dress, though it is likely she may have changed clothes, as she is much given to dressing in finery. Smart and active in the house and market. Speaks plain but has two missing front teeth and scar on right cheek. As she can write a passable hand, she may try to pass for free. As she is well known about Charleston as a seamstress, it is believed she may have returned there. Masters of vessels bound for Georgetown or the Waccamaw are particularly cautioned against taking her away, for she has people at The Oaks plantation. Reward will be paid to anyone who will deliver her to me or to the warden of the Workhouse. However, let it be known amongst Negroes of her acquaintance that she will be forgiven if she return of her own accord.

Eliza Hilliard

Who were these people who left her? George, first, and unexpectedly of a bloody flux, in the autumn of 1842. In the span of seven days, he slipped from the prime of full, manly health to the stitching of the linen shroud, the clipping of the hair, the planing, joining, and smoothing of the pine coffin, and the weeping of the Negroes gathered under the oaks that surrounded the family cemetery on the bluff overlooking the Edisto River. That winter, in December, Mary died of the ulcer in her breast and Alwyn was sent to live with Mary's sister and her family near Beaufort, so Eliza's motherhood was done. I see that morning, the low-lying fog in the rice fields, the winter birds, the tide turning. The sun as it rose would have thrown the shadow of masts and sails over the river and across the fallow rice fields. The morning the girl boarded the sloop for the voyage to Beaufort, Eliza cut off a thick hank of her own hair and, tying it with a white ribbon, gave it to her niece and received, in return, Alwyn's tearful vow that upon Eliza's death, she would weave the hair into a bird or a cross and wear it in memory of her aunt so that she would not be forgotten. And she has not been forgotten; that much we know. Her niece kept her promise and I have seen that memorial of her life, a cross woven of faded auburn hair streaked with silver, and it is enough for any life, is it not, to keep promises to one another, to remember and to be remembered, to be remade in the stories of others, to live in their words?

That spring, the spring of 1843, Mary and George's sons, George and Francis, came home from South Carolina College to manage Fairview and see to the care of their aunt Eliza. With the exception of a bad tooth that dripped poison into her bloodstream and the parasites that disrupted her bowels, a thick milky membrane over one eye that smeared her vision so that she moved sideways, head turned as if listening, in order to keep the good eye facing forward, Eliza Hilliard enjoyed sound health. She almost never passed the day in bed, pierced by startling pain. Most nights, she slept soundly, deeply. And yet, the blackness was growing in Eliza Hilliard, from the edges in, from the center out. Sometimes, surely, she thought of Alexander Seabrook, the man she would have married, and of his bones and the gold coins scattered among his bones at the bottom of the Stono River. What stirred in her, remembering him? I don't know, of course I don't, but whatever I bring to this imagining, I bring from my own time spent steeping in the particular womanly darkness that grows and spreads when a woman begins to meditate on life as a broken promise and herself as the one betrayed. On the failure of life to give her what she deserved. Whatever she felt, it was neither purely satisfaction nor regret, but some amalgam of the two, with a drop of vengefulness stirred in. She might have remembered the money she'd thrown into the harbor at the end of that terrible summer, when Thomas was dead and Diana sentenced to the Workhouse. She did not wish to recover it, but, rather, to have it count as payment against some debt and also, perhaps, to be relieved by the memory of that sacrifice of a growing hardness of heart.

Letter from Francis Hilliard, Fairview Plantation, to (illegible — perhaps Mr. Frampton Wyman, the Hilliard family's factor in Charleston?), March 1843

*I shall be grateful for any advice you might be able to for-
ward to me concerning Aunt Eliza. My own wife is made
so timid in her presence, she can barely speak or raise her
eyes. Every encounter between them ends in my wife's
weeping under Aunt Eliza's sharp reproaches, which strike
my wife's tender heart with such force as to leave her weak
and bedridden for days after the conflict has subsided. I
fear for her health, which, as you know, tends to the delicate, if these quarrels do not end. Only old Nancy has any
sway with Aunt Eliza, but she must be coddled and
coaxed, humored and bribed and promised an extra ration
of molasses or a bolt of cloth, tobacco for her pipe, and all
manner of other privilege besides before she will* consent to
placate our aunt! *I fear I am a poor master to be so at the
mercy of old Negro house servants. Would that I had
learned more from my father before he died concerning the
management of Negroes. Quite early one morning last
week, I went out, thinking to consult with the trunk minder
concerning a weak spot I had noted on one of the dikes,
when I encountered a commotion down at the landing.
The sails of our sloop were being rigged, and on deck a half
dozen of our boat Negroes made ready to set sail with the
tide. Aunt Eliza stood on the landing, issuing orders, and
when I reached her and inquired about her intentions, she
informed me that she was en route to Charleston, where —
so she said she had heard — her property, a slave wench
named Diana who ran away this past fall, had been recovered. She must, she said, go personally and attend to it. I
only convinced her to desist by persuading her that the sky
did not look auspicious for travel, but, rather, promised a
storm. We hear so often of the loss of this girl, her vexed
property, that I am tempted to buy a mulatto sewing
wench to ease the poor soul's suffering and bring peace to*

the household. I do not believe she would know one from
the other.

Letter from George Hilliard to Laurens Seabrook [a cousin in
New York City, undated]

> *In repairing the house, it being necessary to remove the*
> *doors that open between front parlor and adjacent room,*
> *Aunt Eliza became quite delighted to the point of agita-*
> *tion. She said it recalled her childhood to her mind when*
> *her father and mother occupied these rooms and passed*
> *freely between them. Only later did we learn that she had*
> *recently sought the factor's advice, as she thought to sue me*
> *for attempting to deprive her of her house and to withhold*
> *money from her, neither crime of which I am in the least*
> *guilty. Family trouble is a long road that has no turning.*

At last, in June of 1843, George and Francis installed their aunt
Eliza in the house in Charleston, along with Nancy and a boy to
look after her. Next door, Mr. and Mrs. Legare had died and the
house was leased to a French hatmaker named Aimar, and his
family, who kept a shop on the first floor and lived in the upstairs
rooms. Eliza could hear someone singing there in the early after-
noons, accompanied by a piano. From time to time, Rachel
Hayne came to town to check on the family property, sometimes
accompanied by the child for whom the christening gown was
sewed but not delivered, owing to the epidemic and the flight of
the Legare family soon after the child's birth during the terrible
summer of 1837. Now, of course, the child was too large for the
gown, the gown too small for the child, but whenever Eliza
Hilliard saw Rachel Hayne, it jogged her memory and she pulled

the gown out of the trunk at the foot of her bed and sent Nancy next door to summon Mrs. Hayne, who sent her compliments and a promise that she would come later and then did not. Rachel Hayne had grown into a matron: her face wide and soft, her thick body packed into dresses. Hearing a tapping, she glanced up and saw Eliza Hilliard at the window of the house next door; she waved distractedly and hurried on.

The dress reminded Eliza Hilliard of Diana, her runaway slave, and the idea of finding the girl, recovering her property, began to consume her. Maybe she went out into the streets with old Nancy hobbling along beside her. Down near the market, black people thronged, so many that the white people looked out of place among them. They carried baskets of bread and loads of wash in baskets on their heads. Slave or free? It would have been difficult to tell without stopping each one and questioning her until her answers satisfied Eliza, but she studied every light-skinned black woman closely. She might have carried the baby gown with her, hoping to startle a look of recognition onto some girl's face. The slaves wore copper badges that named their occupations— BAKER, SEAMSTRESS, COOPER—but not every Negro without a badge was free. At last, she petitioned the legislature for compensation. Hadn't Mrs. Legare herself petitioned the legislature after Minda's death and been awarded the sum of three hundred dollars for the loss of her valuable property? But Eliza's petition was denied. No one was being compensated for the loss of slaves anymore, and over the next year, she placed ten advertisements in the newspaper, each one more threatening than the one before, the last, a month before her own death in the summer of 1844.

Charleston Mercury, June 1844

Absented herself from the subscriber at Fairview Plantation, Edisto District, these two years past, my Negro, DIANA. Very artful and clever and may likely try to pass as

free, as she said she would call no man master. Well
known in Charleston for her impudent tongue, of which
I have had numerous complaints. Leave is hereby given
to any person to flog her (so as not to take her life) whenever she is found and to deliver her to the warden of the
Workhouse.

Eliza Hilliard

After that notice, she wrote no more, and in July of that year,
she died. There is, however, one last statement she made, and that
is her name sewed into the hem of the baby gown. How did it
come to be there, this last will and testament? I will tell you because I have lived it myself. And what I have not actually lived, I
can imagine, having lived in this city my entire life and also having lived a life longer than my own through the stories of others
who lived before me, and, having at last found an ending that lies
a short distance beyond the place where the old stories usually
end, I offer this scene.

In my scene, it is early in the summer in which Eliza Hilliard
will die, and the first spell of intolerable heat has descended upon
the city. Eliza Hilliard has returned from another search for Diana, she and old Nancy, driven home by the glare of the streets,
exhausted by the heat, which, it seems, you must push through as
though it were a thicket or a jungle.

Inside the house, it is no cooler. The ocean breeze has been
still for a week and the house seems packed with heat, floor to
ceiling. Thomas is dead and Mary and George are dead. Alwyn,
her niece, writes to her once a month at best, and Diana, her
property, is still missing. She sits in the chair near the window in
her room, the gown across her lap, and studies its knots and vines
for clues to Diana's whereabouts. Because property cannot decide
to remove itself from you, or else it is no longer property. And if it
is not property, what is it? As she ponders this question, the agita-

tion begins to build inside her, as if something whole and straight were being twisted and deformed out of its comforting and familiar shape. Ungrateful, traitorous, disloyal wretch. To quiet herself, she takes out needle and thread and begins to sew that series of careful stitches that form letters into words and words into claims: *Property of Eliza Hilliard. Done by her hand, June 1844.* Stitch by stitch, she feels herself grow calm, as though something that had been destroyed was being rebuilt and restored before her eyes. When it is done, it looks true.

Uncollected Mysteries
Known to No One on This Earth

Diana (20 items)
Includes a Letter, Speculation, Invention
and Silence

Letter written to the slave Diana at Fairview Plantation, by
Daniel, a boatman on the Waccamaw, and never delivered

My dear wife,

*I will write you a few lines to tell you that I am well, and
still in the land of the living. I am not married yet and
there is no probability of it yet and I think sometimes that
I will never take another wife, but you know we don't always know what we may do after a while. Write word to me
if you have taken a husband and who he is. I want you to
take good care of my firstborn child. If you can't do anything more, try and bring her up in the fear of the Lord and
pray with and for all of your children. It is my constant
prayer that the Lord would bless and take care of you all. I
am getting along first-rate. I have had a good many difficulties to contend with, but I got along with them very
well. Cuffy has taken a wife, a smart nice young woman.*

Give my love and respects to all of my friends and if we never meet in this world, may we in heaven.

> Your husband,
> Daniel

Some nights before she ran, maybe Diana went out into the oak grove below the quarters, tucked herself back among the low, swooping limbs, and let her mind run, seeing how far it would carry her. Maybe as she sat there she felt the dark settle around her and its weight was the weight of miles of woods and swamps. Whenever she tried to picture a path and follow it, as she'd followed the twisting trails that ran all over Fairview, every path ended in water, deep woods, or swamp.

In this country, they outnumbered the white people, but they did not outweigh them. She would have known that; she would have felt that weight above her head, always ready to fall. She might have recalled Charleston's beating drums and the tolling bells that ordered them back to their masters' houses, then the sound of horses going up and down the streets all night, the white men on horseback, their faces and their guns. She might have remembered a noisy crowd of Negroes near the market one morning, angry voices rising, white men galloping to the scene. Who would have thought that so many white men could gather so quickly, rushing out of every street and alley as though they'd been waiting there? Maybe she remembered the horses' bunched haunches and rolling eyes, the sun on gun barrels, or how the men had fired into the air, how the people crouched and screamed, the boy who was trampled under the hooves of a plunging horse.

She would not personally remember—it had happened in 1739—but she might have heard stories of the black heads set on the mileposts along the King's Highway out near Stono where the man, Jemmy, gathered other slaves at the river and broke into a store, stole guns, and killed twenty white people, then set off marching toward Spanish Florida and freedom before they were caught and killed. She'd heard about Gullah Jack, her father, the one who put his magic powers to the service of Denmark Vesey and the rest, who blessed crab claws and parched corn and handed them around to protect Vesey's slave army from the white man's bullets while they utterly destroyed the city as the prophet Joshua had foretold. He was hanged up on the Lines in July and left hanging in the heat. Vesey's body, so they said, had been cut down and given to doctors to dissect. What did they find, picking through his organs? Lifting out the looped guts, weighing, measuring, searching his heart for the deformity where the plan had been spawned in which they were to rise up and smother, hack, shoot, and poison every white man, woman, and child in the city, then sail to the West Indies and freedom? Did they find anything that did not resemble their own livers and lights?

Maybe she recalled the story Mrs. Legare's Negroes told about how the white people had taken the woman Minda out and hanged her in her apron and white head wrap, flour on her apron and cheeks. Perhaps she remembered how it was to stand up to her knees in the stinking black mud, her skirt tied up between her legs and her belly heavy, under the pale blue sky, while the thunderheads piled up along the horizon and the water moccasins swam by and her skin crawled with heat and insects, cutting rice with a sickle, looking out over the endless stretch of field and water, water and field, and field and field to where the river shone.

Or maybe she remembered felling trees, working the draw knife with another woman, making planks for the Charleston road. If not the draw knife, then the yoke hung with buckets of water, or buckets of dirt to repair the causeway or the ditch embankments surrounding the rice fields. Work and heat and night, and then more heat and more work before another night came and she and Abby slept and her young son, Scipio, slept between them, his mouth making small sucking sounds. Or maybe her daughter slept while she sewed all night and she let the girl sleep past the first blowing of the conch and offered bacon, vegetables, cloth to the woman who tended the children to buy her daughter an extra portion of milk and bread, a good spot at the trough in which the children were fed. As they flexed and pulled, the long muscles of her upper arm wore grooves in the bone. If you found her bones, you could see the grooves now. Man or woman, they worked you the same; they killed you the same—that is where her thinking might have carried her. There was no difference between men and women except for the body's soft places; the pockets in the spirit into which fear burned its mark were the same. Women had children and husbands to be sold, and men had wives and children. And women didn't often run away, for all the reasons that women have always not run away: the weight of children, the weight of uncertainty, doubt, and fear; the weight of the certainty of what waits for them when they're found and brought back. Surely she remembered the grip and the taste of the iron tongs that had pulled her teeth from her mouth, the blood that poured down her throat.

So it would not have been reason that carried her away. Surely what she remembered was reason to run and tether at the same time, but she disappeared anyway; no one knows where. She ran. Not from her family, surely not from her children, though when the time came, she left them, too, and she vanished, leaving behind on the pallet next to her sleeping daughter the head scarf that had so enraged Eliza Hilliard, that had come to stand for all things flagrant, willful, and ungovernable in her slave.

Maybe someone knew the way and drew a map for her on the ground with a stick, then wiped it out, whispered names, pointed in a direction. Or did she go by boat or canoe, hidden under a load of sweet potatoes? She'd managed to be down on the plantation wharf whenever a particular sloop, the *Voyager* out of Charleston, docked there, bringing barrel staves, tar, nails, bundles of cholera medicine, bottles of laudanum and jalap and calomel. She sold the captain produce from her garden, and in this, she was not alone. The people knew that this captain was involved in commerce with Negroes. Meat, vegetables, horseshoes, and money; he traded with slaves up and down the river, and there were rumors of other services he would render for goods or money. Once Diana gave the captain a dress she had sewed for his girl child. She had never worn a finer dress. Fine sewing was some of what the captain took away on the *Voyager*.

Or did she go overland? And where? What dangerous water, deep and running with tides and currents, did she cross? Did she find her way to the Combahee Swamp, a place where runaway slaves were known to hide, where they propped sticks and branches into lean-to shelters and ate their food raw because fire makes smoke and smoke is a sign of human beings keeping warm, cooking, surviving? Did she die there? Not everyone had fled there just to be free. Not everyone cared for others or saw them as more than prey. Sometimes old human bones turn up in Low Country swamps, but there are also many places where people die and their bones are never found. Maybe her bones are among the bones that animals have scattered or the bones that lie hidden in thickets and buried under leaves where they are stepped over or walked past and never noticed. Or did she find her way to Philadelphia? To Baltimore or Washington? In the 1840s, a Negro seamstress advertised her services in the Philadelphia newspaper: fine needlework and regular sewing.

And so this story ends in silence, the way her imagined paths all ended in water, a silence made of flight and absence, of the fact that she was never found nor heard from again, that her daughter, Abby, and Scipio, her son, grew up without a mother, that she did not come back for them or send word or try to find them after freedom came. Maybe she was dead by then and never heard the news. Maybe she sewed and saved her coins and bills and trained other quick, ambitious girls to sew for her and profited from their work and allowed them to profit and rise. Or maybe she was greedy and took so much from them that they were always in her debt and never rose. Maybe as she walked the streets of Baltimore or Washington, Philadelphia or Oberlin, Ohio, and waked and slept and sewed, the faces of her children and the sound of their names flowed like blood through her heart, through her body. Maybe each beat of her heart named Abby, Scipio, Scipio, Scipio, Abby. Maybe she had plans for them all.

Evelyn Pope
1990
Edisto Island, South Carolina

❧

"She can't pick up the phone and ask is this a good time to come out?" is what Son wanted to know when Evelyn told him that Miss Louisa Marion had showed up *in the flesh* at the packing shed that morning. "Miss Marion's *old*, Son, not about to change. She didn't mean harm by it. I don't dwell on these things," she'd tried to say, to head off the tirade on Caucasian arrogance that she felt building, but there was no use in trying to reason with Son once he got on the subject of the Marions or the Hilliards, of white people in general. What you'd get then would be the weeping and the wailing and the gnashing of teeth. Spit would fly, and venom, too. White people were the thorns in his crown, sure enough. And him a preacher now, supposed to love *everybody* and to spread the Gospel of love throughout the earth. But it looked like the buckra vexed Son more than almost anything. Sometimes he dug up the word's African roots and held them out for her to see. Long ago on the Cameroon coast, he said, buckra had meant "devil."

Well, the buckra had paved the broad highway on which the devil had ridden straight into her boy's heart, for sure. He'd even taken her picture of Jesus—the white Jesus with the soft eyes and long auburn ringlets—down off of her living room wall and out onto the screened porch, where He sat to this day, His sweet Savior's face turned to the wall of the house between two pots of dead begonias in their dried-out dirt. She called it the price of peace with her son to put the Lord out of her house that way.

Once, in the year before she died, Son had even gotten onto Mother Mamie herself, his own great-grandmother, for serving the Marions and living in their yard and keeping his mother in bondage there, too, instead of moving out to Edisto Island with her own people, but she'd darted back at him right quick: "Boy, you better look out who you talking to, come around sassing your great-grandmother like that." She had her friends and acquaintances in town. Had her church there, Mt. Zion AME. Had her voter-registration drives, and every election she worked at the polls. The last five years of her life, the idea got stuck in her head that they couldn't hold an election without her. On election day, she was *going* to the polls. Somebody better be there first thing in the morning to pick her up or she'd take off walking and wind up in the projects back of King Street or wandering around the College of Charleston campus, asking students what time the polls opened and if they were going to vote that day.

Even after she had all those little strokes and got so confused that she was as likely to quote Scripture to the voters as she was to check their names off the voting rolls, they used to sit her down beside another poll worker and let her tear the stubs off the ballots and point the way to the big padlocked wooden box where the ballots belonged. And when she decided it was time to vote, one of the other poll workers would escort her straight to the front of the line with no apologies. "This Aunt Mamie. Y'all stand aside."

But Evelyn knew Son's heart; she knew he prayed to be delivered from the violence of those feelings. Many a time, he'd gone down on his knees, with his head in her lap, and wept while she stroked his hair and prayed with him. And now, thank the Lord, he had a wife to walk with him through life and share his burdens. Joyce was a smart girl from Charleston, a graduate of Morris Brown

College in Atlanta and a fifth-grade schoolteacher over on James Island. She'd gone to his church one Sunday to hear him preach and fallen in love with him right on the spot. And since there wasn't much that Joyce wanted that she didn't eventually get, three months later, they were married. She'd been teacher of the year last year, and talking about going back to graduate school. She'd be principal someday—you just knew it. Or senator, or chair of the Board of Education, or president. That girl was bound for the top. She could do any sum in her head, quiet a classroom with a look, teach the ones that no one else could reach, and get herself appointed or elected chair of any committee she joined.

Truth to tell, Evelyn had been pricked by resentment, and a touch of panic as well, when Miss Louisa opened her door and walked right in, but she wasn't about to tell Son any of that. It was the middle of July when Miss Louisa Marion showed up, and Evelyn was juggling more messes than usual, even for this time of year.

Cassandra was one of the troubles she had on her mind the day Louisa Marion came to call. The girl had gone and gotten herself stationed at Fort Bliss, way out near El Paso, Texas. Been there six months and had two and a half more years to go. It had been hard enough when she'd been stationed in Columbia, at Fort Jackson. Those days, when Evelyn missed her daughter and her grandbabies, she could pack a ham or fry up a chicken, whip together a pie and get in the car, be at Fort Jackson in a little under three hours. Now when the army tells you to move, you pack up and move—Evelyn understood that—and Cassandra was going places in the army, about to be promoted to lieutenant, smart as a whip when it came to computers. But taking the babies, too, that was what had just about grieved Evelyn to death. She'd pleaded and pleaded with her daughter to leave the babies. Here they were, herself and the mother of that man she used to be married to, the father of those children, right over there on Mt. Pleasant, both of them falling all over each other wanting to keep those children, to love and make over them and see that they got to school and to church and knew their relatives. But Cassandra said no, said her children belonged with her.

She'd been to visit her daughter once, the spring before this one, right after her girl had been sent to Texas. El Paso was like the beach, but with the ocean nowhere in sight: a windy desert split by a jagged black mountain, a wide, shallow river and Juárez, Mexico, on the other side, a sprawl of shacks. Everything there had looked temporary and dried-up. When the wind blew hard, sand whipped through the air and stung her face. Out there, people decorated their yards with rocks and cactus and the sun was always in the sky, high and brutal, like something you wanted to run from, only it was too hot to run and there were no trees to shade you if you did.

Cassandra had taken her across the Rio Grande to Juárez, where she'd seen Indians curled up asleep under cars, like dogs. Some of them had been practically naked, wearing cut-up tires for sandals. In the marketplace, woozy from the enormous margarita she'd drunk with lunch, she'd seen piles of plucked chickens, and everywhere she'd turned, a thin child had tried to sell her a cigarette, a stick of gum, a ballpoint pen, and Cassandra had stopped her, finally, from buying whatever they offered. In the cathedral, a bloody Jesus hung in twisted agony on an enormous cross behind the altar. Statues dressed in black lined the walls, and their hands hung with silver charms: tiny arms and legs, automobiles and babies that glittered in the light of hundreds of candles that flickered in front of the statues. When her eyes had adjusted to the candlelight, she'd seen that she was standing near a glass coffin with a body laid out in it. She'd jumped then and grabbed Cassandra's arm. Then she'd seen that the body was another statue, a haggard, bearded Jesus, robed in black. "They carry His coffin across the Rio Grande at Eastertime, Mama," Cassandra had explained. "It's part of their religion."

"Where'd you get so grown-up?" she'd asked. She'd held on to her daughter's arm the whole time they'd been inside that church. What kind of religion was this? Who were these people? Nobody she'd ever had any dealings with. Their strangeness frightened her. Their religion belonged someplace deep underground, in a cave that was lit by fire and smelled of blood and raw meat, like the marketplace, out of sight of the civilized world.

Well, she was proud of her girl, really; she would have taken her children with her to the ends of the earth, too. But Jerome, the baby, had strep throat now and Cassandra was out on night maneuvers in the desert, and she couldn't get a clear-enough answer from her daughter to ease her mind about who was looking after those children. Half the time, nobody answered the phone at Cassandra's; other times, a woman named Maria picked up, but she spoke with such a heavy accent, Evelyn could hardly understand her. Every night last week, Evelyn had waked at three and tossed and turned till dawn, fretting about those children. She'd get on an airplane and fly out there to check on them personally, only it was July now, the peak of the packing season, and there was no sense in even asking Mr. Eubanks for time off, because she already knew what he would say. Sometimes, just thinking about those babies growing up way out in that desert was enough to make her shut herself in the bathroom at the packing shed, sit down on the toilet lid, push her glasses up and press her fingers hard into her eyes, and cry.

Then last week, the storm had come. At daybreak that morning, it had felt as if the heat had gotten up hours earlier and had been working hard ever since. The window fan sucked hot air into her bedroom, and by the time she was dressed, she was damp with perspiration. When the sun rose, sunlight slanted through the oaks in her yard in big smoky slabs. Driving to work, she'd known they were in for a thunderstorm before the day was out.

Sure enough, all day the clouds stacked high and turned dark and the air kept getting heavier and hotter, the pulsing rasp of the cicadas grew louder and sharper, until just about three o'clock, that storm cut loose. Sheets of rain swept across the tomato fields surrounding the shed, pounding the plants flat, and the pine woods bordering the fields disappeared behind the downpour. Rain thundered on the tin roof and beat on the ground, and you had to shout to the person next to you, and sometimes even then they couldn't hear you.

In his usual high-handed and stubborn way, Mr. Eubanks decided early that they weren't shutting down for some little storm, and so her job had been to keep everybody calm, to keep them working while the lightning walked closer. Across the tomato field, where the field met the woods, a bolt of lightning sizzled down and for a second after it struck, its path hung in the air like bright powder. Everybody kept working, though, because Mr. Eubanks said they had to. "Nothing but a old summer storm," he said, shouting over the thunder and the drumming roar of rain on the tin roof. "Everybody here's been through a million of them."

So she'd seen to it that the Mexican boys, migrant workers from the camp out on the highway, kept emptying their boxes of tomatoes onto the conveyor belt, and that the women standing beside the winding belt kept culling and sorting, and that the Mexican boys at the other end of the line caught the fruit in boxes as it tumbled off. Just the same, everybody looked over their shoulders while they worked, keeping an eye on that storm.

Then lightning struck a big pine a hundred yards away and sent the top of it crashing down in flames. One of the women on the grading line screamed and started to sway as if she was going to faint, and the women close by turned to help her. That was when the fruit started to pile up and spill onto the floor and Mr. Eubanks came out of his office in his khaki work clothes, his glasses in his hand, his mouth pressed tight and his face red. He'd just started toward the group of women gathered around the woman who felt faint and Evelyn had just stepped up to tell him that they ought to shut down the line until the storm passed, when there'd been a white flash, then a crack, *pow*, as though a bomb had dropped on the roof of the shed. Blue fire shot out of the electrical boxes on the light poles; then the lights went out and the conveyor belt stopped. People touching metal got a jolt. Knocked one lady down. She came to screaming for Jesus, with three people fanning her; then it sounded like everybody was screaming and praying. Mr. Eubanks brought some water in a Dixie cup to the woman who got knocked down and then checked to see that everyone else was all right. Those that had been shocked, he had them sit down and he went to call 911, but found both their phones melted. When he ran out through the rain to his truck and drove off to find a working phone, people just got in their cars and went home.

A dozen people quit that day, and in Evelyn's opinion, Mr. Eubanks was lucky they didn't all walk out. Trying to bully people into going back to work when they were terrified like that, especially the older ones. Telling the ones that weren't hurt, just scared and asking to go home, that if they walked off this job, they could collect their pay and not bother to come back. With the power off, there wasn't any work to do anyway, but once Mr. Eubanks got an idea set in his head, there was no knocking it loose. Plain, blind stubbornness had always been the man's downfall. In a week, the power company got the power back on and they'd repaired the wiring and the electrical boxes and replaced the phones. They were ready to roll again, but the whole run of tomatoes had been spoiled. There were yellow jackets everywhere, sometimes a dozen of them on one tomato or drinking from the puddles of sour juice that collected under the rotting fruit on the conveyor belt. Flies, too, and the thin, sour smell of rotting tomatoes. Between the firings and the quittings, there weren't a dozen people left to clean up and get the place rolling again.

Evelyn had had to make a special plea in every Sunday school class and stand outside after services for two Sundays in a row before she'd hired enough people to run the shed. She'd had to see about the last paychecks for the ones that quit and get time cards and paperwork set up for the new ones, show them their jobs or pair them up with somebody who could teach them. Under Evelyn's supervision, the new help had to shovel the rotten tomatoes off of the conveyor belt and into buckets, then carry them out and dump them. Then they had to clean the belts and machinery.

On the day Louisa Marion came, Evelyn had been working at top speed all morning, finishing the paperwork on the new people. So all of that was on her mind, plus Cassandra and the babies out there in the desert, so far from home, when her door had swung open and she'd looked up to find Miss Louisa Marion standing in the doorway, big as life. When Evelyn didn't speak, because she couldn't, just sat there with a roll of adding machine paper in one hand and her mouth open, Miss Louisa came right on in and plunked herself down in the straight chair across the desk from Evelyn and started picking up her pictures. First she picked up Letitia's picture, then the plaster cast of Jerome's little handprint, then the picture of Cassandra in fatigues and earphones, standing beside a rocket launcher, grinning, with the desert all around her, and finally, Joyce and Son's wedding picture. "Oh, and there's our sweet Mamie," she said, bringing the picture of Mamie on the beach up close to her face. She was dressed so smart, too, in a peacock blue dress and a scarf, a nice gold pin, alligator shoes and purse, and Mr. Eubanks himself bringing her coffee, while Evelyn was caught in blue jeans, a T-shirt with the name of Son's church printed on it, and a vest stained with tomato juice.

"Look at your grandbabies," Louisa Marion said. Now that she'd gotten over the shock of seeing Louisa Marion again, Evelyn sized her up. Old now, older than she should be. A withered face and bright eyes, a mist of white hair and the wispy look of the old, as though they had air in their bones instead of marrow. It made Evelyn proud that she'd kept herself up. She'd always been tall and lean, and she'd stayed that way. Her hair was white now, but she kept it cropped close to her head. Over the years, she'd added glasses and a cane, but not an ounce of flesh. Her glasses were smart, though, wire rims, and even her cane was stylish, a birthday gift from Son and Cassandra, polished black wood with an African mask for a handle. Louisa Marion still had the same sweet smile that Evelyn remembered, though, and she flashed it at Evelyn. "Haven't they gotten big?" she said, pointing to the grandbabies. "I'll bet they're just as smart."

In spite of herself, Evelyn softened, gave her own sweet smile back. Smart? I mean to tell you. Don't get her started about those children. "Letitia's not even three years old yet and she can say the whole alphabet along with Big Bird," she said, looking down at the girl's face in the photograph, two fat braids with colored balls at the ends framing the sweetest cheeks in the world, so plump and soft, just right for kissing. And Jerome, his little bright-eyed baby self. She could almost hear the laugh that told her that watching the tide come in with his grandmother was the biggest fun he'd ever had.

"Well, I know you're proud," Miss Marion said. She'd brought them each a book. *Curious George Flies a Kite* for Jerome, and for Letitia, *Goodnight Moon*, she said as she handed the presents to Evelyn. All wrapped up nice, too, with a blue ribbon for Jerome, a pink one for Letitia, a little pink or blue felt elephant cut out and glued to each package. She'd done it herself, you could tell; she'd put some time into it, too.

"Well, isn't that sweet?" Evelyn said. "Aren't you nice to think of my babies?" It was the kindness that always confused her. She wouldn't dare tell Son that, though, and risk setting loose the demon he carried inside him to rampage up and down, shouting and laying waste to his spirit. Neither did she want him to get righteous with her, fall into pride, another snare the devil always had shaken out and laid open on his path to cause his feet to stumble. She was his mother, supposed to help him carry his cross. She'd stopped, a long time ago, trying to explain to Son about the kindness, how she always got tangled in it, how she couldn't forget that it was Louisa Marion who'd driven Mother Mamie to Spartanburg for Evelyn's graduation from South Carolina State, about how the Marions had made such a big contribution toward Mother Mamie's casket that they'd been able to buy the most expensive one in the undertaker's storeroom, white with gold handles and trim, lined with thick white quilted satin. How, during Mother Mamie's last years, if nobody came to take her to church, she'd go up and knock on the door and Louisa would throw some clothes on and drive her there and pick her up when services were over, too, bring her home. Son hadn't been part of all that. He'd been off running the streets, gambling, drinking that liquor, chasing those women. Then he'd been in Vietnam, or trying to make a go of the Royal Peacock Club the year after he got back. It had only been in the last seven years that he'd settled down at all, and Mother Mamie had been dead for eight years by then. He hadn't really known her, or the Marions, either. He hadn't felt the kindness or the hidden stinger buried in the kindness that got you every time: the way it didn't come across to you, ever, friend to friend; the way it always seemed to come *down* somehow, like a favor. How they could be good to you and still let you know that this was their money, their time, their sympathy, and in order for you to have it, they had to decide that you deserved it and give it to you.

So Son was right in a way; he always was. No sooner had you thought up some hard and hateful thing to say about white people when along would come one of them to prove you right. It seemed like they just weren't able to humble themselves; they were always looking into the glare of their own importance till it blinded them, same as happened when you drove down a road after a rain when the sun had come out again and the pavement shone like metal, dazzling you, and you tried to duck and see around the glare. But when did just being right ease anyone's pain or make it any easier to live together in this world? Best to sit back—she'd told Son this a million times—let them have their say and go on about your business. Half the time, if you told them what they wanted to hear, if they got the answer they were looking for and could feel the way they needed to feel about themselves and whatever they'd done, that would be the end of it anyway.

Miss Louisa Marion hadn't driven all the way out there just to slap mosquitoes and smudge her fingerprints all over the pictures of Evelyn's grandbabies or pass the time in idle conversation shouted over the clank of the conveyor belt. What was she doing here?

"You'll excuse me if I go on wrestling with these numbers," Evelyn said. "We're on a tight schedule here these days." She punched a few keys on her adding machine.

"You go right ahead," Louisa answered. "Your family, how are they?"

"Son's married now. He's preaching over there on James Island in his own church, doing real well."

"A preacher. Well, isn't that wonderful. And Cassandra? The children?"

"Living in El Paso, Texas, right now," she said. "Can you believe it? All the way out there."

Louisa said she couldn't believe it, couldn't comprehend those distances. Finally, she got around to it. She wanted Evelyn to go with her to the Charleston Museum.

You drive all the way out here and can't drive yourself up the street to that museum? was what Evelyn said to herself, but what she said to Miss Marion, as she held up the adding machine tape and frowned at the numbers, was, "You need me to drive you to the museum?" cool and slow, and she felt her eyes squint and her mouth begin to pooch up. Times like these, she could feel a thick wad of anger forcing its way up from her belly toward her throat. Stand a member of the Marion family, man or woman, it made no difference, in front of her and she saw Mr. Hugh Marion, Jr., again and remembered the way he'd come sniffing around her when she was young and lived with Mother Mamie in that little house in the Marions' yard.

The summer she'd turned sixteen, as soon as Mother Mamie was out of sight, he'd come in their house without knocking and stand close to her, breathing all trembly. Miss Louisa had caught him once. She'd had her hand raised to knock on the screen door when she'd seen them inside, and she'd looked from Evelyn to Hugh and back. Then she'd turned away and started walking. "Hugh, come away from there," she'd said over her shoulder, and he'd followed her. Once he'd come into their house drunk, thinking her grandmother was gone, and Mother Mamie had picked up a piece of stove wood from the bucket beside the fireplace and threatened him with it. That's when Evelyn had told her about his other visits. "He comes sniffing around here like I'm a dog" is what she said. But Mother Mamie had shushed her, rough hands smoothing down her hair. "Quiet, baby," she'd said. If Evelyn was a dog, Mother Mamie asked, what did that make him? Nothing but a old nasty dog his own self. After that, Mother Mamie sent Evelyn out to Edisto Island to live. And now, all these many years later, with her own life lived, her children raised and grown, her husband loved and buried, she couldn't look at Louisa Marion without seeing her brother standing right behind her, smiling that nasty smile, and a whole line of brothers, uncles, cousins, sons, and fathers behind him, stretching clear back to the beginning of time.

"No, no," Miss Marion said. Do I not speak plainly? she asked herself. Whey do they never understand what we say? Do we speak different languages? "I want to take you there and show you something of interest to *both* our families." Without meaning to, she raised her voice, leaned closer, and pronounced each word distinctly, as if Evelyn were hard of hearing or slow.

With great care, Evelyn slid her desk drawer open and re-arranged some pens and paper clips while Son's voice shouted inside her. *Mama, you better watch out now. When they say we all the same, we family, they fixing to mess all over you.* Well, I must have been raised right, Evelyn thought. Mother Mamie raised her to be polite and to be kind. To keep her mouth shut and her eyes open, to work hard and to be satisfied, and if she wasn't, not to be sulling up and poking out her lips over her discontents or letting everybody know about them.

Was this another invitation to come to work for her? Evelyn wondered. But no, once they got it untangled enough to understand each other, it turned out that what Louisa wanted was for Evelyn to go *with* her to the Charleston Museum. She pulled a little pocket calendar out of her purse and paged through it. "How does next Saturday sound?"

Evelyn flipped the pages of her desk calendar. "I don't know. Looks like I might have something or other planned for that day," thinking that would be the end of it. Half the time, those promises and invitations were just talk anyway, something to make them feel good so they could go away satisfied that they'd done the right thing, or tried to at least. But Miss Louisa called and then she called again, and finally Evelyn ran out of excuses; she had to go.

At the museum, there was some awkwardness at the front desk, a struggle over who would pay the admission fee, which Louisa won, because the woman taking the money they both held out to her took Louisa's. Evelyn was dressed as smartly as Louisa this time: Louisa in her teal raw silk shirtwaist and Evelyn in a khaki pantsuit by Liz Claiborne, with a blue scarf knotted just so at the neck. They climbed the steps to the second floor, following the signs to the Low Country exhibit, passed under the whale skeleton suspended from the ceiling by wires, walked past the mummy with its unwrapped, petrified toe. Evelyn realized that she'd been looking at that ancient toe since she was a girl and Mother Mamie had taken her to the old museum.

The Low Country exhibit occupied most of the second floor of the museum. The area was dimly lit and cool; on the walls, glass cases displayed eighteenth-century satin coats, fine English plate and silver. Other cases held West African trading pieces found at the bottom of the harbor, a model of trunk gates, rice fields, and old soft brown-and-white photographs of women in white head wraps, leaning on hoes; a small dugout canoe used to travel through the rice fields at Willtown Bluff plantation; a milepost from the King's Highway, and a wooden yoke—USED TO CARRY WATER BUCKETS ON HOPEWELL PLANTATION, the card beneath it read. Pieces of the past. Evelyn wanted to linger and study these things. She hadn't been to the museum since her children were in school. She wanted to stand for a while and study the edge of the yoke, worn thin from steady use, and contemplate the years it had taken flesh to wear wood down to the grain, but Louisa Marion was waiting for her in the doorway that led into the next area, and Evelyn obliged.

Around the corner, there it was. As often as Louisa had seen it, she was never quite prepared. In the glass box on the pedestal, lit from below, the gown appeared to fly: one sleeve raised in a gesture of greeting or good-bye, the rest spread out behind, as if an invisible wearer were running or flying. Yellowed and stained, it was still alive with flowing forms: the smocked bodice and the gown that fell away from the bodice running with leaves, flowers, vines, an airy scribbling of thread; featherstitches and backstitches punctuated with French knots, all flowing down the cloth to the hem, which was held to the gown by a fine web of openwork stitches and strewn with leaf shapes stiffened with a precise and exquisite whip stitch.

A card attached to the pedestal read BABY GOWN SEWED BY

ELIZA HILLIARD, 1844. LINEN, EMBROIDERY, AND DRAWN-THREAD WORK. Louisa studied the photographs of the Hilliard babies as far back as her great-grandmother, each one six months old and dressed in the gown. Even as a baby, her mother had looked haughty. Hugh seemed eager and bright, craning like somebody peeking over a fence at something he wanted on the other side. Her own baby face looked serene, alert. And she was the last of the line.

Looking at that gown, Louisa felt the pull of the familiar story—*our Eliza's famous handiwork*—and the tug of the old, blind greed that had led her ancestor to claim what she touched and mark what she claimed so that no one would ever mistake her possessions for those of another. All the babies, herself among them, stared back at her from their photographs: "Tell the story, Miss Louisa," they seemed to say. "Tell us again what's ours." The pull was strong, and she almost gave in. To tell another story might spoil the past, and if you spoiled the past, you'd spoil the present, too, because the past led to the present and made it true.

With effort, Louisa wrenched her mind away. She'd been baptized in that gown, but she was grown up now, and the story of the christening dress had become too complicated to bring the consolation of comfort. She felt another kind of will begin, a promise that in what was left of her life, she would not hand the story on unchanged. It was little enough, she thought, but it was something. So, she forced herself to look at the hem of the gown, turned back to show the signature: *Property of Eliza Hilliard. Done by her hand, June 1844.* She pictured her ancestor, her straight back, her long, mournful face, sewing her name into the hem. Then she made herself look and remember not just the beauty of that gown, but how it came to be: Diana sewing, the missing teeth, all the rest of it. But she couldn't hold that picture steady, either: the slave girl on the low stool who worked in order to go on living to work another day. The picture dissolved, and Diana was gone again.

She could not chase her down and bring her back the way her mother had always been able to do with Mamie; she was still missing, but the effort of trying left her so weak, she had to make her way to a bench against the wall and sit down.

Evelyn had wanted to stand there alone anyway. Now, with Louisa Marion snatching a little nap, she approached the pedestal, feeling wary. With her hands clasped behind her back, she bent over to read the card: BABY GOWN SEWED BY ELIZA HILLIARD, 1844. LINEN, EMBROIDERY, AND DRAWN-THREAD WORK. She studied the photographs of the Hilliard babies dressed up in the gown and wondered what was expected of her now? Was she supposed to go on about how beautiful that old yellowed dress was? Reminisce about the good old days when her grandmother had starched and ironed it? Or was she supposed to talk about her affection for the little white babies she'd known among the crowd of them clustered around that skirt? "Isn't that something?" she said, and waited, feeling her pulse beat in her temples and throat, the blood packing in behind her forehead, a sure sign that her blood pressure was climbing.

From her seat against the wall, Louisa, who was not sleeping, spoke. "Evelyn," she said. "I've come to the conclusion that Eliza Hilliard might have done the everyday sewing on that dress, but most of the sewing, the fine sewing at least, was done by one of her slaves, a woman named Diana, who ran away and disappeared around 1842. Could she have been related to you?" At the sound of that name, such a feeling came up in Evelyn, a whole clump of sorrow, a blaze of possessive joy, a jolt of fear, too, as if she needed to hide the woman. She felt her son rise up in her, and he'd made his mark sure enough: She was mad at white people for everything. But she tugged her jacket down over her hips and quieted herself. She would tell her son what Louisa Marion had told her and she would also tell him this: "She didn't have to go to the trouble of taking me there and telling me that," she would say. "She could have kept it to herself all the rest of her born days. Her mother wouldn't have bothered, believe you me. Things do change, Son." Maybe that would ease his heart. She would tell Cassandra and the grandchildren, too; she would bring them here to see this and tell them why it mattered.

She thought about times when she'd gone into the tiny hot pantry at the Marions' house and found her grandmother ironing that dress, flattening its creases and folds, her forehead beaded with sweat. How the heat and the cramped room and the sight of her grandmother ironing, tongue clamped between her teeth and the back of her dress soaked with sweat, had come to stand for everything hateful about working for the Marions and living in their yard. Now it turned out that she'd been ironing her own great-great-grandmother's dress, and though that did not cancel the pain, it blunted it to know that her grandmother's work had been for something more than the white people's ease and pride. To know that the care her grandmother Mamie had taken with that gown she would have taken willingly, and more, if she'd known whose knots and vines and leaves had passed under her hands. Filling a basin with cool water and swishing the Ivory soap flakes until they dissolved, squeezing and dipping and rinsing the gown, then rolling it in a thick towel, laying it out to dry, ironing every crease and wrinkle: She'd done all that for them, as well, her own family.

And then that long-ago woman, Diana, whose story had blown like smoke through their lives—a name, a scrap of story, *one of our people way back when used to sew*, a run for freedom—had hands, eyes, ambition, will, a will so strong, it had carried her away and never brought her back. That same woman had made this gown, and made it so well, it was still here, and she was here, too; she'd been here all along, and closer than Evelyn had known. These flowers were hers, and the vines, the knots and leaves, and Evelyn's, too, by blood. She felt a longing that she hadn't felt in years:

to find the woman who had sewn that cloth, and tell her how it is to go motherless through this world. Never to feel the touch of the hands that had made such beauty, or to see yourself reflected in the eyes of the one who'd dreamed it up before her needle ever pierced cloth. Most of all, never to know that the story she was telling in those knots and running vines was the story of how much she loved you. To accuse her, all the way back there and out of reach, of leaving them again. And that longing roused another one: for her own mother, of whom she remembered sharp thighbones, hands plaiting her hair in front of a fire, a narrow, solemn face, and the breathing that was work to get done.

"I know her name," Evelyn said. "I'm told she was my great-great-great-great grandmother. A whole lot of greats between now and then."

Then Louisa Marion was standing beside her, all brisk business again. "Have Letitia and Jerome been baptized yet?" she asked. "They should wear it if they haven't."

A very old, slow, deep anger began in Evelyn then, so old and so deep that she didn't feel it start; it was just there and she stumbled over it. Just like white people to be making plans for you, making plans for your children and your children's children, trying to give you something that belonged to you in the first place so you'd have to humble yourself and thank them for it. To look at your grandchildren's pictures not two weeks past and forget what size the children were, or how old, think of them smaller than they were and younger because it served your purpose to think of them that way. "Be a little small for them, don't you think?" Evelyn asked, and she kept the rough edge to it, felt the weight of that anger, and the weariness that had come from dragging it with her all these years.

Louisa looked startled. The way they get, Evelyn thought, when you've been rough on them. Well, so be it.

Why do we always get it wrong? Louisa thought. Sooner or

later, no matter what we do or say, we always get it wrong. But she had more to tell, and a long drive to tell it. Most of the way back to Edisto Island, Evelyn listened to Miss Louisa Marion talk about how she was going to see to it that the museum changed that card. Said she was going to fix it so that the card told that Diana, a slave, was most likely the one who did the fine sewing on that dress. Said she would arrange for a reception to celebrate this change, at which Evelyn and her family would be guests of honor. "Well," Evelyn said, "looks like that certainly would be the right thing to do." Louisa frowned at the word *right*, straightened her back.

Then Evelyn waited to hear that the change had been made, and for the invitation to that reception to arrive. Not that she *thought* about it every day. But every now and then, when she went to the mailbox and pulled out her mail, she'd catch herself sorting through the envelopes a second and a third time, as though something that should have arrived by now was still missing. Once, almost a year after her visit to the museum with Louisa Marion, Son and Joyce took a Sunday school class to see his grandmother's gown. Son called her as soon as he got home; she could tell he couldn't wait to tell her that nothing had changed with that dress, not a thing, and how he'd had to explain to the Sunday school class how the card said that Eliza Hilliard had sewn that dress, when really it was the slave woman Diana who'd done it. It was the triumphant, bitter mockery in his voice that she hadn't heard in a while that pained her to hear, so first thing that week, Evelyn went down there to see for herself. Sure enough, the mummy's toe was still unwrapped, the whale skeleton swam through air, the edge of the yoke was still worn thin, and it seemed as if the baby gown and all the little white babies dressed in the gown had entered that eternal world as well.

From the museum, she drove directly to Louisa Marion's

house and found her down on her knees, puttering in the garden. She called through an openwork section of brick wall, "You keeping all right, Louisa?"

"Oh Evelyn," she said, climbing to her feet, "come in." A year had taken her down; Evelyn could see that. The climb to her feet winded her, there was a papery look to her skin, and her color was bad, too: a thin blue sheen around her temples and lips. She opened the gate and let Evelyn in, the same sweet smile on her face, but after the first glance, Evelyn couldn't bring herself to look Louisa Marion straight in the eye because of what she saw shining out at her.

What she reported to Son about the visit was that Miss Marion had said that this was harder than she'd supposed. Said she'd been working on it but the museum had dug in its heels about changing that card. Said the gown had been willed to them by her mother; it was their property now, and until it could be proved otherwise, the facts about the gown, as conveyed to them by her mother and written on the card, were true. She'd tried to explain to them about the diary, she said, but the museum people told her they'd have to give it to an expert to read before they could make an informed decision. She told him, too, about how Miss Louisa had wanted her to see the kitchen house apartment and how she'd said she guessed she'd wait on that for another time. And how Miss Louisa had offered her an old brown-and-cream-colored picture of Maum Harriette. How she would have taken it, too—she had a faint memory of her great-great grandmother sitting at a card table under the chinaberry tree in the side yard of her house out on Edisto Island, her yellow dog asleep at her feet—only she didn't want to live with that girl in the picture, Louisa Marion's mother, her hands folded and her chin tipped up like a little queen's, looking down at her every day from Maum Harriette's lap.

But what she didn't tell Son, what she vowed to herself she'd take with her to her own grave, was what happened next. They'd sat on the first-floor piazza drinking iced tea, two old ladies talking about church and the weather and how the hurricane had beaten them down sure enough but they were coming back upright again. That was how their city was, and the people who lived in it. They'd been talking along like that when Miss Marion had all of a sudden put her head down in her hands and started to cry, making little bitty mewing noises, kitten sounds. How she'd said she was all by herself and everything was so hard to do, she couldn't do it on her own. How Evelyn had moved over next to her then and put her arm around her and patted her until she quieted down. She didn't tell him any of that, because she didn't have the heart to listen to Son get going about how they'd been comforting white people at the expense of their own families for way too long. It was easy to talk about *the white people this, the white people that* until one of them you'd known for a long time was crying on your shoulder and it was just the two of you sitting there on the piazza. It wasn't so easy or so simple then, to walk away when it was another human being, not an idea, that you'd turned your back on.

When Louisa Marion died a year later, in the spring of 1992, Evelyn dressed in a navy dress and hat, her best navy and white spectator pumps; she carried her fancy cane with her initials engraved on the silver handle, and she went to the funeral at St. Philip's Church, because that's how decent people behaved when someone close to them died. There must have been a hundred people there, and hers not the only black face, either. She was surprised to see three generations of the basket-making women from the market, a delegation of firemen, and the new black doctor from the medical college among the mourners.

The preacher talked about Louisa Marion for a long time. He talked about her forbearance, her intelligence and wit. He spoke of the depth and rigor of her Sunday school lessons and her abiding interest in the children of the church. He got a laugh when he talked about the generations of young women brought up on the correct way to write up sales slips at the Bargain Shop. And he talked about her handiwork, about the altar cloths and banners she'd sewn. They'd all been brought out and hung around the altar and they stirred in the cool air that flowed through the church. They were a beautiful sight to behold, too: sheaves of wheat and Nativity scenes, Easter lilies and lighted candles. Her most beautiful creation—the long banner stitched with the Paschal Lamb—hung on a stand at the head of her coffin. When the minister had finished and the prayers had been said, six men carried Louisa out into the sunshine in a fine polished wood coffin covered with Susan Simmons's spray of lilies, then slid her coffin into the hearse. Evelyn turned her headlights on and fell in line with the other cars following the hearse out to Magnolia Cemetery. At the cemetery, Louisa's friend Susan spoke to Evelyn. She wore a big black straw hat and was crying, streaks of mascara running down her cheeks, and she had the Paschal Lamb banner folded over one arm. Her daughters stood next to her, and they were crying, too. "Oh Evelyn," she said as she smoothed the Lamb's woolly fur. "We're going to miss her, aren't we?"

"Yes, we will," Evelyn said. Then she sat with Susan in the tent beside the grave, because Susan had taken her hand and wouldn't let go of it, and the minister gave Louisa Hilliard Marion back to the dust and she was laid to rest among her people, her mother and father and brother, in a pretty spot with a little stone bench beside the grave and a willow tree brushing the ground over her head. That's when Evelyn cried a little bit, standing there with Susan until everyone was gone, helping her to drape the Paschal Lamb over the casket, watching the vault go down into the grave and the dirt begin to fall, remembering the Lamb's curly fur, all those little bitty knots her hands had made.

That fall a lawyer called her, said Miss Marion had left her five thousand dollars, somebody's old diary, and a letter asking her to go down to the museum and see if she could work on them, convince them to change that card. She'd go down there, too, she thought, maybe in the winter. Until then, she had enough troubles to keep her busy. In July, Mr. Eubanks had had a stroke. He wouldn't be coming back to the packing shed for another six months, if he came back at all. She'd been to visit him every week, and now here it was early September and there'd been no change in him. Week after week, he sat there with no expression on his face, tied into his wheelchair with a wide soft sash.

She was running the packing shed now, and if Mr. Eubanks didn't get up and come back to work before the slack season came, she was going to be the one to lay people off, instead of putting her foot down as she had every year and making Mr. Eubanks do it. Virginia, his wife, was too much of a refined lady to hire and fire, and his son, Rembert junior, wasn't able. He was a sweet boy, bless his heart, thirty-five years old now and never been married, still living at home, so shy, he couldn't look you in the face when you talked to him. Ever since they'd lost their girl at seventeen— speeding toward Edisto beach in her Chevrolet convertible, she'd lost control on a curve and slammed head-on into one of the big oaks beside the highway—he'd stuck close to home, where his mother could keep an eye on him. Then, last week, in their Wednesday-evening talk, Virginia had as much as said that the packing shed was Evelyn's if she wanted it, and Evelyn had lain awake every night since, running down lists of names in her head, subtracting some and adding others, thinking like an owner.

We just don't know what we'd do without you, Evelyn. How many times had she heard that? It looked like nobody could do without her, unless it was Cassandra. Lord, Lord. This time, she was just going to set her burden down and move out to El Paso, Texas, where her daughter had settled in and decided to stay. She had a good job working with computers and she was going to college part-time and talking about starting law school in the fall.

The week before, she'd invited Evelyn again to come live with her. "Mama, I wish you'd come on out," Cassandra had said. "You won't have to do a thing but look after the babies when I'm gone. We can drink margaritas every day and drive out to the Little Diner and eat a big plateful of *gorditas* anytime we want to. You can go back to school, too, Mama, think about it. UTEP has classes in just about anything you'd want to study."

She'd promised Cassandra she would think about it, and the truth was that she was tempted, strongly tempted, just to pull up stakes and go out there. She sure did miss her daughter and those babies, and there was nothing holding her here, with Son married now and standing on his own two feet. She'd leave all this mess and go, leave it all and not look back and not miss a thing except for the early-morning quiet and the big crane out in the creek; just him out there and her inside, enjoying the dawning of the day from the screened back porch of her own house, where nobody was going to come peering in her door, calling for her. The thought of living too close with other people worried her. Some-times, even the grandchildren's sweet sticky fingers on her hand, their warm cheeks pressed against her own, made her want to push them away, but worrying about that was different from think-ing of what she'd miss here. Which wasn't much except for the early-morning light coming through the gray moss on the big oak next to her carport, or Albert's oyster boat still sitting right where he'd last pulled it out of the creek, Albert's grave in the church-yard, which she visited on the last Sunday of every month and swept clean of moss and twigs and trash. Or maybe the feeling she got—like walking out of a small, cold place into wide, warm sunshine—when she walked into church on a Sunday morning and saw the faces of her friends. Or the look of the creek across the road from the church where they baptized on the ebb tide so the water would drag their sins out into the ocean. Her job on baptiz-ing Sundays was to dry the women when they came out of the wa-ter, and every time she wrapped a towel around another shivering sinner, she remembered the morning her own sins had been washed away and how the first thing she'd seen when she'd wiped the water from her eyes had been Albert, standing at the front of the crowd on the bank, a satisfied look on his face, holding Son in his arms.

Walking Tour of the Historic District
Charleston, South Carolina
Site No. 3
The Hilliard House
1993

The woman who takes the money and hands out tickets at the table in the hallway has popped in to tell them that the one o'clock tour is sold out. The hallway is filled with guests, she says. Actually, the people are tourists, but calling them "guests" is more gracious and welcoming. And actually, it's 1:25, but there's no hurry. This is Charleston; it's spring again, warm and hazy, smothering under flowers. Through the iron gates that lead to the gardens beside the historic district houses, you glimpse the new green of ferns, hear the trickle of water, and everything is slow and soft and blurred, like the pastel colors of the scenes on the note cards in the gift shop at the Historic Charleston Foundation. And since this slowing and softening and blurring is what people come here for, they don't mind waiting.

Back in the kitchen of the Hilliard house, the volunteer docents from the Preservation Society sit around the table, finishing their coffee and trading sections of the morning paper. Someone has brought a lemon pound cake, low-fat but delicious, and

since most of the women there are also members of the Junior
League, they're discussing how they will update the next edition
of *Charleston Receipts*, which the League has published since
1950. The silhouettes of mammies in their aprons and caps that
mark the top of each page will have to go, but they'll leave some
of the old extravagant recipes for historical interest. The Carolina
Housewife Wedding Cake of 1850, for instance. Reading the
recipe, you don't need a picture; you can see a whole household
staff talking and laughing together as they cream twenty pounds
of butter, sugar, and flour, crack two hundred eggs, sprinkle forty
pounds of currants into the batter, stir in twenty glasses of wine
and brandy, grind twenty nutmegs to spicy powder.

Today, it is Louisa Marion's goddaughter, Susan Simmons's oldest daughter, Ann Simmons Culp, who will lead the tour. She is
wearing a linen jumper over a crisp white blouse, flat linen shoes.
She has heavy blond hair and clear skin, good straight white teeth,
and she smells of her mother's citrusy perfume, which she has
adopted as her own signature scent. "Good afternoon, and welcome," she says to the crowd: Midwesterners mostly, judging from
their open faces and bright nylon jogging suits; a few male cou-
ples, too, architects, no doubt, or art historians or interior decora-
tors.

"You are standing in the foyer of the Hilliard house, one of
Charleston's most distinguished historic homes," she continues.
"The Hilliard family were prominent rice planters of the antebellum period, and this house and its furnishings reflect their status in the community. A house on this site was continuously
occupied by a member of the Hilliard family from 1725, when
Isaac Hilliard came to the city from Barbados and built the original wooden structure, until Miss Louisa Hilliard Marion's
death in 1992, at which time the house was willed to the Historic

Charleston Foundation, with the requirement that it be maintained in perpetuity as she had left it.

"Follow me, if you will. There's so much to see in a house this old. If we're quiet, we can almost hear the brushing of hoop skirts against the floor and the sound of long-ago laughter, can't we? If you'll step in here and gather behind the rope, I believe everyone can see." She unhooks the red velvet rope and steps into the room, clips it back onto the hook on the other stand. "It was in this room, called the reception room, that guests traditionally were received. Notice the couch: One side of the back is high and the other side low. Why do you suppose that is? Well, it was to accommodate the lady's hoop skirts," she says when nobody answers. "The gentleman would sit on this end with the high back and the lady on the other, where she could drape her skirt and hoop over the back of the couch. Notice the fine oil portraits of Isaac and Amelia Hilliard painted by the Colonial portrait painter Jeremiah Theus, who often portrayed the aristocracy as you see them here: dressed in silks and satins and adorned with pearls and perukes. Imagine living in a place this old, surrounded by your family's possessions. It would be comforting, don't you agree, to feel yourself part of something that had been going on for so long?

"Now," she continues, "our Miss Louisa herself died right here, in this little room where you all are standing. We call her 'our Miss Louisa' because we feel that she lives here still; you can almost feel her, can't you, in the family memorabilia with which she surrounded herself, and in the furnishings and appointments which made this her home?

"Miss Louisa was sewing when death came to call. Sewing was her passion, and she was very good at it. Notice the fine embroidered doily under the table lamp on the table with the photographs on it there in the middle of the room. That is her work. St. Philip's Church owns another collection of her needlework, her altar cloths and banners, which are still in use there. If you visit the Charleston Museum during your stay in our city, you will also

see the handiwork of another Hilliard, Eliza Hilliard, Louisa's ancestor, who embroidered an exquisite baby gown that is part of the
permanent textile collection there. Miss Louisa was found in that
chair next to the window with her needle in her hand and a
peaceful smile on her face. She was embroidering an Easter altar
cloth for St. Philip's Church, and that was resting across her lap.
Here is the unfinished cloth she was sewing. And here is her
sewing box beside her favorite chair. Notice the mirrored lid that
allowed her to see the contents of the box and to select a spool of
thread without having to get up. Notice, too, the needle and
thread, the silver thimble and fine silver scissors shaped like flying
cranes, tools of the seamstress's art, of which she was a consum-
mate practitioner."

All replicas, she does not tell them. The sewing box, the needle
and thread, even the scissors and thimble. The originals have disappeared, no one knows how, and the rare silver pitcher known
among local antique dealers as the Hilliard trade winds piece
turns up smudged with fingerprints inside its locked glass cabinet.
Who would have stolen those things, smudged that pitcher? Miss
Louisa left no living relatives. Ann and her mother had come here
after Miss Louisa's death to sort through her belongings, and they
certainly didn't steal or smudge anything.

Neither does she tell them that the things *keep* disappearing.
No sooner do they replace a pair of scissors or polish the pitcher
than the scissors are gone and the fingerprints return. During the
last year, since the house has been open for visitors, she's come to
believe that either they have had an unusual number of thieves
among the tourists or else the house has a ghost, and since the
ghost makes a better story, she's begun to make one up. So many
of these old places are haunted. Peopled by pirates, or beautiful
brides, or children, or Confederate soldiers. Her own house on
Orange Street, for instance. Up in the attic, an old straw garden
hat sometimes disappears from the hat stand and turns up on her
daughter's bed, or the kitchen table. It makes a charming story, a

ghostly girl and her hat, her giggly playfulness. This ghost is the ghost of Eliza Hilliard or Elizabeth Hilliard Marion or Miss Louisa herself, any one of them as a girl, on the eve of her St. Cecilia ball, looking for a needle and thread and a servant to mend a rip, or tack up a hem, or tighten a loose button. When she has it worked out, she'll introduce it into the tour and it will make a nice touch. Her friends, the other docents, on whom she's tried out the ghost story, agree. It's charming. She is the most creative writer in the Preservation Society, always asked to write copy for the radio spots that announce the annual candlelight tour of historic homes. *The holiday season takes on a different aura when viewed in the candlelight of more gracious times.*

She already has several nice touches in her talk, especially the one about death coming to call for Miss Louisa. She can almost picture death pulling up to this house in his carriage, the driver jumping down to open the carriage door. A thin, handsome man steps down and walks up to the street door. Meeting Miss Louisa, he bows low.

And really, death did come to call, or death's scout. In the spring of 1992, the spring that she died, Louisa Marion had hired a woman named Addie, the aunt of Susan's maid, Alberta King, to help her with her spring cleaning. Until that year, she'd done the work herself. "I'm not dead yet," she'd tell her friends as she refused their offers of help. She could still drag or carry or shove furniture out of a room, roll up the rugs and send them to be cleaned, scrub a room down to the baseboards. But that year, after she'd dragged the settee out of the reception room, she hadn't been able to catch her breath. She'd felt so weak, she'd lain down and slept until lunchtime. That's when she'd given in and hired Addie.

One morning during the cleaning, she'd been in the dining

room, cutting out shelf paper for a sideboard drawer, when she'd heard Addie's angry voice from the kitchen: "How come you to be in this yard? Get on away from here, boy. Don't be setting your foot to this step."

When she went into the kitchen to see what the trouble was, she'd found a thin boy in a dirty white T-shirt and black pants cinched tight with a cracked leather belt standing outside the kitchen door, offering a piece of paper to Addie, who held the screen door shut with one hand and flapped a dish towel at the boy with the other.

"Excuse me, Addie," she said as she stepped past and pushed open the door. Taking the note that he handed up to her, she looked at his bony, starved face, looked into his eyes, and stepped back. The note he handed her was printed in thick black letters on soiled white paper that had been folded and unfolded many times. "My name is robert davis," it read. "I cannot talk. I was born like this. I can hear and do sign language school on King Street. I have no ID. I have no food in 3 days. Please may I work for $6 to get a room at the Salvation Army on Calhoun Street. Thank you. God bless you."

"Don't be giving that boy nothing," Addie said, watching his hands, his face, his Adam's apple when he swallowed.

"We have to help him, Addie. He's starving—can't you see that? Wait right there," she said loudly. Then she went into the kitchen and packed a paper bag with a new jar of peanut butter, a box of saltine crackers, cheese, apples, and six dollars for the room, while Addie fumed and bustled, slapping the dish towel around the countertops and muttering to herself.

The next day, Louisa's cat died. When Louisa looked out of the kitchen window at dawn and saw the old orange tom, she knew without going out to it, by the deflated and utterly still way the cat lay on the bricks in front of the kitchen house, and by the flies around it, that it was dead.

"I told you not to give that boy nothing," Addie said when she came to work at nine and heard about the cat.

"The cat was old, Addie. Cats just die like that, you know. That boy didn't kill him, if that's what you think."

"Yes'm," Addie said. The next day, Louisa found salt on the hearth, salt in the fireplace. A week later, she died in the reception room, and the story Addie told about how she'd come in and found Miss Louisa twisted up and pop-eyed on the floor, the cloth she'd been sewing flung clear across the room as if it had *flown* there, that story always began with the ragged boy with the empty eyes who'd come to the door begging food the week before.

Louisa Marion passed away as other Hilliards and Marions had died. The genes of the members of the two families possessed a common flaw, a fraying of the DNA strand, which drew them to one another and perhaps compounded the error's potency, because for generations they'd married one another, and in every generation, at least one of them had dropped dead. On an ordinary day, without warning, their hearts had simply stopped as suddenly as if a hand had pinched them out the way Louisa's father had amazed and frightened his young children by reaching out at the dinner table to snuff the candles with his fingers. They always missed the quick dip in the water glass or the lick he gave his fingers, moistening them before he pinched the wick and doused the flame, so they thought the trick was miraculous, another sign of the hard, solid health of which he was made. To the end, his face had been wide and heavy and pink, his blue eyes sharp, his white hair full and swept back, a man whose energy was like a storm, whose roar everyone had to shout to be heard above. His heart had stopped while he was walking down Broad Street one day after lunch. He was whistling and calling hellos to his lawyer friends across the street when he fell, scattering all over the sidewalk the peppermints he carried in his pockets to give to pretty secretaries and old Negroes.

Eliza Hilliard herself had also died this way: collapsed on the floor of the kitchen house in this very yard. And Louisa's heart went the family way as well, but before she died, two things happened to her. She'd looked up from her sewing and out the window at the ferns beside the front gate, when she realized that the spot she was looking at, the spot she *always* glanced at first, was the place where she'd planted the priest's mustard seed thirty-two years ago. And it came to her then that she was still checking to see if it had sprouted, and that if she were checking, she was also waiting, and she felt the length of that waiting settle, coil on top of heavy coil, inside her.

She had just finished a French knot and pushed the needle up through the cloth and looped the thread once around it to begin another, when a tender voice she'd never heard but recognized instantly as her mother's spoke from a spot just behind her right shoulder. "Well, isn't that lovely, Louisa?" the voice said. "I see you have finally mastered the French knot," and at the sound of her mother's approval, her heart filled with more than it could hold, and it stopped. In the seconds before she tumbled from the chair, she felt the silence begin, and as the current drained from her nerve endings and the small fires stopped firing in her brain, a feeling came over her body that felt the way the sun looked as it spread light across the whole visible width of ocean, and she wanted to go there; she welcomed what was about to be, and so passed from this world in a state so close to grace as the fear would allow. Because that came, too: one last terror, an animal *no* that clawed at her. She tried to twist away from it, threw her arms up to ward off the blow, which sent the altar cloth sailing across the room, then grabbed the table beside her chair and turned it over as she fell. Though you won't hear about an overturned table, a flung altar cloth, or signs of struggle in any story but Addie's. In all the other stories, what you'll get is a portrait of an old woman with her head bowed peacefully on her breast and clutched in her hand, an altar cloth with half a Holy Ghost stitched on it.

In the dining room of the Hilliard house, Ann Culp continues: "In accordance with Miss Marion's wishes, the house has been kept just as it was and has always been. What is comforting in life is the memory of life's finer things, wouldn't you agree?" The dining room table is laid with silver and fine plate, as if for a dinner party. Locked up in the glass-fronted corner cupboard are silver candlesticks, the silver cruet stand, each with a story, a history. As they walk from room to room, she points out the crown molding, the family's fine furniture, the chests of drawers that came apart in sections so that when the family moved from their plantation house to their town house, their furniture could come with them.

The first room they visit on the second floor, the drawing room that extends the length of the second floor, is her favorite. A unique room to find in a Charleston double house, a mark of the family's individuality, with the tall windows across the front, the view down the street and across the harbor that always brings a gasp from the crowd. What a view! They must have believed they owned the world, she thinks, that this was their personal ocean. That there was no stopping them, and whatever they saw belonged to them. They could step out and be carried away and come and go like the wind and own the world. In the corner beside the tall windows stands the exquisite ladies writing desk made of French walnut; over by the fireplace, chairs are grouped around a harp on a stand, and Thomas Hilliard's violin lies in an open case on one of the chairs. She gathers the tour near the fireplace. "No doubt the Hilliards spent many long and pleasant hours here," she says. "Second-floor drawing rooms were popular gathering places because they kept the family above the noise and dirt of the streets. They might gather here for an evening of music and conversation. If Eliza Hilliard wanted to make toast for her guests, she would call a servant to make it on this ingenious little brass toaster," she says, holding up the small appliance and working its latches.

"These are the upstairs bedrooms," she says. "Notice that the beds are turned back as if someone will come up and sleep in them tonight. This was also done in accordance with Miss Louisa Marion's explicit instructions for preserving this house." And what an odd document *that* was, she does not say. Miss Louisa became stubborn and eccentric in her last years of life. The sugar caddy was to remain always unlocked, the beds turned down. "Please notice the heads of rice embroidered on the pillowcases, the handiwork of Miss Eliza Hilliard. Notice the exquisitely carved bedposts on the bed, as well. Those are the stalks and heads of the rice plant. If you'll lean closer, you'll see they are carved with such dimension that the individual grains of rice stand out from the seed head itself. This is an example of a Charleston rice bed and it was made in Thomas Elfe's workshop in this city in the late eighteenth century. Today, only a few of these beds are left in existence."

Now Ann Culp's tour has left the house and assembled outside the door to the kitchen house. "One of the things that makes this house so special and unique is the presence of this fine kitchen house. Not many of these buildings have survived the centuries. When kitchens moved inside, most of the outbuildings were torn down. Step inside, if you will." The wide floorboards are silver with age, charred patches show in front of hearth and oven. She stands next to the deep fireplace in front of the heavy, splintered chopping block with the cleaver stuck in the middle of it. She has made this her area of special interest: the preparation and serving of food in old Charleston. As they study the tools and ovens and hearth, she says, "We can't imagine life without our microwaves, our stoves and refrigerators, our can openers and salad spinners, can we?" And the women in the group exchange looks and sigh, roll their eyes and shake their heads: women together, united by their chores and tasks, their burdens. "Open-hearth cookery required constant skill, vigilance, and agility," she says. "And kitchen injuries ranked second to childbirth as the leading cause of death among women in the antebellum South. Just look at these implements." She points to them one by one: an iron rod with a hook at the end for hanging pots, swinging them in and out of the fire; a cast-iron waffle iron; the domed bread oven; iron forks; tongs to grip and drag food from the fire.

"Notice that all the tools are bent, sprung, or otherwise ruined. Now, your General Sherman never got here," she says. She always throws in that *your* for the benefit of the Northerners in the crowd, to remind them that the people of this city have *not* forgotten, that defiance and long memory are part of the city's heritage and always will be. "He was prevented by bad roads, and by our swamps and rivers, from ever reaching Charleston," she says. "Besides, he had bigger plans for Columbia. But other Union troops came, and they are probably the ones who broke these tools, out of pure spite and vindictiveness, a fine example of Sherman's policy of punishing South Carolina and its people for their role in the war." That's the story they tell, because only outsiders would have been this wasteful, this vengeful. "Now, Sherman did make it to Columbia. My great-grandfather hid under the porch of a house there and threw rocks at his troops," she tells her crowd of solemn tourists. A few of them look down at the floor. The color rises in her cheeks as she says this; she holds her head higher. "This concludes our tour of the historic Hilliard house. And now please exit through the gate in the garden, and do come back to see us if you should return to our city."

She led her tour on Friday and now it's Sunday. Her own house is in the historic district, too, on Orange Street, but she's walking fast away from her house now, walking toward the Hilliard house, where she intends to shut herself in for some peace and quiet. She is dressed in linen overalls and a white T-shirt and sandals, and as she walks, she tucks her blond hair behind her ears. These are the things that are on her mind as she walks: On Friday, a letter had come from Ashley Hall, stating that her daughter had been placed on academic probation. The braces will come off the girl's teeth in time for her St. Cecilia ball next year, but they will *not* use the florist who did the flowers this year, because he was so careless with the lilies. He left the stamens in the flowers and the red pollen from the stamens fell onto the girls' gowns and stained them permanently. She has written a letter, and the mothers of next year's debutantes have signed it, informing the florist of the reason they won't be using him again. Her son has a cowlick that won't lie down, and his hair is getting shaggy. Last week, he cut off a perfectly good pair of new khaki pants and made them into shorts, and her husband has been after him ever since. He is a methodical man, her husband, Porter Culp. Generally, in lecturing to their son, he starts with the shorts and works his way up to the hair, but this morning, he started at the top and worked his way down. Then he lost his temper at all of them for bickering at the breakfast table about the shorts, the lily stains, the letter from Ashley Hall. That's when she'd just gotten up, left the breakfast dishes on the table, walked over to the Hilliard house, and let herself in with the key she'd been given. She's head docent now; she has one of the two keys in existence.

It's always quiet there and she loves that quiet: the quiet of finished stories and settled lives, of a family that is gone from the face of the earth, nothing left to complicate and trouble their existence any longer. No one to shout or shove back his chair or weep or lie, slam doors or sulk. She likes best to sit at Miss Louisa's dining room table, which is set so beautifully with china and silver, and listen to the house be quiet. The sunlight comes in through the old wavy glass and shines on the wide polished pine floorboards and on the silver, and there is an order there that never changes.

If it weren't for the ticking of the clock on the sideboard that she winds once a week, the house would be completely still, and even the clock's ticking sounds muted; as though it were measuring long lengths of peaceful emptiness, hours in which nothing happens nor is expected to happen, hours that lead only to more quiet, more peace. *Miss Louisa*, she whispers sometimes, and listens to the silence answer.

When she's soaked in the quiet long enough, she gets up and goes out to the kitchen house to practice her cooking demonstration for the garden club from Spartanburg that's coming next week. She can give a demonstration, and a very good one, of cooking in the old city. She can cook bacon in a skillet over an open fire and not burn it; she can even cook biscuits in a cast-iron skillet on legs set over the coals. She's always surprised, opening the door of the kitchen house, that the place still smells faintly of food. Squatting in front of the hearth, she builds the fire: paper first, then small sticks, and while it sprouts flame and begins to burn, she imagines Eliza Hilliard, the sternly beautiful woman in the portrait that hangs on the reception room wall, feeding her own fire.

But lately, another thing has begun to happen, and now it's happening again. When she comes here, she remembers things. It used to be that she could imagine the house entirely, or almost entirely, peopled by white people. But now, no sooner does she try to imagine Eliza Hilliard squatting in front of this fire than she knows it did not happen. White women of Eliza Hilliard's class and time did not cook, did they? Only if they had to. The blacks did this work: slaves first, servants later. *Servants* is what they're encouraged to call the Negroes of that time; it sounds less harsh than *slaves*. But lately, ever since she's been coming here and making the biscuits, she can't reel off that story; it sticks in her throat. It's getting harder and harder to keep them apart, the black story and the white one; they pull toward each other, merge, and tangle.

With her back to the room and her face to the fire, she is struck again by the feeling that she's being watched. It happens every time she comes here and lights the fire. She turns slowly and looks behind her: nothing but shadows thrown by the fire playing on the brick walls. As the fire burns down to cooking coals, she makes up her dough in a huge scarred wooden bowl, then rolls it out on a cutting board on top of the splintered wooden block table in the middle of the room and cuts out rounds of dough, tucks them into the skillet. When the coals are ready, she sets the skillet over the coals and slips a small piece of slate under the leg of the skillet that had been bent in that vicious spree of destruction the Yankees visited on the city, so that the skillet sits evenly over the coals on the floor of the deep fireplace. "You can't turn a fire up and down, like a stove, can you?" She needs to write down that line and work it into her next tour. People like the personal details that include them, that reach out from this older world and touch their own. As the fire heats the iron skillet, she feels its heat on her face. By midsummer, the building will be as hot as the iron skillet, packed so thick with heat, you won't be able to think there, much less work.

So she squats there, hugging her knees, watching the coals glow, the biscuits rise and fluff and brown. She's not thinking about anything; she's remembering Girl Scout camp or her grandfather's Irish setter, Flag, and how he'd looked, running through the broom sedge at the family place out on the Stono River. She's thinking of the dress her daughter needs for a dance at Porter-Gaud next month; then, without knowing where she made the turn, she's not thinking about those things anymore, but about herself at the kitchen table at the Stono River house, mashing shredded wheat into milk with the back of a spoon, then her grandfather coming into the room, throwing his keys down onto the kitchen table. "Those nigras have paid for what they did," he said, and no more.

Three months ago, her grandfather had died; her grandmother had died years earlier, just after her son was born. It wasn't unexpected: He'd been gone for years—the slow erasure of Alzheimer's disease. But she'd been his favorite among the grandchildren. For the last two years, she would walk into the house on Bull Street where he'd always lived and there he'd be, propped up in his recliner in front of the television set, with the woman they'd hired to be with him sitting beside him. He'd look up at her, his entirely familiar face blank. "Hello, who's this come to see me?" he'd say. She'd told herself that she was ready for him to die, that his death would be a blessing, all the things you tell yourself when someone is still alive and you practice how you'll feel when they're gone. But when it finally happened, she couldn't bring herself to walk into the house or allow anyone else to, either. She'd even closed and latched the shutters over all the windows, as though she were readying the house for a hurricane. *Wait, wait, wait.*

When that feeling had finally subsided, a month after his death, she'd gone to work. One day, she'd been taking a break from the dreary work of cleaning out the bedside table drawers, pulling out handfuls of Father's Day cards, her grandfather's Book of Common Prayer, envelopes full of newspaper clippings. Had he ever thrown anything away? She'd felt dusty all over, tired and sad, thinking of her grandfather and his stubborn accumulations, the weight of all those things with which a person pins himself to earth. How light and wasteful those things felt when the person who'd gathered them was gone. Thinking of her mother's house and its accumulations, of her own house and her children sorting through her sewing notions until all that was left was one pearl button, such as might have fallen off a fancy cardigan sweater, rolling around an empty drawer.

At her grandfather's house that day, she'd been drinking a glass of iced tea and sitting on the floor in the front hall, looking through the heavy glass box of photographs that had sat on a table there for as long as she could remember. There was the photograph of her father as a boy, and another of him as a father, lifting her over the waves on the beach at Sullivan's Island. There she was in her gown before her St. Cecilia ball, and then with her husband and their daughter, their first-born. And then, there it was. A photograph in an embossed paper frame, of men in white shirts and dark trousers, hats pulled low. Men with torches standing on either side of two bodies, which hung from the limb of a water oak, the trailing moss blurred in a breeze.

She'd turned it over, her heart beating hard. On the back there was a date written: August 1939. Where had *that* come from? She had no one to ask now but herself. She'd looked at those photographs all her life. When she was old enough not to tear them anymore or put them in her mouth, her grandmother had let her look through the pictures anytime she wanted, and throughout her childhood, she'd done that. "You could sit there for hours," her grandmother once told her. "Sometimes you'd sort them into girls and boys, or colored people and white people." Three months ago, only three months, after her grandfather's funeral, when they'd all come back to the house, she'd looked through theses pictures again with her brother and sisters. She'd looked at them so often, they'd become part of her memory, so that she placed herself in scenes she'd never been in, standing next to people she'd never known. The picture of the hanging had not been there. It had not. And the worst thing about that picture— beside the decorative paper frame, the general air of deliberate commemoration about it—was that down in one corner, just coming into the frame, a white hand held the ankle of one of the black men's bodies (though *men* wasn't exactly right for who they were; the one being held was not much older than her son), as though steadying it for the long moment when the shutter opened and the light rushed in.

Now as she squats and hugs her knees in front of the kitchen house fire and watches her biscuits brown, that photograph joins with her grandfather's words about the nigras who'd paid for what they'd done and she can't pull them apart. Since she'd found that photograph, something has pushed into her memory of her grandfather and it will not leave.

She watches the fire and thinks of their family place out on a bluff above the Stono River. In the house, on a French trading map from 1698, their bluff is marked with a tiny cross, smudged and rubbed and worn where many fingers touched it. When she was a child, old people still lived in the slave houses. They walked around, smoking pipes, trailed by mopey dogs, gathering twigs for their stoves and carrying them in bundles on their heads, sweeping their sand yards clean with twig brooms. During the hospital strike, the civil rights disturbances, her family spent a lot of time out there. Her grandfather had put in a tennis court, and her friends had come out. They'd played and played and listened to music on the radio, and to the news bulletins from town.

She'd been dating her husband-to-be during the hospital strike. The wedding was set for that fall. He'd come down from Columbia, where he was in law school, and in the summer house above the river, one night when the light of the full moon spread on the water, they'd watched four dolphins swim up the river, and they'd made love for the first time. On their wedding day, he'd given her a gold pin, a leaping dolphin, which she wears every year when they go out to dinner on their anniversary.

And for the first time now, squatting in front of the fire, she lets herself know (it seems to radiate from the fire, this knowledge, from the fire or the air or the ground) that her grandfather had been there when the picture was made, standing outside the camera's view. And if he was there, what part did he play? Did he light a torch? Throw a rope? Was it his hand that reached out to hold the dead boy's ankle? She refuses the answers to these questions as quickly as she might slam a door she'd opened into a familiar room, expecting light and warmth, and finding it pitch-dark and cold. Then she thinks about her children and knows she cannot refuse. She thinks that if she could tell them the story of the dolphins in the moonlit river and the story of their own great-grandfather at the lynching and make them into one story in which every part touched and influenced every other part, she would have given her children something that they might use to save their lives from blindness and repetition. But where was the thread that tied the stories together and made them necessary to one another? How would she find it? Where did it start? There was nothing to do now but to begin.